THE ION RAIDER

ALSO BY IAN WHATES

THE DARK ANGELS:
Pelquin's Comet (2015)

THE CITY OF 100 ROWS:
City of Dreams and Nightmare (2011)
City of Hope and Despair (2012)
City of Light and Shadow (2013)

THE NOISE:
The Noise Within (2010)
The Noise Revealed (2011)

COLLECTIONS:
The Gift of Joy (2009)
Growing Pains (2013)
Dark Travellings (2016)

Co-written with Tim C. Taylor
THE HUMAN LEGION:
Human Empire (2015)
The War Against the White Knights (2016)

THE ION RAIDER

Book Two
of
The Dark Angels

Ian Whates

NewCon Press
England

First published in the UK May 2017 by NewCon Press
41 Wheatsheaf Road, Alconbury Weston, Cambs, PE28 4LF

NCP 117 (limited edition hardback)
NCP 118 (softback)

10 9 8 7 6 5 4 3 2 1

ISBN:

978-1-907069-37-8 (hardback)
978-1-900679-38-5 (softback)

Cover illustration by Jim Burns
Cover layout by Storm Constantine

Book layout by Storm Constantine

One

The man strolled along cobbled streets, past sleepy villas and gardens where tough grasses rose in bristling clumps from the parched earth and tall yellow flowers sprang up in haughty isolation, bursts of colour that came as welcome relief among the white painted walls and sun-baked brown of the earth. The walls reflected the sun's warmth back at him, while the occasional raised voice drifting out from open windows provided scant evidence that he wasn't the sole person alive in the village, merely the only one foolish enough to venture out when the sun was at its zenith. A donkey watched him disconsolately from the shade of a tatter-roofed lean-to, and a pair of scrawny chickens pecked at the dust by a wall. All else was still. Even the flowers' stunted shadows were straight and motionless as sentries.

Soon the cobbles gave way to concrete and he left the village behind, climbing a narrow lane that led into the hills beyond.

His course was bracketed by solid but irregular stone walls that bordered the road, guiding him between fields of golden cereal on his left – doubtless modified to flourish in this arid environment – their crowns unmoving in the absence of any breeze, and olive groves to the right. Scythe-winged birds patrolled the skies, making nimble turns and graceful swoops as they harvested the abundant insects. Their occasional shrill calls were the only sound and their busy energy belied the heat, seeming deliberately designed to taunt or perhaps challenge the two much larger black birds that huddled on a section of wall. The roosting birds ignored them, the epitome of indifference, but flew away on lazy wings at his approach.

At the top of the hill he paused to take a sip of ice-cold water from his flask and look back at the village where it nestled in the shallow valley below, the mix of flat and pantile roofs gazing back at him through a ripple of heat haze. Two days it had taken him to get here from Opal, the capital. The first spent in comparative comfort on an air-conditioned train, the second less so on a trio of aged buses that grew more dilapidated with each change of vehicle, until it seemed unlikely that the last and smallest could complete the journey. The ebb and flow of passengers getting on and off as the bus wound its way from village to village ensured that travelling conditions varied between mildly uncomfortable and borderline intolerable.

His journey had ended at last in a wheeze of hydraulics as the bus drew up in a vast building that had obviously started life as a barn. This was the end of the line. Two tired-looking vehicles, indistinguishable from the one that had brought him here, stood idle, offering the promise of escape back to civilisation at some point. He wondered if the terminus might have been a factor in the choice of location. It was easy to imagine a person getting this far and simply lacking the will, the energy, to go any further.

Even so, he could understand the attraction of this backwater, this refuge from the modern world; low on convenience, perhaps, but there was no denying the setting possessed a certain charm. Life didn't so much slow down here as stumble to a halt and take a break. It was beautiful, languid, tranquil – the sort of place a person might come to retire. Or to hide.

Putting the flask away, he shouldered his pack and resumed walking. Not far to go now.

The way dipped briefly downward and then up again. From the crest of this second rise he could see his destination for the first time: a little ahead a group of low buildings clustered beside a track that led left from the lane he was treading. At the heart of this cluster stood a substantial sturdy-looking cottage, its white walls blazing in reflected sunlight. Two barns and a smaller, squat building completed the set, but they were of no consequence.

Beside him, a wall branched off from the one he had been following; stretching away from the road at an approximate right angle, it marked the divide between two fields. A single tree bearing sparse foliage grew a little way along its length. He left the road, scrambling over the wall and following the field divider as far as the tree. Here he stopped, knowing that the sturdy trunk would help mask his outline against the skyline should anyone in the cottage happen to glance this way at the wrong moment. He shucked his backpack and took out a pair of binoculars – slim, matt black, and lightweight, with exaggerated eyepieces that cupped the side of his face. The cottage jumped nearer, its whitewashed walls similar to those of the buildings he had left behind in the village. An adjustment to the focus and the walls lost their solidity, becoming semi-transparent. He scanned from right to left, ignoring the ghosts of furniture that scrolled across his view, until he reached what was evidently the kitchen.

Here he found them: two people, both seated at a table, presumably eating. The view wasn't clear enough to distinguish detail, but he was sufficiently practiced to determine that one was likely male, the other female. Another adjustment to the focus and the figures acquired a red glow that pulsed in time to their heartbeat and the flow of blood being pumped around their bodies. The binoculars completed their assessment. The man was unknown, presumably the husband – too insignificant to be detailed in the brief he had received – but the woman returned a ninety-two per cent probability that she was his target.

More than good enough.

Placing the binoculars down on the top of the rough wall, the man lifted a compact valise from his pack, carefully took out the first components, and began. He worked with calm, unhurried efficiency, and the gun swiftly took shape in his hands.

The final piece was provided by the binoculars, which split when given a gentle twist, one half clipping onto the stock to provide a targeting scope.

He loaded two bullets, rested the barrel's support on the wall, and sighted. There was no rush. Time was still on his side. He rehearsed the sequence in his mind, picturing every aspect of his actions: two rapid shots, the gun recalibrating automatically, not giving enough time for the second victim to react. He calmed his breathing, cleared his mind, and focused. The gun was a part of him, an extension of his limbs and senses, his actions smooth and efficient.

He acquired the designated target first – if either of them were likely to beat the odds by reacting in the split second between the shots it would be her. He fired, moving immediately on to the secondary target. The gun was dampened so that it was almost silent, a mere whisper, and there was little recoil, which enabled him to get both shots away in well under a second.

The bullets tore through brick and mortar without discernibly slowing.

Two hits. Both targets fell, the man tumbling from his chair to lie on the floor, the woman collapsing over the table. He knew immediately that everything had gone to plan, but sent in a spyfly just to be sure.

The tiny drone sped across to the building, gaining access via the hole made by one of the bullets. There the fly hovered, surveying the scene and relaying images and telemetry back to him. He focused on the woman, his target, visuals confirming her identity, but his assessment went beyond that, taking in the whole scene. Something niggled. He lingered, having the fly scan every aspect again, trying to dampen that small sense of disquiet. Everything appeared to be as it should: two bodies, still warm from residual heat – not yet having had a chance to cool by any noticeable degree. Neither heart was beating, no indication of ongoing metabolic processes. They were dead. As they had to be.

So what was it about the scene that bothered him?

He kept the spyfly in position for a few seconds longer, searching for anything out of place, but if there was an anomaly he failed to spot it.

Perhaps it was merely that this had all been so straightforward. You would think that killing an Angel would be tricky, that such a momentous achievement should be marked by ceremony or at least a degree of difficulty, but this had been a quick, clean kill; unremarkable in every regard.

Aware that time was passing and lacking anything tangible to justify his concerns, the assassin dismissed the vague sense of unease and recalled the fly.

Now it was just a matter of disguise, of passing the incident off as something mundane and every day, a tragic accident.

Hacking the building's domestic system proved simplicity itself. In many ways this was the phase of the operation that carried the greatest risk, the aspect most liable to leave a footprint, so he was careful. An investigator would have to be extremely suspicious and highly skilled to gain any hint that the farmhouse's routine had been compromised.

Natural gas: a primitive form of energy for a primitive setting, and so volatile. He instructed the four rings on the cooker to open. While waiting for the fumes to gather, he dismantled the gun, placing each component into the appropriate couching and slipping the valise back into his pack. Once that was done, he waited a while longer. Finally, judging the time to be right, he sent the signal for the two bullets to detonate – there would be no tell-tale slugs left behind to give him away. The explosion, triggered by the bullets' sparking, was as satisfying as expected. The windows went first, blowing out in a blast of fire and glass and a bass thrum of detonation.

He didn't linger to watch the roof collapse or the walls crumble, instead shouldering his pack and strolling back towards the village.

Every care had been taken, from the scheduling – the operation had been carefully timed to coincide with a blind spot in satellite coverage for this area – to the clean-up: the lining of the valise containing the gun's component parts would even now be treating those parts with a chemical wash designed to remove all trace of his DNA while leaving the weapon perfectly serviceable. He wasn't about to compromise such meticulous planning now.

As instructed, he deposited the valise in a storage locker at the bus station, paid for in advance by a shell company. The binoculars could always be passed off as innocent, the spyfly hidden if need be, but not the gun. He neither knew nor cared what the weapon's fate might be from here. Exiting the terminal building, he peeled off the transparent polymer 'skin' that had coated his hands and provided him with false prints in the unlikely event that anyone might trace the valise. Even before he dropped the residue into a disposal chute it had started to break down into gelatinous ooze.

There was still an hour to kill before his bus left – the delay unavoidable as this was the only bus scheduled that day which would take him in the direction of the capital. The return trip should prove a little shorter than his outward journey due to the vagaries of transport timetabling, but it would still account for more than a day.

A private vehicle – an *unfamiliar* vehicle – was certain to have been noted and remembered by the locals, so that had never been an option. There must be nothing to mark him out, nothing to draw attention; he was simply a tourist who had ridden to the end of the bus route on a whim.

He had spotted a café earlier – two white-painted metal tables with a cluster of attendant chairs standing outside an open door. It seemed as good a place as any to wait, and now that the job was over he could justify the luxury of a beer. He chose to make the call then, as he walked back to the café, secure in the anonymity that inhabited spaces afforded, knowing that his call would be just one among many should anyone bother to check for digital signatures, rather than standing in damning isolation if made in the environs of the farmhouse at around the time of the tragic fire.

"This is Price," he said into the silence at the other end. "Just checking in to say that all is well. It's as restful here as anticipated, and I should be back, fully recharged, in time for the meeting."

Having ended the call he paused, troubled by the sense that he was still missing something – the same unease that had bothered him immediately following the shooting. He replayed things in his mind one more time, reviewing the scene the spyfly had shown him. Perhaps his subconscious had been working on the problem, because this time he had it, he knew the source of his disquiet.

The interior of the kitchen had been dingy despite the brightness of the day, the windows comparatively small and shaded; *so what had caused the strong, distinct shadows cast by the two bodies?*

Attempting to remain as casual as possible, he stretched, flexing his right arm in a specific way, feeling the weapon grafted to the radius shift in response. Designed to fool any scan, to be indistinguishable from the bone itself, the polymer blade housed there slid forward, emerging from a narrow slit on the inside of his wrist.

For all his skill something must have given him away, because part of the shadow on the wall next to him, the part that had no right being there, moved, detaching itself from the white brickwork and lunging towards him. As it came, the shadow gained substance and definition; it developed a face. The face of his target, of the woman he had just shot, the woman he had just *killed.*

He reacted instantly but she was fast, faster than he would have credited. She was on him before he could fully grasp his own blade and offer a defence. Pain exploded in his right arm as she cut him, a slash that severed tendons and sent the polymer blade spinning away from numbed fingers and clattering to the ground. Pain blossomed in his left forearm too, which he had raised instinctively to ward off the attack. Two knives; and she knew how to use them.

He sprang backwards, trying to put distance between him and his attacker, to gain a precious second to think, but she was relentless and gave him no quarter, following his move and closing immediately.

"Murder us in our own home would you? You cowardly bastard!"

She struck again before he could gather himself, her blade slipping past his attempt to block and plunging into his stomach. The pain was excruciating. He gagged, spitting up blood. His legs buckled as he folded in on himself, the wound becoming his centre, his focus. He sat down heavily, looking up at her, squinting against the sun as she loomed above him, trying to make sense of what was happening.

"Didn't you stop to wonder why they call me Shadow?" she said. "Or didn't they bother telling you that?"

It was becoming increasingly difficult to concentrate. *Who sent you, who are you working for?* he thought he heard, but her voice was fading. Everything faded, even the pain, until nothing remained.

Jen stood panting over the body, rage still coursing through her, spurring her on to kick him, to cut him again, both acts pointless but that didn't matter. Then reason won out. She stared down for a split second longer before crouching to clean her blades on his clothing and then search him. ID that matched the face but was almost certainly false, a slim perminal – the same one she had watched him make a call on... She hesitated over that. There was every chance it might contain all manner of information if she could access it. His reservation on the local bus – assuming that was how he'd intended to leave – perhaps the identity of his employer or at least a clue as to who had sent him... Tempting, but the device would be too easy to trace; the risk outweighed the potential gain, so the perminal went back into his pocket. She held on to the binoculars from his backpack – they were an expensive and potentially useful toy, but ground the spyfly beneath her heel, crushing it: too many painful associations.

Her search was professional and swift, completed in less than a minute, and she strode away from the corpse without being seen. There was nowhere to hide the body and she didn't bother trying. One more scandal to add to the tragic events at the farmhouse – fuelling the local gossip circuit for weeks, no doubt. She was officially dead, unfortunate victim of the explosion. So long as she could escape the village unnoticed, no one would make the connection.

People were abroad now, the community stirring, but all attention was focused in the opposite direction, where a plume of smoke rose lazily into the air. She slipped past unnoticed.

Dark glasses, hair tied back and hidden under a hat, this hardly constituted a disguise but it was a start. She reclaimed the bike from where she had left it and rode out of the village. Powerful, light, and durable, the bike's electric motor took her towards the distant capital. As she went, her thoughts turned to Robin, who should be riding an identical machine in the opposite direction at that very moment. For a brief while she allowed herself to feel guilt and regret, the first for what she had put him through, what he had been forced to endure simply by being close to her, and the second for the fact that she might never see him again; but then she shut that part of her life away, aware that she couldn't afford to indulge in self-pity. Robin had gone into their marriage with his eyes open. She made sure he knew all about her past before she would commit, and they had prepared for this sort of contingency from the off, while hoping they would never to have to act on those plans – simulacra convincing enough to play dead and with enough organic components to fool cursory forensic investigation if necessary, sophisticated surveillance to alert them to anyone out the ordinary leaving the village in the direction of their home, and the bikes, always charged, always ready.

It was vital to her that Robin should be safe, and right now the safest place was as far away from her as possible. If – *when* – she came back, she'd know how to find him.

Jen rode through the afternoon without stopping. Taking a far more direct route than the bus would have followed as it provided a service to outlying villages, she arrived at Sharford and its train station just before sunset. As hoped, she was in time to catch the overnight express to Opal, and booked a seat using an account that had never been touched before in a name she had never wanted to need. The train would deliver her to Opal early the following morning. She had no idea who was hunting her, or the level of resources they had committed to the field, but she would find out. Was the assassin working alone or had he been part of a team? Best guess was that he was a solo operative reporting to someone in the capital. For a brief while the assassin's natural furtiveness would work in her favour. The bike would put her ahead of the dead man's schedule, which ought to give her enough time in the city to discover what was going on before anyone missed him.

Of course, her best guess could be wrong.

As the train made light work of the distance, slicing through the night as quickly as any vehicle could without taking to the air, Jen did her best to relax and let the world slip past in the anonymity of darkness. She had almost forgotten what it was like to live this way, and didn't relish being reminded that she ever had. She tried to sleep, but succeeded only fitfully. There were too many things to consider, too many unknowns.

About the only thing she did feel confident of was her destination. On this entire planet just one person other than Robin knew who she was: Sketch. The only way anyone could have found her was through him. Sketch had some explaining to do.

Two

Jen paused to get her bearings, ignoring the tide of commuters that flowed around her without once touching or bumping, as if she existed within her own bubble, warded by some powerful protective force. Gathered from the suburbs and beyond, these disparate people were united in their desire to put distance between themselves and the sleekly engineered tube that had carried them at high speed into the very heart of the capital. Jen was wary of standing out and drawing any unwelcome attention, so she only paused for a second before moving on, going with the flow, drawing the crowds around her and holding them close.

She didn't like Opal.

The decision to name the world's major cities after various gemstones presumably struck someone as a good idea at the time – perhaps the original settlers were sponsored by a cartel of jewellers or something, she'd never been bothered enough to find out – but to Jen it seemed an overly twee affectation. Certainly the city's name in no way matched her experience of the place. Her memories of the city contained nothing gleaming or beautiful, in fact, quite the opposite. Opal epitomized everything Jen despised and had turned her back on. Thankfully, coming back here didn't feel as strange as she had feared it might. She still felt like an outsider, but the air of impatience, the sense that everyone had somewhere important to be, had become a source of wry amusement now that she could step back and view it from a slight remove. She couldn't deny, though, that returning here stirred something in her blood, as if a long dormant part of her relished this re-acquaintance with the bustle of competing priorities that urban living entailed.

After so many years of living at a different tempo, she found the sheer volume of people a little bewildering, but that was only to be expected and she felt confident she would soon adjust. Less predictable was the degree to which that prospect saddened her. She couldn't shake the conviction that by adapting so readily she risked losing a part of herself that might never be reclaimed.

The sultry sense of heat seemed less pervasive here; the air a little cooler. Perhaps it was – the train had brought her a fair way north and closer to the coast – or perhaps the gauntlet of towering buildings somehow leached warmth from the sun's rays, robbing them of potency before they could reach street level. That seemed counterintuitive, the inverse of what she would expect, but the imagery appealed to her.

Jen left the station on foot, shades on, head down, hair tucked snuggly into her hat, careful not to glance up at where the cameras lurked. The datafield of her specs flagged the waiting ranks of fully automated bubble cabs. She ignored the advice, caution prompting her to be circumspect – she would rather overestimate her enemy's capabilities than underestimate them, and the station was the first place anyone would think to search for her, the taxi ranks an obvious starting point. Every journey taken, every destination given, would be logged: a record to damn the unwary. Sketch's place was far enough away that she would have to resort to a cab at some point, but not from here.

Instead, she walked ten minutes in the wrong direction, away from Sketch's. Only then did she set the perminal in her glasses to hail. A cab peeled away from the traffic a moment later to stop at the curb beside her. This one had a driver, but he paid scant attention to his fare while she was perfunctory in turn, giving an address five minutes beyond her actual goal. None of this would make tracing her impossible, but it should at least help muddy the waters. She set the windows to opaque, keen to blank out as best she could this city that had been forced upon her again. Her first stay had not been a happy one. Psychologically exhausted, no longer a Dark Angel, cut off from everyone she knew, the teeming streets of Opal had promised obscurity but proved instead to be a harsh and intimidating place. In the six months she lingered here the city had never felt like home, merely a place to stop off at while waiting for the next phase of her life to begin. Robin offered a way out, an escape to a rural idyll which she jumped at. Since leaving, she had never once felt the inclination to return.

As soon as the cab stopped and the fare had been transferred, Jen slipped out with a curt 'thank you'. Here she paused, taking in her surroundings. Time's passage had robbed her memories of substance. She *thought* she recognised this place, this corner, but couldn't be sure.

Her glasses provided the certainty that recollection lacked, a display at the left margin of vision informing her that the store she was currently gazing at had first opened three years ago, listing the names of the business' owners and the employees currently registered. Had she wished, it could then have gone on to detail what had stood here prior to the current shop, but she wasn't that bothered.

She walked forward and the glasses' focus shifted, identifying the intersection in front of her and enabling her to get her bearings.

It would have been easy enough to confirm that Sketch hadn't changed address by checking the local directory, but Jen didn't want to risk triggering any alerts that might lie in wait against just such an inquiry. Besides, it was hard to imagine Sketch moving anywhere; his place was too established, too much *him*: a labyrinthine geek's lair, a private kingdom filled with a jumble of equipment and dismantled components, half of which she suspected even he didn't know the purpose of. In the unlikely event she found him gone, she would reassess and start tracking him down from there.

She took an indirect route, approaching the apartment block from the rear and choosing the moment to slip into shadow with care: an alleyway, unoccupied, not covered by any apparent cameras and with no windows overlooking.

Perception shifted. The world became duller, as if a cloud had crossed the sun. Sound took on a flat, muffled quality, losing directional definition in the process, while all sense of smell deserted her. A trade off: by crossing into shadow she took a step away from the world and distanced herself from reality.

On first becoming the Dark Angel known as Shadow, Jen's nights had been troubled by a recurring nightmare, one in which she was forever trapped in this twilight existence, unable to cross back. She screamed for help but no one could hear, and reached out to touch people only for them to walk on past, oblivious to her presence. The dream faded with time, as she grew accustomed to the Elder-borne abilities, and had rarely troubled her since, but it did now, returning with a vividness that shocked her. Once more Jen felt the horror of exile, of being cut off from all she knew and doomed to observe the world without ever interacting, without even being noticed.

She hesitated, calming herself, resisting the urge to flicker back into the physical world just to prove that she could, and refusing to consider the flashback a bad omen.

She determined her own fortune, good or bad, omens be damned.

Hell, I'm out of practice at this sort of thing.

Nerves once more under control, Jen moved forward, instinctively choosing a path that took her from shadow to shadow, rarely exposing her shade-self to clear and brightly lit spaces. In this fashion she reached the battered basement door that gave entrance to Sketch's world, slipping inside via the paper-thin crack between door and jamb.

Within, things were pretty much as she anticipated, though if anything even more cluttered than memory recalled. The air was thick and still, the heat oppressive. A single naked lightbulb dangled old school from the ceiling close to the door. It was unlit. A crude alarm, triggered, she knew, by the door's opening. A wan glow emanated from somewhere towards the centre of the spacious room, its source and nature hidden thanks to the clutter of gadgetry and equipment that lay in between. Directly in front of her rested the disembowelled torso of a PoD, a Police Drone, its body tilted at an angle, empty eyes staring at the door, and the drone was just one among many. Piled haphazardly on tables, workbenches, or simply on the floor, set-aside oddments of technology formed a protective maze that required visitors to make their tedious way back and forth across the room in order to reach the centre. Most visitors, at any rate.

The entire space formed a labyrinth of shadows, which Jen crossed in a matter of seconds, merging with the existing darkness to flow smoothly over the mounds and across the irregular corridors, until she reached the hub, where Sketch sat before a bank of screens. He occupied a recycled chair that had been pimped excessively: an assortment of controls festooned the arms, motorised wheels supported the base, and the customised cushions that formed the seat would, Jen knew from past experience, make it the match of any upholstering anywhere in the city.

"This is where I work, so I might as well be comfortable," as Sketch had once told her.

The chair had been updated since her last visit, but the man sitting within its embrace looked no different. The antithesis of expectation, Sketch brought to mind a financier, a high-powered broker, rather than one of the world's foremost techno-geeks. With his crisp on-message suit, neat haircut and stubble-free chin, here surely sat an individual more accustomed to a penthouse office that afforded a view across half the city than a dingy basement in the bowels of a tenement block.

"It's all about image," he had explained. "I'm a professional, so you gotta look the part."

Bullshit. Much of his work was anonymous and the only contact Sketch had with many of his clients was online, where he could make himself look however the hell he wanted to look. Which made the extreme care he took with his appearance… eccentric; which was fine with Jen.

She stepped from the shadows directly in front of him, between his chair and the bank of screens he was facing.

"What the...?"

Sketch jerked backwards, the servos in the chair exaggerating the movement and sending him careering across the floor towards the bank of equipment behind. He regained control in the nick of time, narrowly avoiding collision.

"For fuck's sake, Jen, can't you just use the door like any normal person? No, cut that – of course you can't."

While he spoke, the fingers of his left hand danced over the control studs built into the arm of his chair. She hesitated, holding back the questions, the accusations that had brought her here, waiting to see what he was up to. All the while she drew the shadows close, ready to flee into their embrace if need be.

Words formed in the air before her, the sort of tightly focused projection designed to be invisible to any hidden observers or prying cameras, discernible only to someone who shared her exact line of sight:

TRAP!!
SAFLIK

There was only one way to read that: Sketch's lair was compromised and under surveillance. By walking in here she had effectively presented herself to the very people she had worked so hard to avoid. That had always been a risk but one she felt compelled to take – she needed answers desperately. Realisation of her error was followed by a question: *what the hell is a Saflik?* Jen made sure none of this showed on her face and concentrated on keeping her expression animated in the right way. "What have you done, Sketch?" Fury: that didn't require any acting. "Someone's found me, tried to *kill* me, and the only way they could have done that is through you!"

The fact that he had devised a means of warning her despite whatever pressure these people had exerted came as a relief – he *wasn't* working against her, at least not willingly – but the fact he hadn't managed to tip her off ahead of the failed assassination attempt was a sobering one. To have compromised Sketch so thoroughly and restricted him so effectively… How much time did she have? The brevity and urgency of those two capitalised words suggested not much. Surely her enemies were nearby.

"What, and you think *I* had something to do with it?"

Sketch was doing his best but he was no actor. Even without the message she would have known that he was hiding something, that he was panicking. His fingers continued to slicker, and a new word appeared in the air before her:

RUN!!

For a moment she hesitated: flight or fight? The destruction of her home, of her *life*, had left her seething, itching to get her hands on those responsible. One assassin acting to orders hardly assuaged her need for retribution, but did either vengeance or her need for information outweigh the threat that clearly had Sketch so spooked? In the end his fear unnerved her. She could sense the noose tightening, knew she had to cut this short and get out of here, preferably without giving away his complicity. Sketch was the closest thing she had to an ally, her only hope of finding out what the hell was going on here.

"Well if not you, then who, Sketch? Who have you told about me?

"No one, I swear." His eyes widened, urging her to follow his advice and *Run*.

"Bullshit! I've got to keep on the move for now, stay one step ahead of the hunters, so I won't hang around." Gods, this sounded lame even to her, but it was the best she could come up with. "Don't think for a moment this is over, though. I *will* come back, and I'll be expecting a name when I do. You'd better not let me down, Sketch – you of all people know what I'm capable of."

With that, Jen stepped into shadow. Whether this little

exchange would be enough to fool any eavesdroppers was debatable, but she couldn't afford to waste any more time worrying about that. The panic in Sketch's eyes had been genuine. His basement lair had become a trap, one that only had a single way in or out; it was confining and suddenly not so spacious, shrinking by the second. She had to get out…

She almost made it too. But haste made her careless. Mounting anxiety drove her to take the quickest route, flowing with the shadows directly towards the door.

With escape just a few precious metres away, the door burst open. Daylight flooded in and the hanging bulb flared to life – a mini-sunburst intended to befuddle any interlopers. Two new light sources, banishing shadows, casting new ones and reconfiguring those that remained: she was caught in their glare and in the open, exposed.

"There she is!" A man's voice.

The two figures who entered knew exactly what they were doing and what to look for. Unfazed by the light trap, one of them had spotted her immediately. Even though she knew she was safe, confident that they couldn't touch her in this form, she instinctively sought to hide, slipping sideways to merge within a bank of shadow to her right. The second figure raised a weapon and tracked her movement, which was ridiculous – she was beyond their reach. Even so, she didn't like having guns pointed at her, so checked her progress at the very edge of the cloaking darkness while the gun's muzzle kept going… And then fired.

An energy weapon. It discharged into the heart of the gloom, striking the spot where Jen would have been had she continued on the same course. And she *felt* it.

That was impossible. Nothing could touch her while she was in shadow, yet somehow this weapon did. Only the backwash reached her, licking out to numb her right shoulder, and suddenly she shared Sketch's fear rather than merely its vicarious echo. Who *were* these people?

"Did you get her?"

"Dunno."

Hiding wasn't enough, not when they could reach into the shadows and hurt her, so Jen switched tactics, charging at her enemy, using the shadows as cover and only emerging where they ended, by which time she was almost upon the gunman who had fired at her. She stepped into the physical world at the last moment, leading with her good arm, sinking her fist into his solar plexus and crunching her numbed right shoulder into his chin.

Not the most elegant of attacks, but effective nonetheless. The man stumbled backwards, towards the other attacker, and then crashed to the floor. He must have dropped the gun because she felt two hands grappling for her, but too late. Jen rolled over him, utilising what remained of her momentum, curling into as tight a ball as she could while praying that her leaden arm wouldn't hamper her. The other man was armed too – she'd glimpsed him trying to bring some sort of handgun to bear.

They had sent just two and both men: typical. Physically stronger, perhaps, but men carried their vulnerability on the outside. Jen ended the roll immediately in front of her opponent, on her feet but still crouching, and close enough to be within his reach, effectively nullifying the advantage his gun gave him. He tried to club her with it, more an instinctive reaction than a trained defensive move, but she was quicker. By the time his half-hearted effort clipped her deadened shoulder she had already punched him in the balls.

He let out a grunt of pain and surprise and started to crumple in on himself, reaching protectively for his genitals.

Jen followed up with a jab to his conveniently protruding chin and then ran, without waiting around to see which of the two recovered first. She was past them and out the door in an instant, diving for the protection afforded by daylight's strong shadows.

Jen ran hard and fast. She could move far more swiftly in shadow than in physical form and concentrated on putting distance between herself and Sketch's before emerging and hailing a cab –

an automated one this time, which at least spared her the need to interact with a driver.

"The spaceport," she instructed.

Feeling had begun to return to her right shoulder and arm, which once again felt part of her.

The short journey gave her mind the opportunity to go places she would have preferred it didn't: Robin. She missed him, the constant ache of his absence a physical pain that refused to be ignored. If she could just know that he was safe… but contacting him wasn't an option – it would be too risky – so she put a lid on those anxieties once more and focused on her own situation.

Of course she wanted answers, of course she wanted to know who was hunting her, but survival came top of the list. These people knew who she was, knew her capabilities and had prepared for them. With Robin on the run and Sketch compromised, Jen was short of friends. Her enemies were capable, determined, and clearly not without resources. She had no choice but to run.

Once in the clear, off world and in the wind, then she could start to plan, to piece together what had happened and determine her next move. One word: Saflik. That would be her starting point. From the clue that Sketch had provided her with she would identify her enemies and turn the tables, making them regret ever targeting her.

All too soon the cab approached its destination. Jen steeled herself, deliberately slowing her breathing. Were her enemies here already? Were they waiting for her, or by acting promptly had she stolen a march? Presumably they would try to cover every obvious escape route – spaceport, airport, bus terminus and the major rail stations, but she was counting on them not having the manpower to do so effectively, not immediately at any rate. There were too many options, and her fleeing the city was by no means a given; she might choose to go into hiding, seek out old friends and wait a few days before trying Sketch again. The hunters had only just learned she was still alive, which must have caught them flat-footed – the pair she had encountered at Sketch's were most likely part of a routine watch kept on his place rather than an indication that they were expecting her at that particular time. It was going to take them a while to mobilise whatever resources they could call on. By then, she would be gone. At least that was the plan.

The port was as busy as ever. Hair once more concealed beneath her cap and head down, Jen sought to lose herself among the multitude, moving with the stream of people being processed for departure. Bright v-shaped arrowheads strobed along the floor and walls to guide the way.

This wasn't the most sophisticated of spaceports. The lighting was too bright, the floors too hard, and moulded plastic seating predominated in areas where a little padding would have made travel so much more comfortable. Parcels of travellers were herded from one area to another in a process that struck her as unnecessarily convoluted, and the whole system had the feel of a work in progress, as if the facility were in the midst of an expansion programme and the current arrangements were only temporary – everything would be smoother once it was all finished... Except that to Jen's knowledge the port had always been like this and very little seemed to have changed since she first passed through here a little over a decade ago.

There was no such thing as a quick departure, not from here. 'VIP Status' cut a few corners if you could afford it, which Jen's newly adopted identity could, but any fast tracking was purely relative.

She booked a seat on the first available flight, not caring where she was bound for, just so long as it was off world.

It was only when she went for a comfort break that she realised she was being followed.

In theory, the automated check in should have been a breeze, the flow of people regular, but somebody's registration was evidently not in order – a middle-aged couple whose neutral clothing gave no clue as to whether they were going on holiday or on business. He seemed willing to stand aside as the gate requested and await assistance but, to his obvious embarrassment, his companion refused, insisting that she was going nowhere until the matter was sorted. Jen left the queue that had started to form as a result, in part because her bladder suggested now would be a good time to do so and in part to escape the man with a fractious child immediately in front of her. Not the kid's fault – Jen was impatient herself – but she was also sufficiently on edge that the prospect of a protracted period in close proximity to a child's irritated complaint didn't appeal.

It could have been a coincidence, the man peeling away from the queue behind her and heading in the same direction at the same time, but she wasn't about to take any chances. She stopped abruptly halfway to the comfort booths, turned to the left, and headed across to a drinks dispenser. As she knocked back a flimsy of ice-cold water, Jen let her gaze wander, noting that the man hadn't completed his walk either, but had paused to gaze at a slender device that she presumed was his perminal, as if reading a new message.

Drink completed, Jen dropped the flimsy into a recycling chute and headed back towards the booths. The man hadn't once looked at her but she felt his scrutiny all the way across the floor. She wasn't looking directly at him either, yet he was all that she could see.

They passed little more than an arm's reach apart. She forced her body to relax, not to tense as if anticipating a lunge, not to show anxiety now that he was behind her and out of even peripheral eyesight.

She continued without incident, stepping through the modesty screen that walled off the entrance to the booths – a cultural affectation that might have been amusing under different circumstances – but hesitated at the first green door. Beside it, another door opened and a young woman in chequered suit stepped out to brush past her with a polite smile. The door slid silently shut again, its surface switching from pale pink to green to indicate that it was now vacant. In leaving, the young woman passed the man from the queue as he emerged through the screen. His gaze met Jen's for the first time and she saw the flicker of recognition there. That sealed it. The pretence was over.

She stepped forward, light on her feet, ready to engage, when two other figures crowded in behind the man, neither showing any interest in the comfort booths. One opponent she would have been happy to face but three... not so much.

She didn't have a choice, of course. She prepared to fight. She prepared to scream, though this would be held back as a last resort, both because she doubted anyone could reach her in time and because she was travelling under a false name and didn't need the attention, assuming she somehow survived this. Jen *had* to believe that she would.

A figure appeared beside the three men, causing them to pause – a traveller in need of a booth.

Jen seized the opportunity afforded by the distraction, attacking the man nearest her. If this group were carrying the weapons that could reach into shadow to hurt her, they had yet to draw them, so she stepped across, instantly emerging right on top of her target. A punch to the kidney followed by a chop to the neck and he was down. Without pausing she took on the second opponent, swivelling to aim a kick at his knee. She missed, narrowly, connecting instead with his thigh a fraction above the kneecap. He was quick, dancing back before she could follow up. The injured leg hampered him but not enough.

She now faced the third assailant, the man who had followed her from the queue. He still had his perminal out. He held it level, pointing directly towards her. There was nothing visible, no sizzle of energy or beam of light to bridge the space between her and the device, but she *felt* something. Not pain, not an injury – it didn't feel as if she'd been shot – this was more akin to a caress, a tingling that coursed through her body, unnerving rather than unpleasant. Instinctively she went to step across into shadow. She failed.

Panic gripped her. Unable to comprehend what was happening, she felt as if the floor had just dropped away from under her. She tried to shift again and again, with no better result.

"Not so smug now, eh, bitch?" said the man whose leg she had kicked. She recognised him now as one of the gunmen from Sketch's.

How had they found her so quickly? Had the backwash from their energy weapon somehow tagged her, enabling them to follow? And he was right, damn him. Having her ability torn away like this was as bad as losing an arm. She felt diminished, unbalanced, and *vulnerable*. Would the effect be permanent or just temporary? That tingling, it had reminded her of pins and needles, perhaps her abilities would gradually come back like the return of circulation to a numbed limb – as her right arm had recovered earlier.

Jen struggled to steady herself, to adjust to the loss of her shadow self. Cornered, her heart racing, fuelled by adrenaline and fear, knowing that she had never faced a greater threat, she backed away, looking desperately for a way out as the three men converged.

The gun that could hurt her even in shadow form, this perminal app that so effectively suppressed her abilities: these people knew her to an extent that nobody should. With that thought, memories of the assassination attempt returned, images of her home gutted by fire. These men weren't here to capture her. Why risk bundling a captive through a crowded terminal building with its security systems and personnel? Far simpler to melt away into the crowd, leaving her body to cool on the floor where it had fallen. They had come to kill her.

They rushed her. She caught a glimpse of a polymer blade and twisted frantically out of the way, feeling a sting of pain as the knife cut a bloody groove across her bicep rather than plunging into anywhere more vital. The knifeman crashed into her, his heavier frame threatening to pin her against the wall. She sidestepped before he could adjust his grip, throwing herself to the ground as the blade flashed towards her once more, to glance off a green door just above her head.

Where is the other one? Jen had forgotten all about him, her attention focussed on the knifeman. Then she saw him, lying awkwardly on the floor, unconscious at the very least.

She was still processing the implications of that when a fist connected with the side of the knifeman's skull. He clattered against the wall and then collapsed, felled by a single blow.

Jen stared up at her rescuer, squinting against the brightness of the ceiling lights, wary of accepting apparent succour at face value. What fresh threat did this newcomer represent? Had her body shaken off the effects of the repressor yet? Could she slip into shadow? She gathered herself, ready to make the attempt…

"Hi, Jen," said a woman's voice she almost remembered. "Long time no see." A hand reached out to help her up.

She looked more closely at her rescuer and recognition dawned. *"Leesa?"*

THREE

Drake was having trouble concentrating. No, that was too convenient an excuse. A more honest appraisal would be that he was struggling to feel motivated. He had a report to file but continued to procrastinate, failing to muster any enthusiasm for the task. In truth, he'd found it difficult to muster enthusiasm for the mission the report pertained to, so the report stood no chance.

The mission had been a bust. There never had been an Elder cache to discover, just a scam to fleece First Solar of funds. If not for his actions they would almost certainly have succeeded. As it was, he had brought their ship back to New Sparta, which meant the bank could enforce their security and would not be out of pocket. No black mark on his copybook then, in fact the opposite, as he had turned a likely loss into a small gain. Nor would Reese's judgement be called into question, since the case had come to him via Senior Advisor Mawson, one of Reese's colleagues. Drake didn't envy him the investigation that was bound to follow.

The fact this was a scam from outset may have gone some way to explaining why he failed to settle in and had never connected with any of the crew, but he knew his heart hadn't been in it even before his suspicions were aroused.

Something had changed. *Everything* had changed.

It wasn't just Leesa. Seeing her again had undoubtedly contributed to the problem and was the catalyst that had triggered his unease, but the cause went deeper than that and was more fundamental. Corbin Thadeus Drake, resident of New Sparta and respected representative of First Solar Bank, was an identity he had established over the course of more than a decade, and in that time he had grown into the role, reaching the point where it felt comfortable and natural, where it fitted him.

Not any more.

Since he'd returned from the cache hunt with Pelquin and his crew, the Drake persona had begun to feel taut and inhibiting. At the same time it had acquired a fragile quality, as if it were paper-thin; the itching of dried skin that a reptile might suffer in the days leading up to a moult, when yesterday's husk was discarded in favour of a bright and newer incarnation. Outwardly he continued to portray the detached, unflappable, dedicated-to-the-job professional he had always been, but inwardly he seethed with impatience and indecision. His carefully constructed identity was beginning to resemble nothing more than a dead man walking.

Is this nasal gazing really helping? asked a familiar voice in his head.

"What?" Drake said out loud.

Nasal gazing, Mudball repeated. *That's what you call it, right: morose introspection laced with self-doubt and a bit of fretting on the side?*

Navel gazing, not nasal, Pelquin corrected, this time choosing to address the alien symbiont by thought. Mudball had been his constant companion since saving him from a particularly resourceful cache guardian some years back, the telepathic link they shared as natural to him now as breathing. *And no, I don't suppose it is especially healthy, not in this instance at any rate. However, there are times when we humans find the practice unavoidable.*

It certainly seems to be for you. Are all humans this broody or did I just happen to pick a sour one?

Keep going with the insults and I'll seal you away in your pouch, just to prove how sour I can be. The alien currently occupied its customary position perched on his shoulder, for all the world a cute and fluffy bright green genpet.

Touchy, too.

Drake reached up, as if to push the furry creature back into the sealable pouch at the top of his back.

All right, all right, I'll behave. Think about it, though, what would you

do if you did *walk away? And that's what you're considering, isn't it –
walking away?*

That was the problem right there. What *could* he do? Drake
had been his creation, certainly, but he'd had help. Without the
collusion of Terry Reese – his boss at First Solar – who had run
interference and helped him to fabricate a convincing legend, a
'ghost' personal history, he could never have integrated so
smoothly into society, and he was under no illusion that another
Terry Reese waited anywhere around the corner. So where would
that leave him if he did choose to abandon this life? The prospect
of starting over again wasn't one he relished.

Take away Drake, and who was he?

No, he responded, *I'm not about to walk away; not just yet, at any
rate.*

Good, because Terry Reese has a new case for you.

"Oh?" This was the first he'd heard of it.

At that precise moment there came a gentle chime and a voice
spoke from the air: "Mr Drake, would you please report at once
to Senior Advisor Reese's office."

"On my way," Drake responded.

Told you so.

It was unusual for Reese to summon him for a face-to-face when
assigning a new case. Not unheard of, but rare enough to pique
his curiosity.

"It's not a cache hunt this time around, at least not in the
usual sense," Reese told him.

Drake sat opposite his boss. The room's sparse furniture – in
this instance Reese's chair and one for the visitor (more could be
summoned if required) – was arranged in a deliberately casual
fashion, which was how Reese preferred it. The chairs faced each
other but at a slight angle to avoid any suggestion of
confrontation. Behind her, an expanse of floor-to-ceiling window
offered an enviable view over the city of New Sparta, the slight
tint caused by the dampener glass – guaranteed to prevent both

visual and aural snooping – barely noticeable.

First Solar's HQ might not have been the tallest building in town but it numbered among them and, rather than spoiling the panorama, the thrusting forms of those others that matched or surpassed it in stature only enhanced the aspect in Drake's opinion. After all, it was the city's trademark cloud scrapers reaching towards the heavens that made New Sparta's skyline such a spectacle. Some of these buildings were architectural marvels of tapering elegance and tinted glass, while others displayed a flamboyancy of style that suggested the designers' imaginations had been given free rein; many of the buildings would undoubtedly have seemed gaudy in a lesser setting, but here in New Sparta they were perfectly at home.

When construction had begun on First Solar's flagship edifice, it was set to be the single tallest structure in the city. By the time it neared completion, two others were already under way that would outreach it. Drake never had understood the competitive nature of such things. High was high, and beyond a certain point a spectacular view lost some of its impact as things on the ground lost definition. The habit of installing windows with adjustable magnification supported his opinion.

Reese's office, on the 45th floor, was quite high enough by his reckoning. More than one hidden treasure stood revealed from this lofty vantage point. He knew from previous visits, for example, that a little below and slightly to their left was a building whose roof had been turned into a compact tropical paradise, complete with waterfall, lagoon, trees and shrubbery, and even some arboreal fauna, while to the right an elaborate rooftop housed a cunningly crafted assault course; an executives' playground given physical form rather than the more common virtual variety. Management played at team building and outmanoeuvring the opposition while the city's populace passed through the streets below, oblivious. The Maitland Building, directly opposite, included a hangar partially sunken into its roof and disguised amongst elaborate sculpting. The hangar housed, or so rumour had it, a super-fast shuttle that didn't feature anywhere among the corporation's listed assets. A handy means of escape for the top execs should the firm's financial house of cards ever come crashing down.

"In fact, it's something a little more straightforward for once," Reese continued, drawing his attention back to where it should have been all along. "This time we *know* the cache is there, its existence is well documented and has been independently verified. You might say that the problems here are as much political as logistical."

There had to be more to this than met the eye. What was Reese up to? What wasn't she telling him? "Why me?" he asked. False modesty aside, Drake knew himself to be the First Solar's most accomplished field agent, having overseen more successful cache hunts than any other. But this didn't sound like his area of expertise at all.

Reese smiled, evidently appreciating his directness. "Because the customer has specifically requested you."

Drake froze, and had to remember to breathe again, hoping that Reese wouldn't spot his reaction but knowing she would. Several alarming possibilities flashed through his mind before he settled on the most obvious and was able to relax. "Someone I've worked with before then."

"Oh no, at least not since you joined us at First Solar."

So much for relaxing. "Oh?"

Her gaze skewered him. "He claims to be an old friend of yours, from before you came to work for us."

The face that then materialised in the air between them did nothing to reassure Drake. He knew his heart rate had increased, his breathing becoming shallower and more rapid; knew too that Reese would note both reactions and interpret them correctly, not that she gave any indaction that she had as she continued speaking.

"He calls himself Martin Payne," she said, "though we can find no record of his existence beyond nine standard years ago, so it seems doubtful this was his original name."

It certainly wasn't the one Drake had known him by, but he nodded. "I remember him." Something didn't look right. "Is this a recent image?"

"Yes, why?"

"He doesn't look a day older."

Was that it, was that what bothered him? He studied the image closely. Same angular features and dark eyes made to seem all the darker by the black close-cropped hair that framed the face. How many years had it been: twelve, thirteen?

"Some people have lucky genes…" Reese said,

"…while others have deep pockets," Drake murmured, completing the popular adage. He refocused on his boss. "So, if not a cache hunt, what precisely is the assignment?"

"Payne is the governor of a world called Enduril II." She glanced enquiringly towards him but Drake shook his head. He'd never heard of the place. "It's a moon that orbits a gas giant -- Enduril. It's in the direction of Xter space but this side of Barnard's. You can gen up on it before you leave."

No room for his refusing the mission then. Could he? Was that an option open to him and did he want to even if he could?

"They have a cache there, one that houses some unique Elder artefacts," Reese continued, "and it appears to be largely untouched. This much we're confident of."

That was sufficiently unusual in itself to be noteworthy. Elder artefacts were too valuable, too much in demand to be left in situ. "Why untouched?"

"As far as I can gather, for cultural reasons."

Drake let that go for now – he could always research the reasons in question if necessary.

"So where do we fit in, if the cache doesn't need locating and the artefacts aren't going to be removed or marketed, what's in it for First Solar?"

"Ah, but the artefacts *are* to be marketed, just not in the traditional sense. The Endurians are set on turning the cache and its contents into a tourist attraction."

"*What?*"

That was a new one, but it did make a sort of sense. Handled properly, a significant Elder cache could prove a big draw to a public who had only experienced such places in virtual reconstructions. The vast majority of folk had rarely if ever seen an Elder artefact first-hand. Initially the financial returns would be tiny compared to the potential profit from selling the constituent artefacts, but over the longer term...

"And what's my proposed role in all this?"

"We need an assessment. Go to Enduril, examine the cache, judge its value, and report back."

Drake stared at her. "And the real reason I'm going?"

"Isn't that enough?"

"Not really, no. All of that could be done remotely from here given appropriate information: a detailed catalogue of the cache's contents, images of each item, a full breakdown of known properties for the various artefacts... Why bother going to the expense and inconvenience of sending an agent all the way there in person?"

"There are... complications."

Aren't there always? said a voice in his head.

Quiet! Reese had no idea of Mudball's true nature – no one did – and Drake was determined to keep it that way. There were too many systems monitoring and assessing him in here to risk regular interruptions from the little alien, who was on strict instruction to shut up in Reese's presence.

"For one thing, the Endurians don't allow any images of the cache to be recorded. It seems to be another aspect of their isolationist philosophy, which some might think of as paranoia and is a pain in the backside however you choose to colour it."

A sensible attitude, though, if they intended to exploit the tourism angle, but how long could they enforce an embargo like that once the general public gained access? Someone was bound to smuggle out images and recordings and it was surely only a matter of time before a virtual reconstruction of the cache appeared. It might not be enough to end their business entirely but it would surely dent it. The Endurians were unlikely to have as much time in which to exploit the place as they were anticipating.

"In addition, there appears to be some local opposition to the prospect of opening the cache up as planned. Also..." and here she drew a deep breath. "We don't know where the cache is."

"I'm sorry?"

Reese held up a defensive hand. "I know, I know, this is a moon, right? How can they possibly hide an Elder cache on something the size of a moon... even a *big* moon? The truth is, we're not sure they have. We know there's a cache hidden somewhere in the vicinity, but every search by every means has failed to find precisely where, and believe me, many have tried. Initial efforts concentrated on Enduril II itself, but when those drew a blank attention shifted to the other four moons in the planetary system. Again, no joy. The current theory is that the cache is somehow hidden within the mantle of the planet itself, using the fluctuating energies generated by a gas giant as camouflage, but that's a pretty massive area to cover and a damned good disguise. And if it *is* there, they don't seem to visit too often, which makes the idea unlikely in my view. The plain truth is that, as yet, *no one* has been able to find the cache."

"So my real mission is to locate it."

"Among other things, yes. Locate the cache, assess the political situation – how strong is the opposition, and is there anyone sitting at the opposite end of the spectrum, who would like to see the artefacts sold for immediate gain? We need you to evaluate the viability of the whole concept – will this really work as a tourist attraction? – and, at the same time, assess whether there are any alternative ways to proceed."

That sounded more like First Solar – looking for an angle to exploit.

"I'm hardly the best qualified to do all this," Drake said

slowly, wondering why Reese was even considering him for the job, irrespective of the clients' request. He couldn't believe the bank didn't have a dozen more suitable candidates on the payroll.

"I know, but the customer has asked for you, which might give you an edge and open doors that would stay firmly shut for anyone else, and you're experienced enough to offer an opinion, which will be taken into account along with other factors."

Come on, Mudball urged, *stop trying to wriggle out of this. It'll make a change from being cooped up on a cramped ship for weeks on end with a bunch of resentful spacers who've forgotten how to use the dry shower.*

Clearly the alien needed a refresher on how to behave in Reese's presence. It had a point, though, which didn't stop Drake from saying, "And if I turn the assignment down?"

"You know I would never insist on you taking a job that you strongly object to…"

"But you would prefer it if I took this one."

The way she raised her eyebrows spoke eloquently enough. Not an order, then, but the next best thing.

"The potential profit here is significant," Reese said, choosing her words with obvious care. "At the same time, the risk appears to be minimal and First Solar's outlay would be minor when compared to that of a standard cache hunt, and it'll be fully securitised."

"I sense a 'but'."

Reese smiled tightly. "Indeed you do. I don't know, maybe I'm just getting paranoid in my old age, but something about this whole scenario doesn't feel right. Everything checks out, and when I run an assessment profile the proposal gets a big thumbs-up, so I've no grounds to reject the Endurians' petition. In fact, it scores so highly that I'd risk being pulled up on review if I *did* pass on this, but my gut says differently. The way this Payne character has requested you specifically for one thing, though in all honesty even if he hadn't…"

"You would have put this one to me in any case."

Reese nodded. "I need someone I can trust, someone I know

can handle themselves if the situation turns sour. If I *am* about to throw an agent to the wolves it should at least be somebody who'll stand a fighting chance."

And here was me thinking she liked you.

"Thanks, I think."

She regarded him for a moment. "Having said all that, you're under no obligation. It's down to you. Should I summon another agent and assign them? I could always make apologies to Payne and tell him you're unavailable."

Drake was surprised by that; he hadn't really expected her to offer him a way out. His earlier doubts about continuing to even *be* Drake resurfaced. If he were going to step away, this would be an ideal opportunity… He hesitated, but only for a moment. If there was a problem here that reached back into his past, ignoring it wouldn't make the issue go away. "No," he said. "That won't be necessary."

Good decision, Mudball assured him. He only wished he felt as confident.

Reese nodded, accepting his decision. "Payne is due here tomorrow morning to hear the bank's decision."

"I'll be there."

"Come prepared for a quick departure."

With the conversation over, Drake headed for the door. He was almost there when Reese said, "Drake!" He paused and looked back. "This isn't like one of your standard cache hunts where you're heading off to the back of beyond. You'll be in civilised regions with established lines of communication. I expect regular reports, come what may."

"Of course," he acknowledged. The fact she even thought it necessary to state this showed how uneasy Reese felt about the mission.

"Miss one, and I'll send in the cavalry."

Maybe she does like you after all.

He nodded, ignoring Mudball's aside. "Thank you."

After sleeping on it, Drake found that his main reaction to this new assignment was curiosity. He and Donal, or Martin Payne as the man now evidently styled himself, hadn't parted on particularly bad terms that he recalled, but Donal's stint as a Dark Angel had ended less than ideally and his time aboard the *Ion Raider* had cost him. He had been forced to leave the Angels after suffering severe injuries in an incident that he barely survived, involving a grounded ship that shouldn't have blown up but did. No telling how that might have festered over the intervening years or to what extent the man's opinion of his former comrades had soured.

Was that why Donal or Payne had gone to the trouble of tracking him down? It couldn't have been easy, and Drake was keen to find out both how the former Angel had achieved it and what had motivated him to do so.

He therefore approached the meeting with Payne guardedly, his grip on the familiar handle of his cane perhaps a little tighter than usual as he stepped into Reese's office. His anticipation of the mission had not been enhanced by a visit to First Solar's medical centre. Enduril II was subjected to frequent washes of lethal radiation – a consequence of being so close to a gas giant – and Drake had been scheduled for a jab.

"There's no such thing as a safe dose of radiation, especially these radiations," the doctor had told him. "The only way to avoid any damage is to stay the hell away from the source."

"Not an option in this case."

The doctor had grunted. "So I gather. This should help a little, as will the radiation suit I presume you'll be wearing."

"Already got it on," Drake assured him, having donned the lightweight clammy-feeling garment under his clothes that morning.

The doctor grunted again. "Good. The only other advice I can offer, then, is to keep indoors as much as possible when the planet's up, get some lenses for your eyes, oh, and leave that genpet at home. Fur doesn't offer any protection against radiation, no matter how green it is."

I'll give him 'leave the genpet at home', Mudball growled.

He's only doing his job.

Drake had come straight to Reese's office from the medical centre. Three people waited for him there. Reese, Payne, and a tall smartly dressed individual introduced simply as Evans – no indication whether that was first name, surname, or the only name – who bore the title of assistant but had the physical presence of a bodyguard. Interesting; why would Payne feel the need for that sort of personal security here on New Sparta?

"Ah, Mr Drake," Reese said. "Thank you for joining us."

Evans stood off to one side, near the wall to Drake's right as he entered, a position that put him close to Payne and slightly behind. Reese was seated in her customary chair, with Payne facing her, though not in the usual visitors' chair. He had brought his own: a slick, blue-black chassis that encased his body from the waist down.

Drake made sure that neither surprise nor distaste showed on his face – distaste not at the disability but at the way Payne chose to display it. The man's smile in greeting seemed genuine enough, but Drake was again struck by how unchanged Payne's face appeared to be; it might have been lifted directly from his memories, matching them in every regard.

Payne had said something but the words passed him by. "Good to see you after all these years," he temporised, hoping that didn't sound out of place as a response.

Reese summoned an additional chair, which emerged from the plain flooring in a smooth and organic manner, almost seeming to grow into place. Drake would have preferred to stand but he sat as indicated, both out of courtesy to Payne and because Reese clearly expected him to. The chair was positioned closer to Reese than he was used to – almost beside her though at an angle, naturally – facing away from his boss and towards the visitors. It felt a little odd to be viewing the room from this perspective, with the window behind him rather than spread in front.

He couldn't resist casting a quick glance towards Reese, but even from this angle the fields of information he knew would be flickering in the air before her, informing her discussion and her decision making, remained invisible.

"As you requested, Mr Drake will represent First Solar Bank's interests in this matter," Reese said, addressing Payne. "He will travel with you to Enduril II and assess the situation, providing us with the level of detailed information we've been unable to obtain remotely."

Payne spread his hands in apology. "I'm sorry about that. If it were up to me we'd be a lot more forthcoming, but Endurians can be a stubborn bunch and we've generations of mistrust of outsiders to overcome. You have no idea how much of a concession this whole proposal is for the diehard traditionalists among us."

He flashed a quick grin at Drake, as if to suggest they were all progressives together here. "It'll be good to work with you again."

Drake's lips twitched in response, but he doubted the smile reached his eyes.

You really don't like this Payne character, do you? Mudball said.

Not a question of like or dislike. It's a question of trust. Until I know why *Donal wants me involved and how he found me...* And he wasn't likely to discover either until the two of them had a chance to talk alone, well away from First Solar's premises. Mudball had a point, though; there was nothing to be gained in letting his suspicions escalate into hostility. Not yet, at any rate. So he did his best to relax and keep an open mind. The next time Payne looked his way he even managed a convincing facsimile of a smile.

"I still find it surprising that a society which has been reclusive for generations suddenly chooses to open itself up the tourism," Reese said.

"The worst of two evils," Payne explained. "We lack the industrial base to be self-supporting, so have to rely on imports in exchange for what we mine. The income from our mining is in decline due to growing competition. We need an income stream to supplement that income while we develop the industrial base to be self-sustaining."

Reese nodded, clearly not fully convinced. "Yes, I've read the reports."

From there on, the meeting amounted to little more than formal reaffirmation of what Reese had already told him in private, and before long Drake found himself in an elevator with Payne and the silent presence of Evans, on their way to the port.

"Governor, hey?" Drake said as the doors closed. "You've done well for yourself."

"Thanks, I suppose I have. It wasn't easy at first, accepting my... adjusted circumstances." Payne's hand fell to stroke the chassis of his chair, the move apparently sub-conscious. "But life is what it is and once I came to accept that I was able to get past that. Now, as things have turned out..." and he smiled, "I can hardly complain."

Mudball chose that moment to fidget, the movement drawing Payne's attention.

"I'm surprised they allow you to bring pets into work at First Solar." His continued smile was presumably intended to rob the question of any implied criticism. It didn't work.

"I get special dispensation," Drake replied, matching smile for smile.

"Funny, I never really saw you as the pet-loving type."

Drake shrugged. "People change."

I'm so going to enjoy taking this bozo down, said a voice in Drake's head.

One step at a time; we don't know that we will have to take him down as yet.

Would you fancy taking a bet on that?

"Oh, indeed they do," Payne said, oblivious to the exchange.

The man's attitude needled Drake, which doubtless prompted his next comment. "The chair's a bit melodramatic, don't you think?"

Wow! You're in a diplomatic mood today.

Payne regarded him for a moment. "Don't flatter yourself. You think this is an affectation, do you? Something I've adopted for your benefit, to prick your conscience?"

Score one for you.

Mudball sounded as smug as Drake felt. It hadn't taken much to crack the veneer of pleasantry and, as a matter of fact, Payne's comment pretty much *did* sum up what Drake had been thinking.

"It isn't," Payne continued. "I need the chair. For reasons no medic has ever been able to explain with conviction, regrowth failed to take, despite several attempts – my body keeps rejecting the treatment, presumably due to residual energies..." Drake was relieved he let the sentence tail off there; whatever his personal grievances, at least Payne retained a degree of discretion. Walls had ears, especially when those walls were within the head office of a corporate behemoth such as First Solar.

Almost before it had begun, the ride in the high-speed lift was over and the doors opened. Payne's chair rose from the floor by a barely perceptible degree and slid forward like a puck over ice. Drake stepped out beside him and matched his brisk pace as they crossed the building's foyer, with Evans a step or two behind.

"And cybernetic grafts proved too uncomfortable, for much the same reason," Payne said. "I do have a set of exo-legs, which I can tolerate for brief periods, but beyond that the discomfort becomes too much. A trip like this requires extended mobility, and for that there's only one practical option." He gestured extravagantly towards the chair. "Besides, if we're talking affectations, what about that cane of yours?"

Drake was so used to carrying the cane these days that he barely registered its presence. At the comment, his hand adjusted its grip on the handle self-consciously.

He was still formulating a response when Payne said, "I haven't noticed a limp so don't tell me you need it for walking."

No, not walking; the cane was more a prop to encourage folk

to underestimate him, as well as a convenient means of carrying a weapon without being obvious – clients tended to react badly to a stranger boarding their ship sporting a blaster, but a man with a walking stick…? Drake had no intention of sharing any of this with Payne. It did cause him to wonder, though, whether the other's chair might not serve a similar purpose.

"No, no limp at the moment," Drake confirmed. "An old wound received during a cache hunt that troubles me from time to time."

He's full of manure, a voice said in his head. *Don't let him distract you with all this talk about your cane. The chair is a deliberate goad aimed at you. I don't care how much he tries to explain it away.*

Drake wasn't about to argue. They hadn't even left New Sparta yet and already this trip was shaping up to be everything he'd feared.

FOUR

"I don't mean to sound ungrateful or anything, but what in the Elders' name are you doing here?"

That wasn't how Jen had intended to start the conversation but the words burst forth before she could stop them. She was still bewildered by how quickly events were unfolding and frustrated at the way she had been swept along, apparently helpless to affect their course.

At Leesa's urging they had bundled the three unconscious Saflik agents into one of the latrine cubicles, rigging the door so that it couldn't be readily opened, and the two of them were now hurrying away, keen to put as much distance as possible between themselves and the scene of the incident.

"I was coming to see you, why else do you think I'd be on this gods-forsaken rock?" Leesa snapped, more than a little defensively.

"And I'm grateful for that, of course I am," Jen said, conscious that her question had emerged far more aggressively than intended. "But how did you know I'd be here, at the port?"

"I didn't. I've just landed on world and was about to head out to that wilderness you call home when I felt you shift into shadow. That was the last thing I expected here in the capital, and I knew it couldn't signify anything good."

She had always been able to do that; a combination of her own auganic nature and the enhanced abilities she enjoyed as Hel N enabling her to sense when Jen shifted.

"Thank you." Her explanation, though, prompted another question. "Are you…?"

"No. *No*, of course not… I'm just me."

"Well whatever you are, I'm just glad you're here."

Leesa's unexpected appearance was the first thing that had gone Jen's way since the assassination attempt. Even so, given all that was going on, Jen was struggling to accept her former shipmate's sudden appearance as happy coincidence. Tempting though it was to accept things at face value, recent events had taught her to be wary. What did she really know about the woman beside her? Was she being stupid to blindly follow the lead of someone she hadn't seen in a decade, to assume that their friendship could simply pick up where it had left off after so long?

She stopped walking, forcing Leesa to do the same, and took a deep breath, far more raggedly than she would have liked. "Okay, before we go any further, would you mind telling me what the fuck is going on here?"

"More than you realise," Leesa said in response, "but let's not discuss it here, all right?"

She glanced around meaningfully and Jen took the hint, in fact she could have kicked herself for blurting questions out in such an unguarded fashion. They were in a public area where anyone might be listening. She was more out of practice at this than she cared to admit.

"Trust me, Jen," Leesa said. "We're both going to have to do that, trust each other, if we want to survive this. It's why I've come here. We *need* each other."

Jen stared at her for a moment, then nodded, willing to give her the benefit of the doubt for the moment at least.

Leesa seemed to sag a little, as if in relief, but recovered in an instant, grasping Jen's arm gently and pulling her along.

"Come on, we've got to keep moving," she urged.

Jen walked in something of a daze, dismayed at how rattled she felt and how relieved she was to see Leesa despite her reservations on the subject of trust. She hated to admit as much but it felt good to relinquish responsibility for a while, to follow someone else's lead. She had always considered herself to be practical and competent, capable of handling whatever life threw at her, but the events of the last couple of days had left her feeling punch-drunk. If she were going to place her trust in anybody, then it might as well be an old friend, though even then she wasn't about to do so blindly.

They succeeded in getting off world without incident, foregoing Jen's original booking in favour of passage on another ship, the *Southern Princess*, a bloated commercial liner of the sort Jen had always detested, but it was the next available berth. Jen sleepwalked through the booking and boarding process, too numb to engage in small talk. To her considerable relief their departure went smoothly, despite her half-expecting to be pulled to one side at any moment by armed security.

She only really relaxed once they had made it as far as the shuttle without the alarm being raised and Opal City was a rapidly receding urban stain soon to be obscured by clouds. The shuttle ride was far from comfortable, the cabin crowded, the press of humanity – the warmth and the stale smell generated by so many people crammed together – making Jen feel claustrophobic. She kept calm by imagining the open spaces of her home, though that made the loss of the life so crudely wrenched away from her all the more tangible. Questions thundered through her mind, but she supressed them while there was the remotest chance of anyone overhearing.

That meant biting her tongue until they were safely aboard the *Southern Princess* and in a private cabin, which Leesa confirmed was secure from eavesdroppers. Jen didn't doubt her; she knew what Leesa was capable of even without Hel N's abilities to call upon.

"All right," Leesa said once they were alone. "Now we can talk."

Their cabin was compact but comfortable, a tasteful arrangement of red and yellow blooms on the small dresser employed to avoid any suggestion of sterile blandness – real flowers, treated with floral stasis to ensure they never wilted and never required fresh water.

"To answer your earlier question," Leesa said, "no, I'm not Hel N. Unlike your Shadow persona, Hel N was never a part of me. The skin stayed aboard the *Raider* when we went our separate ways and that's the last I saw of it. No idea where the skin is now or even if it's survived."

"Chances are that it has."

"Yeah, not the easiest thing to damage," Leesa agreed. "I picture the skin neatly folded up and stored at the back of someone's cupboard like a piece of treasured cloth, without their having the faintest clue what it is."

"Now that's a disturbing thought."

"You reckon? I find it sort of… comforting."

"So you can sense me shift into shadow even though you're not Hel N?"

"Seems like it, yeah. I guess my aug must have learnt how to recognise your shift even without the skin's Elder tech to call on."

"Thank goodness it has…" Jen reflexively touched her bicep, where a patch of nuskin was busily repairing her recent knife wound; in her mind she felt the blade bite anew.

"Jen?" The sharp tone brought her back to the present. "Are you okay?"

"Yes, yes I'm fine."

"No you're not." Leesa sighed and pushed herself to her feet, to start pacing the limited cabin space. "Of course you're not. In the space of a day you've gone from sleepy rural idyll to assassination attempts and hit squads, and been dragged back into a past you thought banished to the dark corners of memory. If you're 'fine' after all of that, there's something wrong with you." She sat back down. "Maybe we should leave this till later."

"No!" Jen spoke more brusquely than intended and felt obliged to explain herself. "I might not be here by choice but I'm here all the same. The sooner I discover what the hell's going on the better my chances of surviving." *And of seeing Robin again.*

"If you're sure…?" In the face of Jen's nod, Leesa said,

"Okay," and activated her perminal, conjuring forth a man's face to hover in the air between them. "Recognise him?"

Jen tried to concentrate, to focus on the image, but she continued to be distracted by recent events and her thoughts kept sliding away. She started to shake her head but then paused. There *was* something familiar about this face: older, yes, but the eyes, those hazel flecked orbs that had always struck her as kindly. "Wait, is this Gabriel?"

"Got it in one."

A panel of text appeared beside the image. Jen scanned it. "He's dead?" A boating accident of some sort, stabilisers failing during a fishing trip, the vessel capsizing – the report was scant on specifics.

"Afraid so, and he's not the only one."

The text vanished and the image contracted until it disappeared, to be replaced by another. This one Jen recognised immediately; a woman: long straight platinum blonde hair, grey-blue eyes and a mouth that had always struck her as a little too broad for such a narrow face, though that face had evidently filled out in the intervening years. "Spirit," she murmured.

An accident again, or so the article claimed; an automotive collision caused by the malfunction of the car's guidance system. Such things happened, but they were vanishingly rare – the systems had so many failsafes and redundancies built in that it took a calamitous set of coincidences for everything to fail at once. Four died in the resulting pile-up, including the woman she had known as Spirit.

"Uha," Leesa confirmed. "How about this one?" but this time Jen shook her head, failing to recognise the man whose image appeared alongside a further article reporting a death attributed to tragic accident.

"He may have been before your time," Leesa conceded. "Do you remember Quill?"

"Oh, right. No, not really; he left just before I joined, but I heard about him. I got the impression no one was sorry to see him leave."

"You're right, we weren't. Quill was a complete arsehole. Now he's a dead arsehole."

A fall while rock climbing, attributed to equipment failure, or so the accompanying text claimed.

"Three accidents," Jen said softly. "Three Dark Angels dead."

And if the Saflik assassin had succeeded she would have been number four. Another accident, improbable but plausible – no one would have bothered looking any further. It only became suspicious when you considered the four incidents together and saw a pattern.

"These are just the ones I've identified," Leesa said. "There are bound to be others. We're being hunted down, one by one. Executed stealthily and quietly, and, because we've scattered and haven't really stayed in touch, no one's any the wiser."

"But why? Who are these people? I mean, who even cares about the Dark Angels after all this time?"

"I've no idea. Well, not much of one at any rate. They're well organised and patient – the three assassinations I've just shown you were carried out over a period of more than five years. I get the feeling these people are going to keep coming after us until they've killed us all, no matter how long that may take."

For some reason the realisation that she was on a list, a name to be scratched out before the killers moved onto the next in line, chilled Jen all the more. This was a clinical process, not a personal vendetta; it was just business to them.

"It smacks of ingrained hatred, of an obsession, she said, thinking aloud. "Is this someone from the old days, do you think?" That struck her as unlikely, though. "What sort of a person holds a grudge for that long?"

"It might be, but I'm not convinced. I don't reckon things are that simple. 'Saflik' means purity in a long-dead language, and I doubt the name was chosen at random. It seems to be a reflection of what drives them."

"Purity? How does that become a motive for killing people?

Cleansing in some way?"

"More or less, yeah. As I understand it, they view us, the Dark Angels, as defilers, as evil personified for the way we embraced Elder tech and used it for our own gain. By killing us, they're purifying."

"So they're zealots."

"Yes, pretty much."

There had always been those who felt that the Elder caches were in some way sacred and should have been left undisturbed, that by invading them and removing the contents humanity were perpetrating a terrible crime, but Jen had never heard of them getting militant before.

"*Everyone* uses Elder tech for their own gain," Jen pointed out. "From governments to technologists to traders to cache hunters... So why come after us now, when we walked away from all of that a decade ago? Cache hunts are still happening, aren't they? That hasn't stopped in the ten years I've been cosseted away on the farm? If you're right, surely that's who these Saflik should be targeting – people who are still raiding caches or making those raids possible."

"I know, you'd think, wouldn't you?"

"So why not hit the finance houses on New Sparta that fund the hunts, or the brokers who specialise in the sale of Elder tech, rather than coming after us has-beens?" Jen persisted. "We're ancient history."

"Hey, I didn't claim to have all the answers here. I'm just sharing what I know, what I *think* I know."

"Sorry, this is all..."

"A lot to take in, yes, I know." Leesa slipped her perminal away and hunched forward. "The thing is, whatever the justification might be, this is happening. The threat is real and hiding isn't an option – these Saflik are not about to go away if we simply choose to ignore them. So long as we stay scattered and oblivious to the threat, every single former Angel is vulnerable. We *have* to track down the others before the Saflik do, to warn them, to make them aware of the danger."

Jen shook her head. "Warning them isn't enough." She could suddenly see things with crystal clarity, surprised at how passionate she felt. "We need to recruit them. Individually, none of us stand a chance against an organisation as resourceful and ruthless as this Saflik." Her own recent experience had convinced her of that. "Our only hope is to reunite, to face them together."

Leesa grinned. "Now you're talking. *That*'s why I came to Opal in the first place, to convince you of exactly that; but let's not kid ourselves, this won't be easy. You've had the incentive of being attacked and seeing your cover torn apart. Finding the others is going to be difficult enough. Persuading them to abandon whatever life they've established over the past decade and come fight the bad guys...?" She shrugged.

"So what do you suggest?"

"Oh, I'm not saying we *don't* do this, I'm just pointing out that it's not going to be a walk in the park. Are you sure you're up to this?"

Jen snorted. "No one ever said life was supposed to be easy. Give me a decent night's sleep and I'm in. My only question is: where do we start?"

"Funny you should ask that. The *Southern Princess* is bound for Jacinta's World in the Awen system, which is only a brief hop away from Callia III."

"And who or what might we find on Callia III?"

"Geminum."

"Ah, so our choice of escape route from Opal wasn't as random as it seemed."

"Well... Perhaps not entirely so, no."

"That's a relief," and now it was Jen's turn to smile. "For a moment there I thought you were losing your touch. Callia III it is, then."

FIVE

In stellar terms, Enduril's system was no great distance from New Sparta and the journey called for just a single extended dip into RzSpace. In one regard the trip already represented a significant step up from any previous mission Drake had undertaken for First Solar. He was used to cramped ship's quarters aboard some aged trading vessel which barely had room for its regular crew let alone an unlooked for guest. Conditions here were a long way removed from that, with facilities aboard *The High Regard* closer to those he might expect to find on a top-end pleasure cruiser. Drake had his own cabin and every amenity he could ask for. Payne clearly liked to travel in style, explaining his use of what amounted to a private yacht rather than relying on commercial passenger services with a dismissive, "It saves on time."

You've been going about this banking agent thing all wrong, Mudball told Drake. *Every mission should begin like this.*

Any joy? he asked, ignoring the alien's quip.

Afraid not. There's no mention of the cache's location anywhere in the ship's systems, not a sniff, even in secure files. I've scoured every layer of the database and there's zilch, nada, bugger all.

Drake grunted. The news came as a disappointment but hardly a surprise. The Endurians hadn't kept the location of the cache hidden for this length of time by being careless; of course they would ensure that any ship venturing into the wider universe, particularly a cultural centre such as New Sparta, would be scrubbed clean of any clue regarding the mysterious cache; just in case some unscrupulous corporate concern succeeded in hacking their systems.

Does that make us unscrupulous and corporate? Mudball said, evidently catching the thought.

It's all a matter of perspective, Drake assured him.

Good. I far prefer being cunning and devious. You didn't really expect it to be that easy, though, did you?

No, Drake admitted. *It never is.*

The journey passed far more quickly than Drake had feared it might; in no small part due to the unexpected company he fell into. While he didn't avoid conversation with Payne, nor did he seek it out, and having his own cabin gave him the perfect excuse not to be sociable when he chose without seeming ungracious. The presence of another passenger on board *The High Regard* came as something of a surprise. As far as Drake had understood matters, the ship's sole purpose in visiting New Sparta had been to seek funding from First Solar and return with the bank's agent – him.

Theodor Ungar, who introduced himself as a cultural historian, was an amiable man whose physique had begun to stray towards the portly. A quick check of available records suggested he was genuine. Ungar proved to be erudite, witty, and an entertaining raconteur.

"Couldn't resist the opportunity to hitch a lift when I learned there was a ship in port bound for Enduril," he confided in Drake as the two of them relaxed in the small but comfortable lounge over glasses of Tarkhillan brandy. Such meetings had developed into something of a habit, as both men sought relief from the monotony of being sealed within a metal tube and the deadening effects of RzSpace. "Had to get permission from that Payne chap – what do you make of him? Seems a bit sombre for my liking. Still, mustn't judge. Anyway, as I was saying, Enduril II is a fascinating world. Started out as a mining settlement, you know."

Drake did, but he was more than happy to indulge the historian. Circumstances had given him limited time to prepare for the mission, so he had taken the opportunity afforded by the journey to learn as much about Enduril II and its people as he could, determined to get a feel for the culture he was about to venture into. The ship's library provided copious amounts of geological information and historical data in various forms: 3D recordings, text, and audio accounts, which enabled him to begin building a picture of the world's history and development. He learned, for example, that Enduril II experienced protracted blackout periods lasting several standard days, caused by a planetary eclipse of the sun. During the blackouts, which occurred roughly once every two years, temperatures plummeted. There was still some light generated by the gas giant itself, but this was a feeble thing compared to the sun, and was primarily of wavelengths towards the shorter end of the spectrum – manifesting as blues and violets. Drake skipped the long sections describing how Enduril II's flora and fauna had adapted to the blackouts, and was just grateful his visit wouldn't coincide with one of them.

The moon was also subject to extensive volcanic and seismic activity, which had made early mining attempts difficult, but didn't appear to have presented a significant problem in the long run. The majority of the mining settlements were concentrated around the equatorial belt, where vegetation was at its densest and the crust was at its most stable.

When it came to the history of Enduril's settlers and their society, the records were a little less helpful. While comprehensive in many regards – particularly the world's early history – there were glaring omissions; pivotal moments that were glossed over or ignored completely.

Drake's attempts to fill the gaps with questions dropped into conversation with the crew proved fruitless. Their responses were as uninformative as they were polite, and he didn't doubt they had been well-drilled regarding their dealings with him; as thoroughly vetted as the ship's library itself. Neither made any detailed mention of the Elder cache, the discovery of which must have had a significant cultural impact, while its continuing presence was surely the most important single factor to shape

Enduril's current society. Not if you were to believe the story told by the library, however. He wasn't even able to discern exactly *when* the cache had been discovered, though the presence of the historical vacuums enabled him to glean a rough idea, as did the cultural changes which the records couldn't entirely disguise. In this way, he was able to construct a tentative timeline – discovery, decision not to plunder, decision to keep hidden, etc. – but without supporting evidence the exact timing of the sequence could never be more than speculation.

The library was far more forthcoming regarding the physical aspects and geology of Enduril II. Drake recalled Reese's comment about not locating the cache on 'something the size of a moon' and wondered how she had kept a straight face. All things are relative, particularly celestial bodies, and terminology can be misleading. Enduril II was a giant moon, not atypical for a habitable moon circling a gas giant, and Reese must have been aware of that. In fact, Enduril II was larger than the 'world' of New Sparta. In order to support life a moon needed to be large enough to retain its liquid water. Greater mass meant increased gravity and also enabled the moon to retain the heat at its core for a longer period, facilitating the generation of a magnetic field. That, with a little help from the gravity of their parent world, gave them a fighting chance of sustaining life. Smaller moons were far less likely to support an atmosphere; he knew that, so the scale of Enduril II shouldn't have come as a surprise.

Just goes to show that in some things size does matter, Mudball commented. At times the little alien had human idiom down a little too well. *I'm impressed, by the way. I never realised you knew the first thing about planetary geology.*

The first thing, yes, but don't press me for a second. I'm liable to disappoint you.

Oh, don't worry, I'm used to that.

Given the sparsity of information sources, Drake was more than happy to indulge Ungar and play the attentive audience. If anyone could shed some light on these matters it was surely a historian, and sitting in a bar nursing crystal bulbs of excellent brandy beat approaching Payne to request a release of information every time.

It's not like you to avoid a confrontation, Mudball observed.

I'm not averse to a bit of confrontation, Drake admitted, *but I prefer it on my terms, not his. I get the impression Payne wants me to ask him about the cache.*

Right, I see; you don't intend to give him the satisfaction.

Not if I can help it, no.

Complicated, isn't it, the way you humans interact.

Always.

"Mining settlements have a habit of surprising you," Ungar was saying. "Have you ever been to Largos?"

Drake shook his head.

"Can't say I blame you. I mean who *would* go there unless they had to? It's a dreadful place – a small world orbiting a giant sun, whose surface is constantly bombarded by lethal radiation – far more than Enduril II is subjected to. It would be hard to imagine a less hospitable hell-hole anywhere in the galaxy, yet people *do* live there, buried deep beneath the surface in a labyrinth of tunnels and shafts, shielded from the radiation by layers of rock… Miners, of course. The extreme conditions have resulted in the creation of an incredibly rare mineral, known locally as sun glare; the planet's sub-strata are riddled with the stuff. If not for sun glare, nobody would go anywhere near Largos, let alone choose to live there."

"So why did you?" Drake asked, primarily because Ungar had paused as if to invite the question.

"For the same reason I'm so keen to visit Enduril II now. Research. Largos is a unique place, as is Enduril."

Drake had noted that 'Enduril II' was often shortened to simply 'Enduril', both by Ungar and in the ship's records. The interchangeable nature was perhaps understandable, given that Enduril itself, the gas giant the moon orbited, was never likely to support life – at least nothing anyone would currently recognise as life – and the planet's closest moon, Enduril I, was equally inimical.

"This is all part of a long-term project I've pursued for much of my life," Ungar continued, "when other commitments permit, of course; a study into how mining has developed and diversified over the ages. What particularly interests me is how the communities that arise to support the industry have had to adapt both to their environment and changing social circumstances in order to do so."

All this talk of mining put Drake uncomfortably in mind of Falyn de Souza and the Jossyren Mining Corporation, whose meddling had so nearly sabotaged the Pelquin cache hunt in fatal fashion.

"Of course, much of the industry is automated these days," Ungar continued, "but there are still some instances, such as on Largos, where that isn't practical and others, such as Enduril, where automation wouldn't be culturally acceptable. These are the communities that draw me.

"I found Largos in particular interesting because of the extremes the miners and their families have subjected themselves to in order to harvest the sun glare. The founding families were genetically modified in order to survive and thrive in the hostile conditions. The adaptations were, of course, passed on to subsequent generations. One consequence has been a shorter, heavy-set but stronger variety of human, better adapted to their home's higher than standard gravity and the physical labour of mining.

"The historian in me finds a certain irony in the fact that many of the oldest myths of ancient Earth depict dwarves as miners, and, here in this modern age, we've created exactly that in order to mine Largos!

"My stay there was not as long as originally planned. The heavy gravity and low ceilings proved too uncomfortable a combination. I must admit, though, that my visit was not without its rewards. I've never encountered a community before or since that was more obsessed with... well, to put it bluntly, sex. I suppose they need something to alleviate the boredom of what must otherwise be a fairly drab existence.

"Bizarrely, men from Largos have become highly sought after on certain worlds as... for want of a better word... studs. Largans might be squat and solid, but they are deceptively strong and have exceptional stamina. This combined with the novelty of their short and stocky physique evidently makes them irresistible in some circles, which means that any young man of Largos who chooses to turn his back on the mining vocation can be guaranteed a comfortable life elsewhere."

"I notice you specify 'men'," Drake commented. "Does the same hold true for the women?"

"Ah, that's very perceptive of you. Sadly, no. As far as I'm aware, women do not have a ready escape from the life they're born into in the way their menfolk do. What can I say? The universe isn't always a perfectly balanced place.

"One further thing I should mention regarding the women of Ungar is that I found them very... welcoming. I was much younger back then, of course, in my prime, and while I might have lacked the strength and stamina of the local males, evidently my height and more slender frame made me as much a curiosity to the Largan women as their men are to thrill-seekers on other worlds.

"That was another reason my stay on Largos was curtailed. My success with the women there didn't endear me to some of the menfolk, who made it clear that my continued presence could prove bad for my health. There are plenty of opportunities for 'accidents' around a mining community, so I took their advice to heart.

"I always promised myself I'd go back there some day, but I'm not sure my body would stand the stresses these days – *any* of the stresses – and, besides, the older I get the less compelled I feel to follow up on the intention."

Drake appreciated the twinkle in Ungar's eye as he told such anecdotes, and he was never sure how much embellishment went into the narration, which only added to their entertainment value.

"So you're going to Enduril instead," he said.

"Indeed!" Ungar laughed and raised his glass, a salute Drake mimicked.

"And Enduril's mining traditions intrigue you in a similar fashion to Largos?" Drake had avoided discussing the mysterious cache directly, fearing that perhaps even Ungar had been warned against mentioning the subject, but an oblique approach seemed innocent enough.

"Oh they certainly intrigue me, though not necessarily in the same way. I've been meaning to come here for years – where else would I find a mining community whose cultural development has been influenced so dramatically by the presence of an Elder cache?"

Well that was easy enough, Mudball said.

"Does Enduril even qualify as a mining community any more?" Drake wondered.

"Oh certainly. Mining is still their main source of income. They've nothing as rare as sun glare to trade but their export trade consists almost entirely of what they extract from the ground."

"I'm surprised Enduril has *any* export trade these days. My understanding was that Endurians prefer to keep themselves to themselves and mistrust outsiders."

"That's true, to an extent," Ungar agreed. "Most of the export contracts hark back to a simpler more open age, predating the discovery of the cache. Some of those historic contracts have been maintained and renewed ever since. If you look at the planet's economic history, you can see what a dramatic effect the discovery of the cache had, with other forms of export being dropped almost immediately, but nobody likes poverty and the Endurians aren't stupid, so the export of minerals has continued without discernible interruption."

He's a 'mine' of information, isn't he?

Keep going at this rate, Drake thought back, *and you might actually get the hang of this 'humour' thing one day.*

You're too kind.

Mudball was right, though; during the course of several conversations with Ungar, Drake was able to fill in many of the gaps in the planet's history with far greater confidence. It was impressive, the way the community seemed to have acted together, their habits changing with apparent uniformity following the discovery of the cache a little over five decades earlier. He suspected this indicated strong governance – though the histories offered no indication of draconian measures – and reflected the fact that humanity had never spread far across the face of Enduril, remaining concentrated in a few mining communities and leaving much of the world a wilderness, as far as he could tell.

As the journey progressed and they drew ever nearer Enduril, Drake found himself warming to Ungar, the historian's gregarious nature rubbing off on him. He had obviously travelled widely, and possessed an apparently inexhaustible repertoire of anecdotes, so much so that Drake began to wonder how any man could possibly have fitted so much into one lifetime.

At least his bullshit is entertaining, Mudball noted on one occasion, as Drake found himself doubting the veracity of the latest Ungar tale.

Twice during his relaxed sessions in the lounge Drake spied Payne, on both occasions deep in conversation with ship's crew or other officials. Payne acknowledged him with a nod but otherwise made no move to come across or otherwise interact, clearly content to leave him in the historian's company. If Drake had anticipated some clue during the journey as to why Payne wanted him on Enduril, it would seem he was to be disappointed.

One thing that became immediately apparent about Enduril II, even before they touched down, was that it had Weather. Drake tended to think of the word as capitalised because, to date, it was the single most impressive aspect of the place.

They had landed amidst a downpour, the ship buffeted by high winds as it braved the atmosphere, and the following day little had changed. In the limited glimpses of their new surroundings he was able to snatch as they were transferred from ship to shuttle to lodgings, Drake gained the impression of a rich, verdant land.

Payne escorted the two visitors – Drake and Ungar – to a waiting car. Evans, Payne's 'assistant', accompanied them across the landing field, helping Payne out of his chair and into the vehicle, but then returned to the ship. Drake had seen little of him during the trip out here and had yet to hear the man speak.

The car was driven by a stolid, dour-faced man the visitors weren't introduced to, who seemed cut from much the same cloth as Evans. As they drove away, Drake noted how empty the port seemed. A shape just at the farthest reach of the lighted area might have been another ship, but apart from that there was no sign of life or activity.

The sleeting rain and overcast skies brought a premature darkness to the world, making detailed observation difficult, but to both sides of the car he could make out the massed bulk of towering trees that suggested forest or even jungle. The treeline began a little way back from the road, as if a strip of land to either side had been cleared. Beyond that strip, wilderness reigned.

Their journey proved surprisingly short. Within minutes of leaving the port the car drew up at the lodgings: a flat-roofed single storey complex which proved comfortable and well-appointed but isolated – it was apparent they were still some distance from the nearest town.

Introduced to them by Payne as a 'guest centre', the facility had all the trappings of a budget-price hotel, albeit one for which the state was footing the bill. There were no restrictions on the guests going outside – apart from the inclement conditions – but even so it felt somewhat like a prison to Drake, or at the very least another layer of bureaucracy put in place to delay him and keep him at arm's length. This latest tactic, coming straight after the limited level of information available to him on the trip out here, only heightened his sense of something being awry. Why specifically request his presence and then hamper his ability to do the job expected of him?

Looks as if Reese was right, Mudball commented, catching the thought.

She usually is.

The first thing that struck Drake as he walked in was the whiff of antiseptic which seemed to pervade everything, suggesting that the 'guest centre' might have been long unused and reopened especially for their benefit. It couldn't quite disguise the smell of disuse that stubbornly lingered. Both aromas soon faded, though Drake suspected only through familiarity.

As they arrived they were greeted by a smiling man bearing a rain repellor, who was introduced to them as Carlos.

"I hope you don't mind if I don't get out," Payne said. He went on to apologise for leaving them here, explaining that he had been summoned to the capital on urgent business and promising to collect them the following day. Drake and Ungar watched as the lights of the car vanished into the rain, both of them wondering, perhaps, what they had let themselves in for.

Enduril II had a total population of a little over two million. The capital, Hamilton, boasted some nine and a half thousand residents.

There are buildings in New Sparta with workforces larger than that, Mudball observed.

Not quite, but I know what you mean.

The populace was concentrated at settlements that had been established around mining and refining centres scattered across the face of the planet though concentrated around the equator, of which Hamilton was the largest and most significant. It wasn't the site of the first landing – that was further north – but it was where the apparatus of government had been established and, despite the mines that had once seen the town flourish having played out long ago, that was where government remained. Due to the small population and the way it continued to be focused around the mining settlements, vast swathes of the planet remained uninhabited and, judging by all that Drake had learnt to date, that included some fairly wild and impenetrable terrain. He couldn't help but wonder how comprehensive and sophisticated the various searches for the cache had been. He knew from experience how well hidden such places often were. Reese had sounded confident of her facts, though.

He, Mudball and Ungar appeared to be the only ones currently staying at the guest centre – a fact Mudball verified as soon as he accessed the building's systems. The complex was largely automated, though it did have one further human on the staff in addition to Carlos: Rosa. While the former was unfailingly polite in a stiffly formal way, Rosa was surly enough to suggest that she would rather have been anywhere other than here and that she held Drake and Ungar directly responsible for her inconvenience.

By late morning of the day following their arrival, Drake was growing increasingly impatient. He had kept himself busy up until that point but had now run out of things to do. As he stepped out onto the veranda that led outside from the lounge he was wondering about the practicalities of walking to the capital.

On an alien planet, in the pouring rain, with jungle to either side and the threat of radiation… Yes, that sounds like a sensible plan.

Not a plan at all, Drake responded, *just idle speculation; you really should learn to tell the difference.*

The veranda provided a good vantage point, offering a view towards the edge of the forest which, on another day, was probably beautiful. In truth, it still was, the prevailing conditions adding a sense of drama to the scene.

He stood on the threshold between the inside and outside, just beyond the reach of the rain which drummed on the terracotta floor tiles turning them wet and glistening and, indeed, drummed on most everything. He watched as the occasional splash from the most ambitious drops speckled his shoes.

The previous evening he had sent a message to Reese confirming his safe arrival. His perminal had yet to gain access to Enduril's internet, something that Carlos was apologetic about, explaining that the service here was patchy at best. Drake therefore had to rely on cruder means of communication, sending a liveLink message via the spaceport, but Carlos assured him it would still get through in proper order.

Following a decent night's sleep and a passable breakfast, Drake had gone for a wander around the guest centre, seeking out the areas he hadn't seen as yet. He found much of the place still mothballed – lights out, furniture absent and rooms empty. Having exhausted the possibilities of exploration without getting wet, he headed for the lounge, hoping to bump into Ungar and gauge his thoughts on their night's accommodation.

There was no sign of the historian as yet, so he braved the automated bar – which possessed all the charm of an elaborate vending machine – ordering and accepting a whiskey before stepping out to gaze at the trees as they weathered the storm. The whiskey was from a distillery he'd never heard of and tasted a little thin to his palate, but it would do. Given current circumstances, he felt the need for some fire in his belly, irrespective of the early hour.

In addition to the forest edge, you could also see the road from here, off to the right. Not in any detail, but well enough to spot any vehicles that might happen to be using it. Few did. Drake suspected that the road ended at the port, providing s direct link from there to the capital. Bearing in mind the Endurians' reluctance to interact with other worlds, it was hardly surprising that the road saw little use. So far he had only witnessed two instances: a car, which had been heading in the direction of the port the previous evening, a couple of hours after they had arrived, and one heading in the opposite direction a short while later. He couldn't be certain given the poor visibility, but he suspected they were the same vehicle. Today, he had seen nothing.

He had hoped to catch a glimpse of the parent planet, Enduril, but the skies were too overcast and the weather too foul. The rain was relentless; perhaps not the heaviest downpour Drake had ever experienced but it didn't show any signs of stopping and the intensity peaked and receded in erratic waves. Just beyond the edge of the veranda there stood a broad-leafed plant that caught his attention. The plant's flat leaves were formed of six splayed and pointed lobes. The leaves bobbed up and down independently under the opposing influences of the rainfall's impact and their stems' support. He found the resulting undulations mesmerizing.

Is this what we've come all this way for? Mudball asked. *To watch a few plants being slapped around by the rain?*

No, but it helps pass the time. Until Payne decides to let us visit this fabled cache or at least brings us to the capital, there's little else for me to do. Any progress your end?

Not much. The systems at this 'guest centre' are isolated, and nearly as carefully vetted as The High Regard's. *I've already told you everything of interest. Anyone would think these people don't trust you, or something.*

As if.

Drake still hadn't managed to connect with Enduril's internet, and he doubted that was a coincidence. Ungar had remarked on the lack of connection the previous evening, adding, "I hope things improve once we reach Hamilton."

Of course they will, Mudball commented. *They can't jam an entire city.*

As if summoned by Drake's recollection of him, the historian entered the lounge, fetching a whiskey for himself and a refill for Drake.

"I've just heard from Carlos that Payne's on his way to pick us up and take us to the capital," he said. "Apparently he should be here in half an hour or so."

"That's good to hear."

"Isn't it just? I won't be sorry to see the back of this

internment camp."

Evidently Ungar was no more enamoured with their current lodgings than he was. "Nor will I."

"This isn't what I've waited so long to come and see," the historian grumbled, his usual bonhomie slipping for once. "Still, hopefully we can put it behind us now and move on."

Drake raised his drink in acknowledgement and they clinked glasses. The reason for this stopover continued to intrigue him.

Once the drinks were finished, the two went their separate ways, Drake heading for his room to gather together the few items he'd unpacked. He wasn't about to give Payne any further excuses for delay and wanted to ensure he was ready to depart the moment the car arrived.

I take it you still haven't managed to get beyond the centre's own systems? He asked Mudball.

No. Everything here is internal only.

They can't keep doing that. Once we reach the capital they have to give us wider access. As soon as you can, find out who has arrived and departed from Hamilton spaceport in the past few days.

Well… There's us for starters.

Apart from us.

Okay, will do. Am I looking for anything in particular?

Yes. The decision to bring him here, to approach First Solar and request him specifically, hadn't been taken on a whim. It had been planned in advance – a strategy put in place – but the stopover at this 'guest centre' smacked of something different, of last minute arrangements made in haste: the smell of disinfectant when they first arrived, the fact that not all the facility was open and operational, the sense that staff had been called in at the last minute and were none too happy about it. Drake was increasingly convinced that their stay here had been improvised, a desperate measure to keep him away from the capital for one more night. The only reason he could envisage for doing that was to prevent him meeting someone – somebody who wasn't supposed to be in Hamilton when he arrived but, for whatever reason, had been.

Such a small population increased the likelihood of a chance encounter, however much they might seek to avoid one; best to keep him out the way entirely.

A single car speeding to the spaceport within hours of their arrival, the same car – probably – coming back a short while later; and now it was okay for him to continue to the capital.

Ah, said Mudball, who must have caught most of Drake's reasoning, *so you reckon they were shipping out whoever it was they didn't want you to bump into.*

Pretty much. Why else delay us here? There are no turn offs between the spaceport and this place, so that car could only have been heading for the port and, presumably, a waiting ship. I haven't seen any other vehicles using the road, so…

Who is this mystery man or woman? I get it. At last, something vaguely interesting for me to do. You leave this to me. I'll get on it as soon as I can.

Carlos escorted them to the car, again holding aloft a small metal wand that generated a field to hold the elements at bay.

Payne was all smiles and apologies. "Good morning. I trust you slept well, and sorry again for having to leave you yesterday."

This time around, Evans drove the car, which enabled Drake to fill in another piece of the jigsaw: Evans had stayed at the port to see off whoever the mysterious visitor had been, and had then returned with the car to the capital.

Drake's perminal vibrated almost as soon as they drove away from the guest centre, confirming that it had finally been able to link with the local internet.

"You should have access to the internet now," Payne said right on cue. "Apologies, this isn't New Sparta and coverage here can be patchy, but you ought to be fine once we're in the capital itself."

The hotel that Payne delivered them to, describing it as, "The only place in Hamilton to stay at," was called The Miners' Retreat.

Seems these people do have a sense of humour after all, Mudball observed.

The two travellers were greeted by a human receptionist. Whereas on New Sparta this would have indicated an ostentatious display of wealth, in this instance Drake suspected it was simply how they chose to do things here.

Before depositing them at the hotel, Payne had arranged to collect them the next day, promising to take them to see the cache. The speed with which this was to be accomplished surprised Drake after the delaying tactics and obstructiveness he had encountered to date. It did mean he would have little time to meet any of Hamilton's political hierarchy in advance and assess how unified or otherwise support for the tourism plan might be. Perhaps that was the point.

He was still settling into the room when Mudball spoke excitedly in his head. *Okay, I think I've got something. You're right, Hamilton spaceport is rarely used these days apart from internal flights and there aren't too many of those. These people really do like their own company, don't they? To be honest, I had a problem finding anything to start with, apart from references to you and Ungar. Whoever the mystery bozo is, his visit isn't listed officially. But…*

Go on. A penchant for grandstanding was something else Mudball had picked up from his exposure to humans.

Well, with travel records proving a dead end, I decided to tackle the problem obliquely. I cross-referenced meetings involving Hamilton's bigwigs, looking for a name that cropped up in recent days but was absent previously – with an urban population of less than ten thousand and power and influence concentrated in a small proportion of those – as you humans seem to like it – that wasn't as onerous as you might suppose…

And you found someone? Drake cut across, suspecting that Mudball was prepared to spend several more minutes demonstrating how clever he had been before saying anything useful.

Yes. There's an individual who attended meetings with many of Hamilton's movers and shakers over the past few days but didn't seem to be around before that.

Does this person have a name?

He does indeed: Bowman.

The name meant nothing to Drake but, as he knew only too well, names were mutable. *Any recordings or images?*

No, whoever this is, they know how to be careful.

Or others know how to be careful for them.

I did find something else, though.

Go on.

This Bowman has visited before. The same pattern of an intense period of meetings followed by protracted absence has occurred a total of nine times over the past eight years. Whoever he or she is, they have to be from out of town.

Or, more likely, off world. Thank you, Mudball.

Hey, a new phrase for my vocabulary: thank you. I'll check the database for a definition. Are you sure you're feeling okay?

Very droll.

You're not going soft on me, are you?

Not likely. And don't milk it.

Eight years. That suggested a plan that had been in motion for a lot longer than Drake had previously suspected, unless this was all coincidence and he was reading conspiracy into something entirely unrelated.

I didn't think you believed in coincidence.

I don't, Drake agreed. *Not until I've ruled out all other possibilities first.*

Six

Colours pulsed and twisted in dazzling profusion, bulbous plasmatic limbs that swelled forward and broke to wash over her body in rainbow globules and a spray of tiny droplets, while light flared and dwindled only to flare again, before strobing without warning, bleaching colour into stark monochrome and transforming smooth movement into stop-start staccato. The assault on her senses didn't stop there, either. Sound erupted in prolonged bass thrums that struck with physical force and reverberated through her being, or tormented her in high-pitched bee-sting bursts. Leesa fought desperately to cope, to make sense of the bedlam and regain some level of coherency, but every time she threatened to do so a new variation of stimuli would tilt her perceptions and send her reeling once more.

Time had become an irrelevance; she couldn't have guessed how long she spent at the mercy of this insane environment before she started to get a handle on it.

Finally, bit by bit, she did so, and began to assert a consistent sense of her own identity, every gain hard fought, every step a triumph. The secret, she discovered, was to tone down the senses; not ignore them completely – it would be impossible to do that here of all places – but to dampen them sufficiently that reason had a chance to prevail. Colours still buffeted her, sound and light maintained their pressure, but she was able to blunt their impact by focussing her attention inward and accepting her situation rather than fighting against it, all the while clinging stubbornly to the concept of self. The more she did so, the easier it became, until she reached a point where she could peer outwards once more without the turmoil overwhelming her.

Slowly, carefully, she began to move forward.

Leesa, are you okay? Jen, contacting her via a link to her aug as they'd planned before either of them knew what Leesa would be getting into.

The distraction nearly cost her. Attention wavered and the chaos threatened to break through, to shatter her brittle progress.

Stow it! she sent back, to curtail any further distractions from that quarter. *Need to concentrate.*

Mercifully, Jen fell silent, allowing Leesa to gather her resolve and continue.

Progress proved anything but easy. It was as if the sensory bombardment intensified the further in she went. She had assumed that, having adjusted to the environment, the hard part was behind her and personal equilibrium would be comparatively easy to maintain. Evidently not; to her dismay, she felt the edges of her psyche start to fray, eroding by ragged degree as if flayed by whips or scoured away by abrasives.

Despite every effort, Leesa was losing it again. She concentrated for all she was worth, clinging to her sense of self, trying to ward off the outside, but this was just more of the same tactic she had employed since arriving here and it patently wasn't working.

For the first time she felt the stirrings of fear. There was no Plan B; she had no idea what else to attempt. As panic threatened to overwhelm her, the part of her that never slept came to the rescue. It offered a solid, unshakeable core, which she clung to, drawing the tattered elements of her consciousness together and curling up in the mental equivalent of the foetal position, centring on her aug and then retreating within it and pulling down the shutters behind her.

By retreating like this she surrendered control to the inorganic part of her and she was glad to do so. There was a sense of detachment – she no longer felt fully engaged with her own actions, more a passenger within her own mind. This was a reversal of the normal state of things, the delicate balance that enabled the two sides of her to integrate and function had been turned upside down, and it was the closest she had ever been to fully becoming an automaton. She found the clinical, unemotional thought processes and decision-making of her auganic mind fascinating, never having observed them from this perspective before, never really stopping to consider them in their own right. She could still sense the outside, but everything was muted, manageable; even her emotions seeming dulled to the point where they were more the memory of an emotion than the genuine article. She did feel relief, and shock at what had so nearly happened to her, but these were watered down reactions and of little relevance, the responses of someone else that she was sharing vicariously.

In this semi-somnambulant state, Leesa was able to make progress once more.

She found him, at last, lying on his back, in repose, much as he had been in the physical world. His skin glowed with colour, a kaleidoscope of shades that danced and swirled and contracted, only to burst forth in a firework of primaries and pastels.

She picked him up. He weighed nothing.

Her aug knew the way, and in the blink of an eye it brought them both home.

She gasped and shuddered and blinked, trying to adjust to a reality that seemed suddenly insipid and watery bland.

"Lees! Lees! Are you all right?" Jen hovered above her. She managed to focus, seeing concern etched on her friend's face.

"Yeah," she managed, wondering if it was true, "but I'm not sure anyone else would have been." She avoided any direct mention of her aug, of how it had been her refuge, conscious of the facility's owner, Pedre, hovering at Jen's shoulder, and a small crowd of onlookers beyond him.

When they first found this place, initial impressions had been less than favourable. It stood open-fronted, the interior cluttered with irregular rows of immersion couches, sensory chairs, quick-jump headpieces and gaming platforms, and as they approached the main signage leapt out at them in crude holographic splendour, declaring "Pedre's Sensory Emporium".

"Amusement arcade," Jen had muttered, while Leesa's immediate thought was *sleaze pit*. "Are you sure he's in there?"

"Yeah, at least his perminal is."

There weren't too many people on this world called Mosi Jalloh and only one on this continent, according to official records. People here didn't realise, or more likely chose not to think about, how vulnerable their perminals were to official monitoring and tracking. Leesa didn't have to hack into the highly secure system that kept tabs on folk to locate Mosi, she just had to hack the network that fed information to that system. Of course, there remained an outside chance that this wasn't *their* Mosi, but she doubted it.

Layers of sterile jangly noise washed over them as they stepped inside, ensuring that second impressions remained as rock-bottom as the first.

The commotion was obvious at once – a cluster of people gathered around one of the couches towards the back of the emporium, alarmed voices calling for medics rising above the tinny background sounds. When she saw who was lying supine on the couch, Leesa's heart sank: Mosi Jalloh, better known to them as Geminum. They were too late. Saflik had got to him before them.

Looks, however, can be deceptive. It turned out that Mosi wasn't dead; comatose, yes, and unresponsive, but still breathing. As Leesa allowed herself a moment to feel relief, Jen had taken charge, pressuring the emporium's owner Pedre into co-operating: "You don't want to have a customer dying while plugged into one of your immersions, do you? What would that do to business? Come on then! There's no time to lose..."

They couldn't simply unplug Mosi, there was too much risk of permanent damage that way, of not all of him coming back. The option was there, though, at the back of everyone's mind, but only as a last resort.

They quickly dragged another couch over to rest beside Mosi's, and while Jen monitored from the side-lines Leesa had settled into it. She lay her head back into the cushioning and let the foam-like headrest surround her, closed her eyes as the tinted visor slid over her face, and the outside world receded. Her consciousness was inserted into the same immersive experience that held Mosi in thrall.

Nothing could have prepared her for what she found here. Leesa had rarely indulged in immersions, the auganic part of her mind being too rigid a judge, preventing her from fully enjoying the experience. The part of her that never slept insisted on seeing through the illusions, refusing to accept the imposed realities that immersion relied on. She didn't hesitate in volunteering for the job of rescuing Mosi, confident that whatever loop of false reality had snared him would prove ineffectual against her.

She realised her mistake immediately.

This was no standard immersion trip; the environment – meant in this instance to sooth and calm – was the antithesis of its declared intent, an all-out assault on sane thought and an individual's sense of identity. From the moment she first immersed Leesa came under attack. There was malevolence here and intent. If this was a malfunction, it was a catastrophic one.

Now that she had escaped back to the outside world, her organic self assumed control once more, the aug slipping back to its subordinate role without any fuss or resistance. She didn't attempt to sit up immediately, taking a moment to reorientate. Jen had turned away to check on Jalloh, who still hadn't shown any sign of movement, but now she was back with her.

"Is he...?" Leesa asked.

"I've no idea. He's still breathing and his pulse is strong, but as for his mind..."

"It's nothing more than an unfortunate accident," Pedre continued to hover in the background babbling inanities as Leesa gingerly sat up, having decided she now could. The man fidgeted from one foot to the other, almost wringing his hands with anxiety. "You can't hold me responsible for a mechanical malfunction, no, not at all. It's there in the small print when you enter..."

"Something's not right here, Jen," Leesa said quietly. "These consoles are designed to give a punter a quick thrill and then spit them back into the outside world with a smile on their face and a lighter balance in the bank, not suck a person in and strip away their mind."

"Yes, I know. The energy levels that immersion was drawing on were off the scale. While you were in there I ran a diagnostic. The system's been hacked..."

Whatever Jen had been about to add was forestalled by a groan from close behind her. Jalloh was waking up.

He rolled onto his side and for a moment Leesa thought he was about to throw up over the emporium's floor, but after a series of exaggerated deep breaths he seemed to bring things under control.

Jen had turned to him again, a hand on his shoulder, offering support. "Mosi, do you remember me?"

He looked up, blinking several times, and then his eyes widened. "*Jen?*"

"Yes, yes it's me," and her relief was clear. "Welcome back, Mosi. Leesa's here too. She brought you out."

"Out from where? What's... what's going on?"

"You see, no harm done. Everything's fine." Pedre had raised his voice, speaking as much for the onlookers' benefit as theirs, Leesa suspected.

She had to fight back the urge to jump to her feet and swat the obsequious self-serving toad. Instead she contented herself with a glare that caught and held his gaze and a few choice words. "Shut. The fuck. Up!"

His eyes bulged but he fell mercifully silent, for the moment at least.

"A bad immersion trip," Jen was explaining to Jalloh, who

had dragged himself up into a sitting position. "Leesa went in and got you. Otherwise…"

He looked across at Leesa. "Thank you. How did you find me, though, how did you know I was going to be here?"

She snorted. "Are you kidding? You haven't even bothered to change your name."

"It's my name, why would I want to change it?"

"All right, all right, the drama's over, folks." Pedre had evidently found his voice again, and was now attempting to shoo away the gaggle of onlookers who continued to linger, presumably for fear they might miss something.

"To hide who you used to be," Jen said quietly.

"I thought that was the whole point of keeping our identities secret. No one knows who I am, so why would I bother becoming somebody else?"

Leesa shook her head in response to the imploring look Jen shot her, seeing little point in arguing against that sort of stubbornness masquerading as logic.

Still not having risen from the couch, she leant forward, saying to Jen, "You mentioned a hack?"

"Yes, and not just a general one. None of the other immersion couches or other devices were affected. This was targeted specifically at Mosi's immersive experience and only triggered when he went under."

"What?" Mosi had joined their conspiratorial huddle but now pulled away as if stung. "No. You've gotta have that wrong. Why would anyone come after me?"

"Keep your voice down!"

"You'd be surprised," Leesa added. "It's why we're here. So they would have to be monitoring what's going on in this place, to know when Mosi went under and which couch he'd picked," she continued, thinking aloud.

"Yes, but they could do that from anywhere once they'd hacked the system, you know that. They could be on the other side of the planet for all we know."

Leesa shook her head. "That's not Saflik's style. They'll be close-by so that they can confirm the kill, and they'll do so in person, if possible..."

"Who are Saflik? What's going on here?" Mosi mumbled, still sounding dazed.

Leesa and Jen ignored him, both looking out towards the street beyond the front of the emporium. Two figures had stopped there and were gazing in, a man and a woman. Their stillness marked them out, as did the manner in which they stared directly towards the three of them, ignoring all else. Leesa locked gazes with the man, and knew. They were Saflik. Whether they had come to check on their handiwork or to finish a job interrupted, she couldn't say, but she didn't doubt who they were.

Beside her, Jen vanished.

Jen didn't doubt the two watchers were Saflik – one predator instinctively recognising another. Having made that connection, a red mist descended upon her. These were the same people who had wrecked her life, who had done their damnedest to kill her, not to mention Robin.

She stepped into shadow and ran, the arcade's garish light displays casting a multitude of shadows that granted her an easy passage. She was on them in an instant, shifting back to physical form as she attacked.

Despite the rage that engulfed her, a degree of reason prevailed. Her knives, which had delivered death so swiftly to the actual assassin back home, were of a unique constitution: metal to all intents and purposes but not recognised as such when it came to security scans. Their edge was keener than any ceramic or polymer equivalent, but they were just as undetectable when it mattered. She had brought the twin blades with her, carrying them through planetary safeguards unnoticed, but she knew that assaulting two apparently innocent bystanders with weapons drawn would have consequences, especially if she killed them, which she would. Brawls, on the other hand, were unlikely to provoke too much attention in a neighbourhood like this.

Therefore it was feet and fists that erupted towards the two startled Saflik, bludgeoning force rather than lethal blades. The man was the more powerfully built. Jen knew better than to make assumptions on that score, but she had to select a primary target and it was his lucky day – he was marginally closer. She aimed a kick at the woman, doing so while still in the air, which meant there was momentum behind the blow but no balance or precision. Her foot connected with the woman's ribcage, perhaps with enough force to crack bone, certainly with enough to send her target sprawling.

It was the man, though, who claimed most of her attention. She was coming in from too high an angle to reach the softer, more vulnerable regions of his body, so she punched him in the face, left-handed, while with her right hand she grabbed hold of him to check her momentum, using his neck as a fulcrum and swinging her body around.

Soft tissue compressed against bone as her fist struck his cheek, and she felt cartilage crumble, guessing that the punch must have broken his nose. He staggered and toppled to the ground as she brought her full weight to bear. She landed, his flailing arm almost snagging her as he fell. Jen spun and stamped, aiming for his genitals, but he rolled out of the way and her heel thudded against his thigh.

She followed his roll. He tried to spring to his feet but she struck while he was halfway up, kicking through the hand raised to ward her off and catching him just beneath the jaw. Blood and spittle trailed from his mouth as his head jerked back. He went down and this time showed no sign of rising again.

Someone was shouting and Jen caught movement at the periphery of her vision as people scurried away. She spotted other movement as well. The other Saflik agent, the woman she had kicked, was stirring, pulling something out from within her clothes.

Jen didn't wait to see what it was. She dived towards the bank of gaming machines the woman had landed against – several of them had tumbled over, carapaces cracked and lights dull – crossing into shadow to emerge beside the woman, who had brought the slender gun clear and started to look around to see where her target had gone.

Jen chopped down on her wrist, sending the gun spinning away, then punched as near as she could tell at the same place she had kicked the woman earlier, to be rewarded with a sound that emerged somewhere between a gasp and whimper. The woman's eyes glazed and her face had turned ashen. Before she could recover, Jen grabbed a handful of hair and beat her head twice, as hard as she could, against the solid stand of the console beside them. The woman went limp, unconscious at best. Jen took stock, her awareness finally expanding to take in her surroundings. The man still hadn't moved, lying where he'd fallen. People were staring at her from a wary distance or simply hurrying out and away. Pedre had his hands to his head and was wailing about damage and the cost of repair. Perminals were raised in several hands, and she had to accept that this 'brawl' might not go as unnoticed as she'd hoped.

She stared down at the woman who lay crumpled at her feet. The urge to finish these two bastards off, to make sure they never killed again, was still there, but it was manageable now, no longer a compulsion.

Then Leesa was there beside her, half leading and half dragging Mosi, who had evidently recovered enough to stand.

"We need to get out of here," Leesa said, "before the police, the medics, the news crews, the gang who claim this emporium you've just trashed as territory or whoever else is on the way turns up."

Jen nodded mutely, and allowed herself to be led away.

"Congratulations," Leesa said. "You've gone viral."

They were holed up in a dingy room Leesa had secured after spotting a random 'room to let' sign, Mosi's place being too risky

81

for them to approach given Saflik's presence. Their refuge was above a gaudy bric-a-brac shop in a street of similar outlets ten minutes' brisk walk from Pedre's Sensory Emporium.

The street outside appeared normal. There was no sign of anyone following or looking for them.

"Sorry, I just saw them and…" Jen felt obliged to say.

"Yeah, I know."

At no point had Leesa given any indication that she blamed her, and that just made Jen feel worse. None of the news outlets had picked up on the fight as yet, but recordings had turned up on the local web and were already clocking up impressive viewing figures. It would just take the wrong people to notice and they could find themselves trapped on Callia III with no easy way out.

Jen hadn't seen any stills of her face as yet, but presumably they would appear in due time, as people continued to speculate about the incident. She wondered whether Leesa was beginning to regret seeking her out; she couldn't blame her if she was.

"We need to get off world now," Leesa said, echoing Jen's train of thought, but at least she had said 'we'. "Mosi, you're coming with us."

He shook his head. "I can't, not yet."

"What? But you know the threat."

They had brought him up to speed, showing him the reports of the other Angels' demise while Jen had related her own experiences in harrowing detail.

"I wouldn't have survived if Leesa hadn't been there for me," Jen said. "And you'd be dead if the two of us hadn't turned up. Doesn't that prove to you that we need to face this together? If we don't, we die. It's as simple as that."

"I know, I know," he said, raising a hand as if to ward off any further persuasion. "You don't have to convince me, really."

"Then what do you mean you're not coming with us?" Leesa said. "Saflik have found you. They won't give up. Even if this team has been thwarted they'll send more, assuming more aren't already here."

"I know, really I do. I'm not arguing with any of that," Mosi said, "but there's something I need to do first. After that, I'm committed to the cause a hundred per cent, but I have to sort this out before I go anywhere, and I can't ask you to wait around. After what happened at Pedre's there's going to be a net tightening for you, and you have to get off world before it closes. Leave word of where you've gone and I'll follow, as soon as I can."

"What could be more important than preserving your own life?"

"A promise. One that I won't break."

"You're kidding us, right?"

"No, no I'm not. I need to do this, and you need to go. That's just the way it is." He shrugged, as if to suggest it was out of his control. "We'll meet up again soon."

Jen and Leesa stared at each other, but neither could find anything more to say.

They went their separate ways, with Mosi again promising to seek them out as soon as he was in a position to do so. Jen couldn't shake the conviction that this was a mistake for all concerned. She felt deflated by their failure to recruit him, disappointed to a degree that even she recognised as being out of proportion with events, but she still didn't understand *how* they were leaving without him.

"Do you think he meant what he said, about joining us later once he's done whatever it is that's keeping him here?" she asked, hating herself for needing that level of reassurance even as she spoke.

"No. Yes. Oh... I don't know." Leesa sounded as despondent as Jen felt. "It doesn't really matter, does it? How will he find us even if he does mean it? *We've* no idea where we're going next ourselves."

Mosi had given them a friend's perminal details, suggesting they use it as a dead drop to leave a message before they left

Callia III, letting him know where they were bound, but Jen had to wonder who was kidding who. They couldn't risk Saflik intercepting such a message and a simple vague destination wasn't likely to help Mosi catch up with them even if they did.

"Hell! We should have been more insistent, refused to take no for an answer," Leesa said.

"We didn't. It was more of a 'yes, but'."

"I know. Even so… Why didn't we go with him? Neither of us even tried to."

Jen shook her head. "He wouldn't have bought it. Whatever he needs to do, it's something personal, and I got the feeling company was the last thing he wanted."

"Yeah, you're right, I realise that. But what if they're all like this – everyone we find? It's not as if we're the Dark Angels any more, inviting them to return to the fold, not really. We're just a bunch of individuals who used to know each other a long time ago."

Jen knew that Leesa had a point. "We need to find something that's guaranteed to unify us," she said, "something that everyone will respond to."

"Isn't the threat of assassination enough?"

"No, clearly it isn't. We need something more, something that every Angel can believe in and trust… There's only one person capable of fitting that brief. We need the captain."

"Maybe you're right," Leesa said, nodding slowly. Then she grinned. "So it's just as well I know where he is, then, isn't it?"

Jen stared at her. "You what?"

"I didn't want to go there, not yet, but… I've seen him."

"And you were thinking of mentioning this when, exactly?"

"Don't get angry; it's not that simple… I didn't know who he was at the time. Come to that, I didn't know who *I* was. Long story," she added in response to Jen's enquiring look. "The thing is, he didn't reveal himself or acknowledge me when he had the chance to, didn't say a thing. Not until afterwards, at any rate, when I was long gone and not likely to be coming back in a hurry…"

"What does any of that matter? It's the *captain*!"

"I know, I get it, truly I do. It's just… He seemed so settled, Jen, so sure of who he's become. What if *he* doesn't want to join us? What if he says no? Where would that leave us? After all, he walked away from the Angels once before."

"That was different," Jen said quickly. "We'd all had enough by then; we all wanted to reclaim a normal life while there was still a chance we could." She certainly had, at any rate.

"Maybe. But I was the closest to him, don't forget, and the truth is that even *I* don't know the full reason he called it a day."

"Is that why you've been holding this back until now?"

"I suppose so, yes. I was hoping that if we approached him later, when there are more of us… he couldn't say no."

"For Elders' sake, Lees! It's a chance we're going to have to take. We can't afford to wait, not after losing Mosi. If we're going to make this work, we need the captain *now*."

"Yeah, okay. I agree."

"So where is he?"

"New Sparta. He's working for one of the big banks."

"You're kidding me, right?"

"Only wish I was. You don't honestly think I'd joke about something like that, do you?"

"No, I don't suppose you would." She turned the notion over in her mind: the captain, a *banker*? Jen doubted anything Leesa might have said could have surprised her more.

SEVEN

I've discovered another thing that might interest you regarding our mysterious friend Bowman, Mudball said the moment Drake started to emerge from the grip of sleep.

Hang on a minute and let me wake up first, will you?

Oh, sorry, I thought this was supposed to be important.

Of course it is. Drake sat up, rubbing sleep from his eyes and steeling himself for the inevitable; his mental processes would have to catch up in their own time. *Okay, go ahead.*

As you know, there's no record of this individual's arrival or departure for what we presume to have been his recent visit, but they weren't always so meticulous. Although no passenger is named, either side of the clusters of appointments that occurred three and four years ago there are records of a ship arriving at the port and departing again. Point of origin for the inward trip and destination on the outward are recorded as... New Sparta.

Really? Drake digested that, coming fully awake in a rush, the muzziness of sleep banished in an instant. Until now he had assumed that, like Payne, this Bowman character was someone from his past – another former Angel using an alias or somebody they'd encountered during that period, but this cast things in a new light. A connection with New Sparta suggested that Bowman could be someone a little more contemporary...

He couldn't help but wonder how long Payne had known who he was and, leading on from that, how long he might have been a factor in whatever was being planned here. Most conspiracy theories were just that – theories; but every now and then you came across one that had some substance. This had all the hallmarks of being the latter.

Drake wasn't sure what to expect from the day's excursion. He wouldn't have been surprised if Payne conjured up some pretext not to take them to the cache at all, given what had happened on the trip so far. He felt resigned to whatever the day revealed, facing it stoically, refusing to get his hopes up, and determined not to show any impatience to Payne. While he was intrigued to discover precisely how the Endurians had kept a cache hidden for so long, he was not about to waste any time speculating about it.

Over breakfast, it became evident that Ungar had no such compunctions.

"So what's your theory regarding the cache? Are we about to be taken by private jet on a short internal flight to a secret location somewhere deep in the unexplored interior of the continent, or whisked away via an unregistered and unsuspected underground rail line to a shielded chamber somewhere deep beneath the planet's outer mantel, or maybe to a shuttle that will blast off from a second concealed spaceport to destination unknown...?

Drake laughed. "I'm trying to keep an open mind on the subject." He wasn't entirely sure how Ungar had talked his way on to the cache visit but nor was he complaining; he enjoyed the historian's company, and any additional buffer between him and Payne was to be welcomed.

"Oh come on, man, you must have *some* theory."

"To be honest, I've considered a dozen possible scenarios, including variations of the ones you've suggested, but none of them explain how the locals have kept the cache's location a secret for so long, so..." Drake shrugged.

"Hmph. Has anyone ever told you that you're far too pragmatic for your own good?"

Many times, Mudball said in Drake's head.

The simple truth was that none of Ungar's suggestions would have surprised Drake – assuming an additional layer of cunning concealment that he hadn't thought of. In the end, though, what actually occurred did.

The car – quite possibly the same car they had ridden in the previous day; the same model and dark grey colour, certainly – collected them from the front of the hotel as arranged. Once again Evans was their driver and Payne was sitting inside. On the plus side, at least the rain had finally stopped. A quick glance skyward revealed only clouds, so Drake was going to have to be patient for a view of the parent planet.

"So," Ungar said as he sat down beside Payne, "a mystery tour."

"Indeed, though it won't be a mystery for long."

Was that a deliberate tease, or did it really mean that the cache was nearby?

Drake had no idea what Ungar was anticipating at this point, but for his part he certainly hadn't expected the car to travel such a short distance. They took a left turn, a right turn and then drove for a couple of minutes before swinging in to face a broad corrugated door – all peeling white paint with green moss at the edges – in what appeared to be a derelict building in a rundown neighbourhood towards the edge of town.

"This will all look very different, of course, by the time we open for visitors," Payne said. "The plan is for there to be a series of cafés and eateries along here. The project will lead to regeneration for this whole area."

At their approach, the door retracted upwards – not ponderously as its appearance might have suggested, but smoothly and quickly. The car slowed but didn't have to come to a complete halt, rolling forward into the building's interior, which proved to be one large, empty space, capable of accommodating a hundred or more cars their size.

Here they stopped, Evans jumping out to hold the door open for Payne, while Drake and Ungar climbed out the other side.

Drake's mind was racing. The cache couldn't be here, not right in the capital. This was the most obvious place to look and where attempts to locate it would have been concentrated. He recalled Ungar's frivolous suggestion over breakfast about a secret underground rail line. Could the historian have been closer to the truth than either of them realised? He began to speculate as to how something like that could be accomplished without being detected: a system built using existing mining tunnels perhaps, keeping modifications to a minimum, and relying on manual labour for much of the work to reduce tell-tale energy signatures...

I thought you weren't going to conjecture, Mudball reminded him.

You may have noticed that consistency doesn't number among humanity's strongest traits.

I had spotted that, as it happens.

No chair in evidence for Payne on this occasion. He stood unaided, without any apparent difficulty, presumably using the 'exo-legs' he had referred to back on New Sparta. If so, they were effectively concealed beneath loose-fitting trousers, and his movements, when he walked, were disarmingly natural.

"Gentlemen, this way, if you will."

He called you a gentleman, Mudball observed. *Your natural charm must be winning him over.*

Payne led the way across the empty room, their footfalls echoing against the unforgiving concrete. Evans brought up the rear, walking a couple of paces behind them as seemed his wont.

"I hope you appreciate how rare this is," Payne said, slowing so that he walked beside the two visitors rather than ahead of them. "Very few outsiders have ever been permitted to visit the cache before now."

Tempted though he was to point out that the proposed venture into tourism would soon change all that, Drake stayed silent.

"This would act as a reception area, Mr Drake," Payne said, gesturing to take in the room. "Here visitors will be processed and any recording devices confiscated for the duration of their visit. Initially, visitors will be taken through in parties, each accompanied by a guide. There will be a series of 3D presentations at specific points of particular interest to supplement the guide's commentary and, eventually, we propose providing each visitor with individual virtual guides, but I'm getting ahead of myself, that won't be until phase three.

"As I'm sure you know, many have tried to discover the location of our cache without success. I have to admit that the various theories as to why have been a source of considerable amusement over the years. Some of them are quite imaginative. I'm still confident, however, that what you are about to see will amaze you."

Likes the sound of his own voice, doesn't he, Mudball said.

Doesn't he just. Drake didn't recall Donal being this vociferous in his days with the Dark Angels, but then he hadn't been trying to sell anything back then. This was the first time since they left Reese's office that Payne had made any attempt to promote the project to Drake, when he had the whole of the journey from New Sparta to this room in which to do so, had he so wished.

There was something else that felt wrong to him. "Will any of your colleagues be joining us today?" he asked.

So far, the only official from Enduril's government Drake had come into contact with was Payne himself. He hadn't expected a state banquet or a red carpet to be rolled out, but maybe a delegation to join them here on what was, after all, his first morning in their capital. If the Enduril government was trying to woo First Solar's representative to their cause, they weren't putting a great deal of effort into it as yet. Assessing the political situation was also going to be pretty difficult if he didn't meet with any politicians.

"Not today, no," Payne replied. "This is just an initial taster, to introduce you to the cache. There'll be plenty of time to meet everyone else later."

Drake couldn't escape the feeling that Payne was putting on a performance; that he had now slipped into a role he couldn't be bothered with on the trip out here. That and the surprising absence of any other representatives of authority lent credence to Reese's misgivings about the whole project, and Drake had yet to discover anything to allay those concerns.

They had crossed the room and now stood before an unassuming wooden door at the far side, which came complete with a very retro-looking manual doorknob. Beside the door stood an incongruously modern security box, affixed to both the wall and floor.

"I must ask you to deposit your perminals and any other recording devices you may be carrying here," Payne said, smiling.

After a brief hesitation, both Drake and Ungar did so, each placing their perminal into the open box.

"Is this strictly necessary," Ungar asked, even as he complied.

"I'm afraid so. They'll be here waiting for you on your return. Mr Drake, your cane too, if you please. Due to its length we'll rest it beside the box, to be collected afterwards along with your perminal, but Evans will remain here to keep an eye on things and I promise you it will be safe."

If he suggests putting me in that damned box I'll strangle him, Mudball said. *Maybe his dismembered body will fit in there even if your cane won't.*

"I'm sorry, but I can't trust my mobility without my cane, especially in an unfamiliar environment with all manner of potential obstacles," Drake said, having anticipated something of the sort.

"Ah yes, that old wound of yours. No need to worry, there won't be a great deal of moving about once we're there. I'm sure you'll cope without it."

"Thank you for the reassurance but I'd feel a lot more comfortable having the cane with me, just in case. I'm sure you can make an exception in this instance. After all, you have your exo-legs, I have my cane."

"I only wish I could, but my hands are tied." Payne reached out, hands extended with palms up, to demonstrate his helplessness. "Our rules are very clear on this. I can't allow you access to the cache carrying anything that might conceal a recording device, such as your cane."

Is this bozo for real? Mudball fumed. *Doesn't he realise that a microrecorder could be concealed almost anywhere on your clothing?*

Probably, Drake replied, *but that's not the point.*

Oh I see. Is this another instance of that macho posturing and point scoring that you humans enjoy so much?

Something like that.

"That's unfortunate," Drake said aloud, all smiles. "However, if there really is no compromise on this, I'll just have to accept the situation." He reached into the security box and reclaimed his perminal before glancing at Ungar. "Enjoy the visit to the cache, Theo. I'm sure it will be remarkable and I look forward to hearing all about it at the hotel later." With that, and a nod towards Payne, he turned and started to walk back towards the car.

He had taken perhaps a dozen paces before Payne called after him, "And I suppose you'll report to First Solar that you were denied access to the cache."

Drake paused and turned back towards the other three men, holding out his hands in an imitation of Payne's earlier gesture. "The current stand-off would seem to render any further negotiations pointless."

His gaze locked with Payne's and for a frozen moment he saw in the other man's eyes naked hatred to a degree he had rarely witnessed before. In that instant he dared hope that Payne might reveal the true reason he had brought him here, but then it was gone. Payne broke eye contact.

"Very well," he said, smiling once more. "If you feel that strongly about your cane, of course you must keep it with you. I'll accept responsibility for the decision and will grovel to my colleagues later."

Does this mean that we won the posturing competition? Mudball asked.

Pretty much.

Go us!

Drake walked back to join the others, managing not to swing his cane in the process despite a strong temptation to do so. He placed his perminal back in the security locker, looked Payne in the eye and said, with all the sincerity he could muster, "Thank you."

"Well, I'm glad that's sorted," Ungar said, in a transparent attempt to lift the mood. "It wouldn't have been the same going in there without you, Corbin."

As Evans sealed the security box, Payne stepped back towards the door, recovering his composure. Judging by the man's grin as he reached forward to open the door, Drake had a feeling that he was about to get some answers, one way or another.

At the last moment Payne paused, his hand hovering over the doorknob. "Please don't be alarmed by what you're about to experience. I promise you it's perfectly safe."

With that he gripped the handle and swung the door open, to reveal... a small plain cubicle.

"An elevator?" Ungar exclaimed, sounding as nonplussed as Drake felt.

"Please, step inside."

Drake and Ungar did so, followed by Payne, with Evans remaining at his station by the security box. There was sufficient room in there for the three of them, though not with a great deal to spare.

Then Payne did something which Drake didn't quite follow, and his entire world turned inside out; at least, that was how it felt. Whenever he was aboard a ship that crossed into RzSpace, Drake experienced a brief flash of expansion, a sense that his mind had spread outwards to fill the whole cosmos. It only lasted for a fraction of a second before his consciousness snapped back into its proper place, but it was perhaps the most pleasant aspect of travelling through that mathematical realm.

This was the opposite.

He felt a brief flash of... not quite agony, that was too strong a word, but of *pressure*. Whereas the transition into RzSpace seemed to send his consciousness racing outward, this was all about going inward. He felt that his vital organs had imploded, as if two giant hands had encircled them and squeezed them together. As with Rz transition, the sensation was instantaneous, gone before his brain could fully register the discomfort, but it left him feeling breathless and disorientated, the memory of the pain infinitely worse than the sensation itself.

Wow, said Mudball, *that was intense.*

That's one way of putting it.

We're not where we were.

No kidding.

When they had entered the small cubicle, a blank wall had confronted them. That wall was now gone. Instead they peered out into what was clearly a sizeable cache.

No, you don't understand, the small alien said. *We're no longer in the same universe.*

What?

"Welcome to the Enduril II cache," Payne was saying. "I do hope the transition from there to here wasn't too uncomfortable." The look he directed at Drake as he spoke suggested quite the opposite.

"You have just experienced the reason the cache's location has proven such a perplexing puzzle to so many people over so many years. The cache was never on one of the other moons, or hidden within the dense jungles of this one. It isn't buried deep within Enduril II's labyrinthine mines or even within the mantle of Enduril itself. It is right here, in Hamilton, which is why the town has remained the capital even when the economic support the community was founded on has gone. The cache is here. Except, of course, that it isn't.

"The cache occupies its own space, a realm adjacent to but quite separate from our plane of existence."

A pocket universe! Mudball exclaimed.

The phrase sent a chill down Drake's spine, and he had no idea why.

"Astonishing!" Ungar said.

"And, as agreed, not for publication until we are ready,"

Payne said sharply.

"Of course, of course."

Drake was starting to recover; enough, at least, to take in his surroundings. He had visited many caches since he started as a field agent for First Solar, but had never set foot inside any that were as large as this one. Most chambers were spacious, but this seemed... cavernous; he could think of no better word. Even the accumulated artefacts, of which there were many, seemed diminished by the setting.

Once you've gone to the trouble of creating a pocket universe, why bother thinking small? Mudball said. *It's not as if you're going to inconvenience the neighbours.*

Really? Drake said. *I'd have thought the bigger you make a place like this the more energy it requires to establish and maintain.*

Not really – you'd be surprised. The tough part is creating the pocket in the first place – or accessing it; that's another of those chicken or the egg questions which you humans love to pontificate over: did we create the pocket universe or was it there all along just waiting to be discovered?

Schrödinger's cat, Drake said, remembering an ancient philosophical paradox.

Whatever; the point is that once you've put all that energy and effort into opening such a universe, the size becomes immaterial, up to a point.

I didn't realise you were such an expert.

Compared to you, of course I am.

Drake's attention returned to the artefacts. What struck him immediately was how ordered everything looked. In his experience, most caches exhibited a degree of messiness, of items knocked over and never righted or heaped on top of each other in careless abandon, tilted precariously, spilling over, or leaning against each other at awkward angles.

There was none of that here. Where he would have expected disorder there was instead neatness. It was as if housekeeping had come in and tidied the chamber while everyone was out.

"Has the cache always been this tidy," he asked.

"Yes," Payne replied. "I understand that other caches tend

towards the chaotic, but I'm assured that such was never the case here, that the contents have been arranged like this, in an orderly fashion, from the very first."

Drake recognised some of the artefacts by general type, but many more were new to him. There were the usual bejewelled trinkets of unfamiliar style and construction – what appeared to be a hollow filigree cube caught his eye, a tiny cage spun from fine strands of bright red rubies – as did an intricate item that looked to be a convoluted Möbius strip, the surface of which seemed to flow restlessly as if formed of a liquid that was subject to the pull of unseen forces.

Not one of these smaller items was placed carelessly or strewn across the floor in casual abandon as previous experience had primed him for. Instead, they were arranged with precision atop other, larger objects; some individually, others in neat piles.

Even the familiar slender rods of unfathomable substance shot through with a sparkle of diamond dust were all gathered together and neatly stacked on top of a long tall oblong box, which itself was inscribed in a flowing pictorial script that might have been a form of writing but – or so experts had concluded after analysing similar finds – was most likely an elaborate form of decoration. Nothing ran free; the scene had none of the spontaneity Drake was used to finding in Elder caches, and as a result lacked some of the sense of wonder. The wonder was still there but it had been tamed, organised, every element in its place.

A cache guardian with OCD, he couldn't resist commenting to Mudball.

Yeah, it's all a bit creepy if you ask me. How can any intelligence maintain this level of control over the course of so many centuries?

Can't help but wonder how it's likely to react to hordes of unruly tourists traipsing through here. The guardian was apparently content to allow the Endurians unhindered access, but would it really accept without complaint an invasion such as Payne was proposing? *Have you made contact yet?*

No. I can sense him, but he's being coy. I'll keep working on it.

Payne had started to lead them down the central aisle – which stretched to the back of the chamber in a perfectly straight line that any designer would have been proud of. "We had the lighting installed decades ago," he explained.

"And the cache guardian allowed that?" Drake asked.

"Oh yes, we have a good working relationship."

Despite his outwardly casual tone, Payne was evidently working to a timetable. He set a fairly brisk pace as they progressed through the chamber, pointing out this article and that but never lingering. Drake determined to test his resolve.

Ahead and to their left stood a trio of artefacts atop a long dull grey lozenge-shaped casket, its surface resembling machine-tooled metal. The three objects were all different and positioned individually, as if on display. Drake had never seen their like before. He broke away from their small group and stepped towards them.

"Please be careful, Mr Drake," Payne said. "Some of the artefacts in here are dangerous. For your own safety I must ask you not to touch anything. Especially not *those*." Both Ungar and Payne had stopped and were watching him.

"Oh, and what makes these three in particular so dangerous?" Drake asked.

"The one to your left," and Payne indicated an irregular black dish, its edges serrated like a leaf's, with silver veins running through it. "We call that the inverter. The name is self-explanatory. Anything that touches the upper surface is quite literally turned inside out. It works on both organic and inorganic objects."

Drake stared at the dish with renewed respect. It didn't lie flat against the casket but curved gently upwards at the edges, like a webbed hand. "I pity the poor soul who first discovered that," he murmured.

"It was quite... messy, by all accounts."

"And this?" Drake indicated a triangle, perfectly formed with a circular hole in the middle. The object seemed to be cast in grey metal but its surface looked slick, almost oily, and as Drake pointed at it the empty hole at its centre began to fill with red light.

"Ah yes, there's been some debate about that. It's either a weapon that disintegrates whatever touches it – though that theory is largely discredited these days – or... it's a matter transmitter."

Drake stared at him. "Are you serious?"

"That's our best guess. Anyone who touches that triangle vanishes."

"Why has the theory about it being a weapon fallen out of favour, then?"

"Because at the moment of contact, of disintegration, we've traced an energy signature crossing back into the physical universe and shooting in an incredibly tight beam into space."

"Where to?"

"That, of course, is the question. If this *is* a matter transmitter, no one's ever come back to tell us where they went. All we know is that they disappear and a beam of energy is created at the same instant, a beam that vanishes the moment it leaves the atmosphere – not dissipating you understand, it simply disappears with no residue."

I wonder how many test subjects disappeared along the way before they reached these conclusions, Drake thought to Mudball, who remained silent.

"And on that evidence you've concluded 'matter transmitter'?" he said out loud.

"Yes. That's our best guess based on what we know. We've extrapolated the path of the beam, of course, but have found no obvious target or receiver. Our hypothesis is that it *did* go somewhere once, via RzSpace or some other means that's even swifter, but as you're well aware the stars aren't static. Where once, in the time of the Elders, there might have been another terminal waiting on signals fired from this one, now there is only empty space, whatever waited at the other end having moved out of range long ago or fallen into disrepair.

Mudball?

No idea, I'm afraid, but my advice would be to listen to the man and don't touch.

Thank you so much for that.

"The third item," Payne was saying, "now that's the interesting one."

And a matter transmitter isn't? Despite the thought, Drake's attention turned to the final artefact in line. This differed from the other two in that it was a bolt of cloth, or perhaps a garment. It was difficult to be certain because the material was neatly folded – of course – making it hard to gauge dimensions or shape.

"The Heben Cloth," Payne said.

Only once before had Drake seen anything like this in a cache chamber, and that was when Leesa had stumbled on the shroud that transformed her into Hel N. The two were far from identical, though; whereas Hel N's skin was of brightest silver, the Heben Cloth displayed a kaleidoscope of colours that seemed to shift as he watched. Purple and mauve predominated but there were also blues and greens and wine red, all twisting around each other in a languid, sinuous dance. The effect was almost erotic and yet as the same time vaguely... unwholesome.

As he regarded the neat square of cloth, Drake felt the same odd sense of dislocation that had struck him at first mention of the cache occupying its own pocket universe.

His reaction was evidently enough to draw Mudball's attention. *Are you all right?* the alien asked.

Yes, I'm fine, Drake replied, clamping down on his thoughts, not willing to share this even with Mudball until he'd had a chance to analyse the implications himself.

"What does this Heben Cloth do?" Ungar asked into the silence left by Drake's distraction.

"It was named after Hebe, the Goddess of Youth in an ancient culture of old Earth," Payne explained. "In essence, the cloth freezes the aging process." He spoke casually, as if this were a matter of little consequence.

"When you say 'freezes'…?" Ungar said.

"Quite literary that. Any organic matter wrapped in the cloth for more than a few seconds will benefit from the halting of the aging process for a period of a little less than a standard year. Cells will not degenerate, none of the biological aspects of aging will advance during that period. The cloak won't return your lost youth, but it does prevent you from losing any more of it."

That explains his unaltered face, Mudball said.

"There are no apparent side effects, and the process can be repeated with identical results once the freezing effect has worn off," Payne added.

"A veritable Fountain of Youth," Ungar said, reverence in his voice. "That is quite remarkable."

"A Cloak of Youth, at any rate," Drake said, having recovered sufficient composure to at least feign interest.

"Now, if we may continue?" And with that, Payne led them forward once more.

Drake paid scant attention, his thoughts in turmoil. He had effectively shut Mudball out, right up until the moment the alien battered his way back in, his thoughts insistent, evidently in a state of high excitement

Done it! Mudball declared. *I've made contact with the guardian and, I must say, I've never encountered a cache entity quite like this before.*

Drake forced himself to focus, knowing the importance of Mudball's news. He was wary of reading too much into the alien's 'voice', conscious of the temptation to anthropomorphise. It was easy to fall into the trap of assessing Mudball's intonation in human terms, especially when 'human' was your only frame of reference, and he suspected that Mudball wasn't above pandering to that. The longer the alien spent with him, the more human his voice had become, or had *seemed* to become. Despite all that, Drake couldn't escape the impression that the alien seemed impressed.

In what way? he asked.

It's so... docile.

Weak, you mean?

No, not that at all, Mudball assured him. *In fact, quite the opposite. This one's strong, but instead of viewing humans as unwanted intruders, it seems to welcome them, to relish their presence. I don't understand. Unless...*

What?

But Mudball was silent.

Unless what? Drake prompted.

Nothing. Let me think this through and I'll say more once I can make more sense of this.

Drake knew there was no point in pressing Mudball. The alien would share its conclusions only when good and ready; besides, the prospect of Mudball withdrawing into his own thoughts for a while suited Drake just fine. It enabled him to do the same. He made sure not to let any of that show, however, as he said: *anything that might give us a handle on what's going on here, no matter how outlandish, I want to know.*

Oh, don't worry, you will. I mean, who else have I got to brag to?

As the brief tour came to an end and Payne led them back to the 'elevator' and hence to the wider universe, Drake continued to be reticent, his thoughts deeply troubled. He knew it was impossible, but so much about this place resonated with something almost remembered that he couldn't escape a nagging conviction that he had visited the Enduril II cache chamber before.

EIGHT

Jen had never been to New Sparta. She'd heard of it, of course, usually as a swear word. Here was the antithesis of everything the Dark Angels had believed in: the financial hub of human commerce, source of the exploitative culture that had spread to the stars to create a pyramid structure of wealth, where money flowed from the broad base to the narrow tip; the elite – usually represented by the words 'New Sparta'. The *Ion Raider*'s crew had, in their own modest fashion, done their best to redress that balance, skirting the edge of legal practice and stepping beyond it when circumstances required. Trips to the beating heart that pumped capitalism around the settled worlds had never been high on their agenda and Jen liked to think there would have been parties aplenty on New Sparta the day the Dark Angels disbanded.

The concept of Cornische being here, of his earning a living as part of the corporate machine was... bizarre to say the least.

"Well, you've got to give the captain credit for hiding in the last place anyone would think to look for him," Leesa said, her thoughts evidently following a similar course to Jen's.

They had no real plan as yet, beyond finding Cornische. Leesa had done well to discover as much about these Saflik as she had, but when Jen sat back and analysed it, she was dismayed by how little that amounted to. They had no notion, for example, who their enemies were or where they were based. They had no idea of how to strike back and hurt them.

Once they had connected with Cornische and informed him of the situation, that wouldn't be her problem any more. It would be his.

If Opal City had come as a culture shock, then New Sparta

was even more so. Traffic here was a nightmare – at least that was her first impression. She had never *seen* so many vehicles in such close proximity moving at such breakneck speed. As she and Leesa emerged from the terminal, Jen simply stopped and stared; she couldn't help herself.

"You get used to it," Leesa assured her. "In central areas like this traffic flow is automatically regulated. That's why you don't see any accidents or even snarl-ups, despite the speed and volume of cars. If a driver attempts to override and resume manual control, their vehicle is shunted out of the flow and parked, with all systems suppressed until they pay a hefty fine. Try that a second time and the fine becomes astronomical; a third, and you're banned from driving in the city environs."

"So you're telling me that this is actually *safe?*" The assessment was counter-intuitive to everything her eyes were reporting, that was for sure.

"Pretty much. It's a lot safer than most traffic systems you'll find, at any rate."

"Do we have to actually go in one of those things?" She nodded towards the passing cars.

Leesa laughed. "No, I brought us out the tube system close enough to First Solar's offices that we can walk from here."

"Thank the Elders for that."

"You ought to try it at least once while we're here, though, if only for the experience."

While Jen appreciated the advice, her response was a firm "Thanks but no thanks." She looked around, a little overwhelmed by the view, having to crane her neck to see the tops of the buildings closest to them. "So, where to now?"

"This way." Leesa set out to their left, with Jen hurrying to catch up. "See the big tiered building ahead, the one that looks to be all tinted glass? That's First Solar's head office."

"A-ha."

That was the other thing about New Sparta. Jen had thought Opal boasted some towering structures, but this place took the concept to another level. "Cloud scrapers," she said softly, recalling the phrase.

"Aren't they just," Leesa said. "Amazing place, isn't it?"

Jen kept quiet. To her this forest of super-high buildings that rose up around her on every side was vaguely disturbing. It brought home just how insignificant she was – *all* humans were – in the grand scheme of things. She didn't feel threatened as such, more… humbled.

She wondered if some of the city's residents felt this too, subconsciously; because while some of the folk they passed were dressed in tasteful elegance that spoke of refinement and cultural confidence, others were clad in flamboyant extravagance, as if determined to ensure they wouldn't be overlooked, no matter how imposing their surroundings.

To reach the First Solar building Jen and Leesa had to cross two roads – the streets laid out on a grid system so that everything bisected at right angles; a pattern that made sense in so many ways but which struck Jen as bland and… soulless. The traffic barely appeared to slow even at junctions, so the prospect would have been daunting but for the abundance of skybridges: gently arched structures that carried pedestrians over the roads on smooth conveyer-belt travellators. The skybridges were essentially transparent, which meant you had an unobstructed view of the speeding traffic beneath as you sailed across the road – a privilege Jen could have done without.

The First Solar building gave the impression that it was entirely constructed of smoky dark glass, which was completely opaque from the outside looking in. The only exception was the ground floor lobby. Here the glass was crystal clear, presumably so that any passer-by could note that the bank was wealthy enough to employ a human receptionist – flesh and blood, not a hologram or a simulacrum, as Jen and Leesa were soon able to confirm.

The receptionist – a woman, tall, slender, with golden skin and hair and a bright red suit – met their approach with a smile and a formulaic greeting. She took their request to see Corbin Drake and confirmation that no, they didn't have an appointment, in her stride, smiling and saying, "Just one moment while I check if Mr Drake is in the building."

Moments later a suited man appeared to escort them to 'Mr Drake's department'. After an overly rapid elevator ride – why did everything on New Sparta have to happen so *quickly*? – they were ushered into an office on the 45th floor. Inside they found not Drake as they'd hoped, but rather a short silver-haired woman with an air of authority and unnervingly intelligent eyes.

"Good morning," the woman said. "I'm Terry Reese, Senior Loan Advisor for First Solar. I understand you're hoping to see Representative Drake. He's not here at the moment – absent on assignment, but I'm his boss. How can I help you?"

Jen and Leesa exchanged glances, neither sure of what the heck they ought to say in response.

Terry Reese prided herself on being able to adapt to any given situation and take the unexpected in her stride. It was a quality that had served her well in a career that had seen her rise to a position of seniority within one of the most powerful financial institutions in human history. It was, she suspected, an ability that was about to be sorely tested.

Perhaps that was why she hesitated, why her thoughts now turned to memories that were usually docile, content to stay locked away in the recesses of her mind: the relationship sacrificed when she first moved to New Sparta – she struggled to recall his face now, though his voice came through clearly enough, as did the cosy sense of warmth that being with him had inspired – and the estrangement from her parents. Her father had always taken pride in her achievements, she knew that; though he would never dare admit as much in the presence of her mother, who refused to forgive her daughter for 'selling out' to the corporate establishment.

Terry sighed. These were issues she had wrestled into

submission long ago, any regrets at past choices appeased. So why were they resurfacing now? Not really that hard to fathom: procrastination; a friend whose charms she had rejected in her teens.

Refusing to be distracted any further, Terry stood up, took a deep breath, and adopted her most disarming smile. "Show them in," she said to the empty air.

The door slid open and two women stepped through. The nearest scowled, suggesting she wasn't willing to take much more of being treated like this. She was lean, muscular, a coiled spring awaiting the chance to be released; young at first sight, but there was a maturity in depths of her eyes and in the way she held herself that belied the assessment. The other woman was darker skinned, lithe of body, and attractive; apparently a little older than her companion but possessing a grace of movement that brought to mind a dancer, or a trained assassin. Whereas the first woman glared at Terry, this one's gaze darted everywhere, taking in the sparsely furnished office, the flickering 'family' faces of the image cube that Terry barely ever noticed, the verdant tumble of the single pot-plant on its tall stand: cosmetic touches intended to put customers at ease. Terry had a feeling they weren't working in this instance.

She saw the uncertainty in both women's faces at news of Drake's absence, so continued speaking, to give them the chance to regroup. "You're Leesa," and she directed her smile at Scowl Face. "You've visited us before. While you are...?"

"Jen," the darker woman said, automatically gripping Terry's proffered hand in a gesture of greeting that predated spaceflight. The grip was firm, strong; there was nothing timid or meek about this one despite her elegant appearance.

"Why the hell are we here?" Leesa said.

"Precisely what I was intending to ask you," Terry replied. "But come, there's no need to stand on ceremony. Please..."

She gestured towards the three comfortable chairs that formed the heart of the office. The two women again exchanged glances. Jen raised her eyebrows as if to say 'why not?' and was the first to move, stepping over and taking the nearest seat. After a brief hesitation, Leesa followed suit. There was no desk here, nothing to separate Terry from her visitors; this wasn't an interview, just three friends settling down for a natter.

"We don't know why you asked to see us," Jen said, smiling, evidently opting for the friendly approach. "We just called in to catch up with an old friend who works at the bank."

"Corbin Drake," Terry said, smiling in turn. "The bank's agent assigned to the successful cache hunt which you were a part of, Leesa."

"That's right." No friendliness from that quarter.

"I'm Drake's boss," Terry repeated.

"And?"

"And… he may be in trouble."

An indiscreet and unsupportable statement; said in part because she believed it to be true but mainly to stimulate a response. She watched their reactions carefully, her own observations supplemented by readings provided by the two chairs in which her guests now sat and hidden cameras trained on their faces. The resulting analyses appeared in the air before her, invisible to either Leesa or Jen. They confirmed her own conclusions: the surprise, concern, disappointment and even fear shown by the pair were all genuine. Terry allowed herself to relax a little, but not for long.

"What sort of trouble?" Leesa asked, but Jen cut across her sharply.

"What are you looking at?"

"I'm sorry?"

"Your focus shifted," Jen said. "For a moment there you were looking towards us but not at us."

She was sharp, this one. Terry had underestimated her – a rookie mistake that she couldn't afford to make twice.

"She's receiving intel we're not privy to," Leesa said.

Was that a case of astute deduction or did she have some

other means of knowing? Terry realised abruptly that she had no idea what Leesa could do, what her *sort* were capable of. She'd heard rumours, of course, but how much of that was exaggeration or scaremongering and how much fact?

In one fluid movement Leesa surged to her feet to stand over Terry.

The threat was unmistakable and Terry flinched despite herself. She was suddenly conscious of being vulnerable and, for the first time since she was promoted to this office, she felt the stirrings of fear.

"Now hang on, wait, I'm sorry." She held up a defensive hand. "I'm on your side here. I just have to be certain of your intentions, that's all."

"Let's hear what she has to say, Lees."

A command hovered on the tip of Terry's tongue, a single syllable that would instantly bring security systems into play, but she wasn't ready to voice it, not yet.

"All right, all right… But whatever she has to say, it had better be good."

The presence above her withdrew and Terry released a breath she hadn't realised she was holding. "Thank you."

Leesa didn't return to her seat but instead started pacing back and forth.

"You placed an alert, so that anyone enquiring about Drake would be referred to you," Jen said.

"Yes, I did."

"But why do that?" Leesa asked, pausing in her prowling to stand beside Jen. "Why would a bigwig executive like you take such personal interest in a mere employee?"

"Because… Drake is in a situation I don't trust, in the company of somebody from his past, a man who came looking for him. I wanted to see if anybody else did the same."

She summoned an image of Payne to hover in the air between them.

"Donal," Leesa said, her voice flat.

"What would he want with the captain?"

"And how did he know where to find him?"

Terry was good at her job; in fact, she was one of the best. These two women were either hunting Drake or trying to help him, there was no in-between. She just had to decide which. Her whole career had been built on assessing risk and deciding when a gamble was worth taking. She trusted her instincts, and right now those instincts were telling her that here before her stood friends of Drake rather than foes.

"Calypso Protocol," Terry snapped into the air, invoking the God of Silence from a long-forgotten religion. "Right," she said, turning back to her guests. "We can speak in confidence now. This room is secure; all monitoring and recording systems are ignoring us until I lift the protocol.

"You see... I know who Drake is, or rather who he was, and that gives me a pretty good idea of who you two are, or at least *what* you are. You ask why I'm taking such an interest in an employee's welfare? In part it's because Drake is the best damned field agent First Solar has ever been fortunate enough to employ, but, on top of that, he's someone I consider a friend. I saw something in him when he first came to me. I knew who he was from the start, which made it a gamble taking him on, a big one, but it's not a decision I've ever had cause to regret. I helped him establish the identity of Corbin Thadeus Drake and then helped him hide in plain sight for more than a decade, putting his past life behind him."

"Trouble is," said Leesa, no longer aggressive but displaying a cold calmness that Terry found equally unsettling, "a past like that has a habit of catching up with a person, eventually."

"I guess you'd know more about that than most," Terry said quietly.

"Meaning?"

"The last time you were here, with Pelquin and his crew, you never got beyond the foyer and its interview rooms. This time, you've come a lot further into the building. Anyone venturing into an exec's office is routinely scanned as a security precaution."

"Is that even legal?" Jen asked.

"So sue us."

"What exactly did these scans reveal?" Leesa asked, that chilling calmness still in her voice.

"That neither of you are fully human, not baseline human at any rate. You," and Terry nodded towards Jen, "show signs of elder tech melded with your body in a way I've never seen before, but every reading insists that you're fully organic... While you," and now her attention switched to Leesa, "possess bionic enhancements of a magnitude that has been outlawed since the Auganics Wars. I am in no doubt that I'm currently in the presence of the two most dangerous women I've ever met in my life. And you turn up here, looking for Drake. That's not a coincidence."

"Which tells you what, precisely?"

"That you've come to either kill him, or to save him."

"It's the latter," Jen said immediately.

Terry nodded. "Your reactions throughout this meeting have convinced me of that. So... I've reached a decision. For now, at least, I'm willing to believe that you're on the side of the angels."

Neither woman reacted.

"I'm going to trust you," Terry reiterated, "and help you as much as I'm able to."

"Good," Leesa said, as if that settled everything. "You can start by bringing us up to speed with the details of the trouble you think Drake might be in. Where, when, what he was doing... Everything you've got."

"Done. Drake is involved in a sensitive mission a little removed from the usual cache hunt. I'll squirt full details across to one of your perminals."

Leesa looked hesitant, which caused Reese to wonder whether auganics were more susceptible to cyberattack and so more reluctant to share perminal access. It was irrelevant to the current situation but she made a mental note to do a little digging on the subject when time allowed.

"I'll take that," Jen said.

Reese nodded. "I'll also erase your scan results from the bank's systems and replace them with something a little more... mundane."

"Won't the alarm have gone up already?" Jen asked.

Terry shook her head. "Only to me, so far. We value discretion here.

"If my fears about Drake prove to be justified, the bank will dispatch a second agent to Enduril II, his last known location, so don't be surprised if another First Solar representative shows up."

It was a gamble, setting these two on the trail of an assignment that might yet prove to be innocent, but a calculated one. If Drake were in trouble, she had a feeling that these two women might be of more help than anything First Solar could muster; besides, their involvement cost neither her nor the bank a thing. What she was about to do next represented an even bigger gamble, but she'd gone this far...

Terry stood up and stepped across to the blank wall behind her. "There's one more thing I can do to help. When Drake first joined First Solar, he entrusted something to me for safe keeping, or against a time of need." Her fingers quested for a moment, brushing across the apparently seamless surface of the wall until they located the panel, which slid open at her touch.

"It strikes me that current circumstances qualify."

She reached in and located what she was after, withdrawing a gaudy-looking bright red chit. Roughly the length of her little finger and apparently formed of plastic, its feel was closer to that of machined metal.

"What's this?" Jen asked as Terry handed it to her.

"An ident tab. Swipe it across your perminal and it will transfer the location of a specific lot within a facility. Hand it across to the attendant and it will confirm ownership and authorise you to access the lot."

"What sort of a facility?" Leesa asked.

"A junk yard."

The two women stared at Reese, who was enjoying herself, deliberately milking the moment.

"To be specific, a ship's graveyard," she then added. "It's located on the far side of the planet."

"Oh," said Leesa. Reese watched as realisation dawned. "*Oh!*"

"Thank you," said Jen, who appeared to have caught on a fraction ahead of her friend.

The sky was a purple bruise punctuated by stabs of golden lightning, and thunder rumbled in the distance.

It was the day following their audience with Terry Reese, and Leesa and Jen had been travelling for much of that time, resorting to a hire car for the final leg of the journey due to the lack of any public transport in this gods-forsaken backwater. The contrast with the high-tech high-paced dazzle they had come from could not have been starker.

"If the city of New Sparta is the beating heart of this world, I think we've just found the arsehole," Leesa quipped as they first sat in the car.

Jen wasn't about to argue.

Two hours spent traversing the flattest and dullest landscape imaginable had done nothing to improve either of their moods, particularly as Leesa insisted on driving the car manually. "One of my first jobs was working on junk heaps for hire like this," she'd explained, "so I know how unreliable the autodrive can be."

The occasional boulder and thin, spiny, cactus-like flora did little to break the monotony, so when their destination hove into view they were both relieved. It seemed to take an age, though, before the irregular crenellations that first broke the horizon took on greater substance and definition.

Eventually, mercifully, they arrived.

"Crud!" Leesa said, bringing the car to a halt. "Have you ever seen so many wrecked ships?"

"No," Jen conceded, "can't say that I have."

They climbed out of the car, Jen glad of the opportunity to stretch her tired legs. The heat struck her immediately, the thicker-seeming air rolling over her the instant she left the coolness of the car's air-conditioned interior.

"This is like a spaceport for geriatrics."

They had travelled halfway around the world, to a barren region of proto-desert on another continent. At no point since leaving the urban sprawl around the small airport they'd landed at that morning had they encountered a town or even a hamlet, and the number of other vehicles they passed could have been counted on the fingers of one hand. Jen suspected that the total population of this area would struggle to fill even one of New Sparta's thrusting skyscrapers. The hire car's pre-programmed navigation had brought them unerringly to the right place but their destination would have been pretty hard to miss in any case, given the scarcity of roads in these parts and the vast area their goal occupied.

Before them spread a field of derelict vessels that stretched away as far as the eye could see. It felt as if they witnessed an assembly of wounded giants. Closest to them lay the remains of an old Leviathan transport, the hull stripped bare to leave the vast hoops of its support frame exposed to the elements. They rose from the ground in an extended line like the ribcage of some long-dead behemoth whose carcass had been picked clean by scavengers an age ago. Only the flared engine tubes at the back and the distinctive snubbed nose of its prow remained to identify the proud craft it had once been.

"I count at least two Comets," Leesa said, the excitement in her voice mounting, "a couple of Dragonflies, an Apex cruiser – bet none of the weapon systems are still in place – a Starbloom, a luxury yacht over there, a couple of Lion Class transports, a Starfish… and isn't that mountain over there an Excelsior passenger liner?"

"Looks like it," Jen confirmed. "And that's a Cloud beside it, completely dwarfed…"

"I'd love to work on the drive of an Excelsior. Can you imagine? All that power…"

"I don't even recognise half the classes of ship I'm looking at, and they're just the ones we can see from here."

"Yeah, it's impressive, no question. Mind you, a lot of these hulks are so dilapidated it's impossible to tell what they might have been in better days. Come on."

Leesa was more animated than Jen had seen her since they first arrived at New Sparta. She led the way towards the only apparent building: a white oblong block of a cabin.

Jen's gaze was drawn back to the wrecked ships, to the blistered hulls smeared with soot and pitted by impacts from micro meteorites and larger objects, to the yawning gaps where sections of plating had been cut away, scavenged for whatever purpose, to the ragged wounds that spoke of fires and other violent events. Each ship here must have a story to tell, and she wondered how many of those stories were even remembered by anyone still living.

Above the cabin stood a sign bearing the words 'Lionel Sanders: Shipyard and Storage'. As they drew nearer, a list of smaller words flickered into life, superimposed in the air across the cabin's walls: 'Spare Parts, Reclamation, Refurbishments, Repairs, Restoration, Renovation'.

"They must have run out of words containing the letter 'r' after that," Leesa muttered.

"Resuscitation?" Jen suggested. "Restaurant?"

Leesa snorted. "Bet that'd go down a treat in these parts."

As they approached the building, the panelled door swung open and a portly man stepped out to greet them. He wore shorts and a white tee-shirt: not the most professional of attires perhaps, but Jen couldn't fault his practicality given the prevailing heat.

"What can I do you ladies for?" he asked.

"Are you Sanders?"

"Yup, like the sign says."

"We're here to claim one of your lots." Jen fished out the ticket Reese had given them and held it towards him.

He eyed the red chit suspiciously but declined to take it. "Is that a fact? Don't get many reclaims… You'd better come on in."

He led the way into the hut's gratifyingly cool interior, which was cluttered with a bizarre assortment of oddments, including a 3-D football game frozen in mid-kick, a tall gunmetal filing cabinet, a trio of ill-matched chairs, an outdated drinks dispenser, a pile of what looked to be model spacecraft in far better condition than their larger cousins that sat outside, a single person hover-scooter thrust incongruously into a corner, and even a wooden rocking horse in need of a fresh lick of paint. While Jen took a moment to absorb her surroundings, Sanders strode across to a desk, over which were suspended several edocs that Jen only caught a glimpse of before he banished them with a sweep of his hand. Behind the desk rose a triple-banked row of small screens, each depicting what she presumed were views of the yard.

"Is that what passes for security?" Leesa asked. "How do you stop anyone from just walking in here and stealing things?"

"Try it sometime and you'll find out," Sanders replied without bothering to look up.

Exhibiting a surprising degree of care that approached reverence, he lifted two yellowed and brittle-looking documents – paper, *real* paper – from the desk and placed them on top of the filing cabinet, to reveal a small flat-screen scanner. He gestured for Jen to hand over the ticket, which she did mutely, watching as he slapped it down onto the scanner's surface.

Sanders grunted. "Yup, it's one of ours all right. Lot 572. Been here a while, that one." He tapped away on a keyboard built into the desk. "Okay, back outside again."

He all but shooed them back through the door.

As they stepped into the heat of the day once more, a gangly youth pulled up on a hover scooter. His eyes passed over the two women with obvious interest before he grunted a greeting to

Sanders. He wore a tee-shirt that bore the mobile 3D image of a spaceship blasting out and upward.

"Are you going to take us to the ship, or what?" Leesa asked, addressing Sanders and ignoring the newcomer.

"Ship?" Sanders laughed. "You might be a little... disappointed; heap of rust more like. No, I won't be taking you, not in person at any rate, that'll be down to Gurney Two here."

As he spoke, a large flatbed luggage trolley trundled into view, multiple-wheeled and evidently self-guiding.

"Hop on," Sanders instructed as the trolley came to a stop. "Navigation's already laid in. Once you've inspected your... ship, the gurney'll bring you back here and we can discuss the cost of transporting your property from the lot. Unless of course you want to sell it to me for parts, which would save us all a lot of bother. Not that she's worth much, mind. Cold drinks are available once you're back here too, at a price, to soothe those pretty little parched throats o' yours."

"So I take it she's not in a fit state to fly?" Jen said quickly, in part to forestall any retort Leesa might have been considering.

The comment inspired another bark of laughter from Sanders. "Not exactly. I've seen industrial freezer units that are more airworthy."

With those encouraging words ringing in their ears, Leesa and Jen climbed aboard the transport.

Despite the distant storm, the air felt hot and dry, as if the weather front on the horizon had sucked in all the moisture for miles around. The two women sat on the gurney's flatbed, initially with their feet dangling over the side but as the strange vehicle picked up pace they both drew their legs in to avoid their feet knocking against the ground.

"If he describes me as either 'pretty' or 'little' one more time I'll take that cold drink of his and shove it where the sun will never find it," Leesa muttered.

"Did you see the top that kid was wearing?" Jen asked,

deliberately changing the subject.

"Of course I did. The *Ion Raider* – that was the logo for a holodrama series that did the rounds seven or eight years ago."

"They made a *series* about us?"

"Yeah, I know. You can still find it if you're curious, but take my advice and don't bother."

Soon after that the trip became too bumpy and dusty for further conversation, with dust getting into mouths, nostrils and eyes despite their best efforts to protect their faces. Forced to constantly squint and wipe away tears and grit, Jen paid scant attention to the hulking relics from various eras of space flight that slipped past as they sped through the vast shipyard.

Finally, mercifully, the gurney slowed and came to a halt. Jen spat out sand and squinted. She dabbed at her eyes, determined not to rub them because she knew that would only make them smart all the more.

"Fuck!" Leesa said, jumping down to the ground.

As Jen's vision continued to clear, she found herself sympathising with the expletive; before them sat a burned out hulk of debris. She slid down from the flatbed, staring up at the excuse for a ship that towered above her. Nowhere could she see a glint of clean surface. Every inch was charred black or blistered.

"This can't be right," she murmured.

Leesa didn't reply immediately. She was staring at the wreck intently, and then started walking along its length. Jen followed, trying to see in this misshapen mass the outline of a ship.

"You know it might be, it just might be," Leesa called back without breaking stride. "It's almost as if somebody's tried to deliberately mask the profile, to disguise what class of ship this is, but with a bit of imagination…"

She came to an abrupt stop.

"If I'm right, the airlock should be about… here."

Leesa stepped forward, reaching up to rub at the burned hull with the palm of her hand. "There's something…" she murmured after a slight pause.

Jen heard it then, a low humming, almost too quiet to detect. The mound of charred junk that might once have been a ship began to tremble. At the place where Leesa had touched it the blistered surface started to peel away, falling to the ground like flakes of dead skin or leaves dropping from autumnal trees struck by a gale.

Beneath the black lay untarnished, corrosion-free hull. Leesa stepped back, looking across at Jen as if to gauge her reaction, or perhaps for reassurance. If so, Jen had none to offer. A seam appeared, widening to form an open doorway. As soon as the shape was fully revealed, a ramp extended, touching ground immediately in front of where the two of them stood waiting.

"Still got some power, then," Jen murmured.

"Enough to lower the ramp, at any rate."

Jen took the lead, stepping forward to climb the ramp, conscious of Leesa at her heels.

Once they were both inside the airlock, the ramp retracted and the door sealed shut behind them. Jen had time enough to worry that this might have drained what little power reserves remained and that she and Leesa would now be trapped in the airlock, doomed to face slow death by suffocation, when the lock commenced cycling. In seconds the inner door swung open.

She hadn't realised how nervous she was until now. This whole experience seemed… surreal. Confronting them was a well-lit corridor, the air musty but breathable. For a moment they both hesitated, and then they stepped forward together, as if by unspoken consent.

"Hello, Hel N. Hello Shadow," said a voice Jen had never expected to hear again.

"Raider?" she said, not quite believing. "Is that really you?"

"Who else?" said the placid, ageless voice. "Welcome home, Dark Angels."

NINE

Jen felt an odd mix of emotions as she wandered around the *Ion Raider's* interior. On one level, being back here brought the comforting warmth of nostalgia and, given recent events, a sense of relief. However, when she stepped away from the Dark Angels a decade ago she had never intended to return, and the fact that she now had inspired a vague sense of disappointment, as if she had failed in some nebulous way by not following through on a commitment. It also acted as an unwelcome reminder of her recent misfortunes. If these various reactions weren't precisely at odds, nor were they entirely comfortable in each other's company.

The ship was exactly as she remembered. Of course it was, given that the *Ion Raider* had been mothballed soon after she left, but, irrationally, part of her expected it to have changed in the interim, even as she had.

Outwardly, *Raider* had always resembled any other comet class trading vessel, but her interior had been drastically reconfigured. In its purest form, the comet was little more than a mobile cargo hold with crew quarters appended almost as an afterthought; there was only one way in or out – the vast cargo doors at the stern – and any thought of comfort had to be set aside the moment you stepped aboard. *Raider* was a little different. The most obvious modifications were to the cargo hold, which had been drastically reduced in size. Still the single largest area on the ship, it no longer dwarfed everything else, and various concessions to human habitation had been installed – the additional airlock giving direct access to the living quarters being one of them. The others included a gym area and a couple of sealed rooms, all encroaching on what would normally be the cargo area. The two rooms, dubbed by the crew 'the cloud chamber' and 'the artefact room' respectively, she shied away from for now. Time enough for them later. She noticed that Leesa studiously avoided the latter as well, which was understandable; the artefact room in particular held a far greater significance for her. They both knew she would have to venture in there at some point.

The two women reconvened in the galley, over glasses of ice-cold water that tasted as cool and fresh as a mountain stream's, for all that their components had been sitting in the ship's systems for more than a decade.

"Well?" Jen asked.

"On the whole, we're in good shape," Leesa said. While Jen had been reacquainting herself with the ship, Leesa had been consulting with Raider, inspecting the engines and running diagnostics on the ship's systems. "The drive is basically sound. There are three parts I wouldn't mind replacing before we attempt lift off, one more vital than the other two, but everything else is in good order."

"Well, if we're looking for spare parts we could hardly have picked a better place."

"Yeah, I know. There are other comets out there, we've seen them, so it shouldn't be a problem."

"But...?"

"But it means dealing with Sanders."

"There is that, but come on, surely he can't be that bad."

"*How* much?"

They were back in Sanders' office, and had just presented him with a list of the three parts they needed.

The portly man sat behind his desk, chair pushed back and clearly enjoying himself. "The comet's an old class of ship," he explained. "Parts are hard to come by, especially round here."

"You've a dozen comets in the yard at least," Leesa pointed out, "and I could get newly minted repros on Babylon for a *fifth* of what you're asking."

"So go to Babylon and get them."

Leesa simply glared, and Jen wondered how much longer she'd be able to restrain herself.

"Better still," Sanders continued, oblivious to the threat, "admit defeat and let me take that heap o' junk off your hands. You seriously think a new fusion filter and a couple of replacement links will get that burnt out husk off the ground? You're gonna need the entire budget of a small country before you see that ol' lady in space again."

He sat forward and attempted to look sincere. "Look, I'm trying to help you out here. I don't know what that ship means to you but she's a lost cause. Quit while you can."

"Thanks for your concern," Jen said, gripping Leesa by the arm and propelling her towards the door. "We'll have a think, bearing your advice in mind."

"Fucking rip off merchant," Leesa muttered as they walked away from the hut and back towards the *Raider*.

"I guess he has to make a living where he can," Jen said. She had no idea why she felt compelled to defend Sanders, except for a vague desire to calm Leesa down. "I've got some credit I could contribute," she added, though in truth the emergency funds she'd set aside under false names were limited and had already been severely dented.

Leesa shook her head. "I can cover it if need be. I've still got a fair bit left from my share of the Pelquin haul, but it's the principle of the thing. I'd rather save my credit for when it's *really* needed."

Jen refrained from pointing out that in the face of being stranded here, that time might be now.

Off to their left, a cage of scaffolding had been erected around the body of an old transport vessel, Projecting from the scaffolding were a quartet of precision energy cutters, which were in the process of carving vast panels from the ship's hull. The finished panels were then being stacked by mechanical arms onto a large flatbed gurney, considerably larger than the one that had first carried Leesa and Jen to the *Raider*.

Two men stood off to one side, overseeing the process. They looked bored.

Clearly not everyone baulked at Sanders' inflated prices, another observation that Jen decided to keep to herself.

The *Raider* continued to impersonate a burnt-out wreck. Even the section of sham charring that flaked away at their arrival had subsequently been replaced by re-tasked maintenance bots.

"Why continued with the charade?" Leesa wanted to know once they were back on board.

"It has been a necessary subterfuge for more than ten years, Raider replied, "and it seems expedient to maintain the illusion for now."

"If you say so. I'm going to see if it'll be 'expedient' for me to buy the filter offsite and get it shipped in here."

"Drones are not permitted to enter the compound without permission," Raider reported.

"Good luck to Sanders enforcing that one over an area this large."

"There's an exclusion field in place to enforce the policy; crude, but effective. Any drone that crosses the boundary drops from the sky. I've seen it happen."

"An exclusion field? Where the hell did Sanders pick up kit like that?"

"Cannibalised, I'd imagine," Jen said. "With this many derelicts to ransack, who knows what he's picked up?"

"Any parts imported into the site have to be to be inspected and cleared by the owner or his representative," Raider continued, "who will charge a levy at their discretion in line with the item's perceived value."

"Seriously?"

"These terms are specified in the contract that enabled me to remain here for the past ten years."

"Great. Whatever possessed the captain to leave you at the far ends of the world in any case?"

"As strategies go, it seems to have worked," Jen pointed out. "No one ever suspected that the *Raider* was here."

"Doesn't help us now, though, does it?"

"Maybe it's time for us to swallow our pride and accept the fact that we have to deal with Sanders, then."

"Like hell. The next time anyone shafts me that thoroughly I want to be a willing participant, thanks all the same."

"Well in that case," Jen said, "I guess we'll just have to go and steal this fusion filter of yours."

Leesa grinned. "Now you're talking."

Raider had identified three potential donors for the vital filter, having hacked the yard's inventory. When it came to cataloguing resources, Sanders was surprisingly thorough, even going to the trouble of grading the various components.

"You're lucky not to have ever been cannibalised," Leesa said.

"Luck had nothing to do with it," Raider replied. "I am not owned by Sanders. I am a private lot that is merely parked here, at considerable expense."

"And you think that would be enough to stop him?"

"That plus the fact Sanders probably thought it wouldn't be worth the effort," Jen said.

"You are quite right," Raider confirmed. "The yard's inventory – which, as I have just demonstrated, is easily hacked and could just as easily be manipulated should it ever have become necessary – does not list me as possessing any worthwhile spare parts. Of course, the inspections by First Solar doubtless helped stay Sanders' hand and maintain my integrity."

"First Solar?" Jen interrupted. "They know about you?"

"It's probably just Reese keeping an eye on things," Leesa said. "Doesn't necessarily mean anything official."

"I am not privy to what First Solar may or may not know," Raider said. "I merely report that on five occasions during my time here individuals claiming to be from First Solar have come to inspect me. On two of those occasions it was Captain Cornische, under the name of Drake."

"Figures," Leesa said.

"On the second occasion, he was not alone," Raider added. "He brought with him... a presence."

"A presence? What the hell does that mean?"

Raider was uncharacteristically silent in response to Leesa's question.

"Who was with him, Raider," Jen asked, calmly.

"Not so much a 'who' as a 'what'," the ship said. "It was something from the Elder days, something a little like me."

Jen digested that.

"I have been pondering the implications of its presence ever since."

"I thought you were unique," Leesa said, "that there weren't any others like you."

"So did I," Raider replied.

"Was this other Elder aspect aware of you?"

"No, I kept myself isolated and did not attempt to communicate with either the captain or this other."

"Cornische knows about you, though," Leesa pointed out.

"Cornische does, yes. Whether Drake does is uncertain.

"What the hell does that mean? They're the same person."

"Up to a point, yes," Raider replied. "Cornische had me apply blocks on certain areas of his memory when we parted. I had not anticipated this particular development, however, and have no idea whether those blocks still hold. It is not something I have any control over."

"Wait a minute," Leesa said, suddenly animated. "The captain had his memories tampered with too? How extensively?"

"Subtly," Raider replied, "to preserve some of our more sensitive secrets without leaving any obvious gaps in his recollections."

Jen was impatient to hear more of the unknown alien the captain had brought with him. "What do you think it means,

Raider, the captain being with this Elder aspect?" she asked.

"I don't know," Raider admitted, "but nothing good I'll venture."

Neither Jen nor Leesa had taken Sanders seriously when he made vague claims of security measures to thwart any would-be thieves. Leesa brushed aside the possibility with a dismissive, "Bluff, pure and simple."

Nonetheless, they waited until nightfall before making their move. Of the three filters Raider had identified as being of acceptable quality, the closest was in the poorest state, according to Sanders' inventory. On the plus side, the filter listed as the highest grade was the next closest, so they opted to liberate that one.

Jen led the way, following the path Raider mapped out for her via her smart glasses. The lenses also enabled her to see in the near darkness, depicting the night-time world in stark greens and greys. Perhaps she should have let Leesa take point – her augmented eyes would doubtless have no problem with the low levels of light – but Jen felt that her friend had taken the lead too often since they'd reconnected. It was time for her to step forward and pull her weight.

The temperature had plummeted since sunset. Nothing too drastic – there was no suggestion of freezing as she had heard concerning some desert environments – but there was a marked chill in the air. The air also felt fresh and clean, which she suspected had little to do with the day's violent storm, which had barely reached them beyond a period of high winds, and was instead the natural order of things here.

Whatever the cause, it made for ideal running conditions. Jen had kept herself fit since leaving the Angels, not only through the sheer physicality of farming – forget automation, she and Robin had run a profitable smallholding, not a corporate factory farm – but also by maintaining regular workouts and runs. She would have been hard-pressed to explain *why* she did so with such dedication – and her husband has asked her more than once – except that this was something she'd always done, and while the daily work routine helped with strength training, it didn't do much for speed and agility, nor for reactions and mental sharpness.

Perhaps a part of her had always expected to be back here doing this again, no matter how much she'd tried to bury the past. Why else go to all the expense and trouble of acquiring simulacra?

Jen had no qualms regarding Leesa's fitness, suspecting her friend's augmented body could maintain this sort of pace all night.

They ran, smoothly, swiftly, quietly, passing beneath and between the towering hulks of ships that would never leave the ground again; not speaking, not needing to. They kicked up a little dust as they went but not enough to be a problem, the sand here compacted and solid beneath their feet.

Jen could have covered the ground more swiftly in shadow form but that would have meant both she and Leesa running alone. They would have reached the same place but by separate paths, and Jen preferred that they travel together. She had missed the comradery, the sense of belonging that being a Dark Angel entailed. There might only have been the two of them as yet, but she was confident that would change. Finding the *Ion Raider* again had more than compensated for the disappointment of failing to recruit Mosi. For the first time since her home had been destroyed around her, Jen felt that things were on the up, and now she was impatient to get after the captain. The sooner they could find this filter and leave New Sparta behind the better.

At last they reached the ship Raider had identified, the familiar shape of a comet class transport squatting on the sand directly ahead of them, the borders of Jen's lenses strobing forward in red as she looked at the ship, confirming they had arrived.

The comet's systems were dead and its carcass was far more

complete than many they had passed, but they soon found a section where the panelling had been cut away and were able to gain access. Leesa took the lead now. This was her territory. Jen activated the lights in the frames of her glasses and followed – the light levels too low and the environment too cluttered for her to rely on the glasses' night vision in this environment.

Leesa had no such problems, moving confidently through the stygian darkness of the corridors, stepping over the occasional obstacle and around open panels that jutted from the wall ready to snag the unwary as readily as she would had they been in broad daylight. Within moments they had reached the engine compartment.

When it came to ships' engines, Jen was out of her depth and knew that her role from here on in was one of support. Leesa had brought all the tools she might need with her, so Jen didn't even have the satisfaction of passing her anything.

It surprised her how grateful she felt when Leesa said, "Shine that spectacle light of yours down here, will you?" Finally she could contribute something. The request also showed that perhaps Leesa's mastery of darkness wasn't as complete as she had always assumed.

In the event, the angle wasn't quite right, so Jen took the glasses off and handed them to her friend, who wedged them somehow behind her and a little above where she was working.

"That's better."

Jen was now plunged into a pitch dark world, where the only things clearly visible were Leesa's upper torso and her hands, plus the small section of grubby, dusty machinery she was working on. Beyond that, everything faded into the murk by rapid degree. Even Leesa's body from the waist down had been rendered invisible to her.

Leesa had always been in her element with engines, doubling as the *Ion Raider*'s mechanic when need be, and it didn't take her long to extract the part they were after. With a final wrench and the sharp snap of something broken, she hefted a small component in one palm, just a little larger than her clenched fist.

"There!"

Jen stared. "That's it? We've run halfway across the yard and broken into a derelict spaceship just to come back with a chunk of metal the size of a kid's playball?"

"It isn't all metal but yup, this is it. Small components keep the big wheels turning, you know. That's how it works."

Leesa reached back to slip the filter into her backpack.

"Without this little beauty there's no guarantee we'd ever make it back from RzSpace, always assuming we could cross into it in the first place."

"Seriously?" Jen said. "So every time we cross into RzSpace from here on in we'll be staking our lives on a second-hand pilfered component?"

"Relax. I'll check it through thoroughly once we're back on the *Raider*," Leesa said, handing her back her glasses. "Besides, how else do you think we've ever done things?"

On further consideration, Jen decided she'd rather not know. Leesa clambered past her and the two of them hurried back the way they'd come. In no time at all they were jumping down through the breach in the hull.

"Once I've given the filter a clean and a complete going over, I'll replace *Raider*'s knackered one and we'll be good to go," Leesa said as she landed on the sand beside Jen. "All being well, we should be able to head out after the captain by late tomorrow."

"Remain where you are!" The words boomed out at the same instant a search light flared to life, its beam centring on the two women. "Place all illegally acquired items on the ground before you."

"Shit!" Jen's glasses opaqued in the sudden brightness, blinding her. She snatched them off.

"I guess Sanders wasn't bluffing after all," Leesa muttered.

By rocking back on her heels slightly, Jen was able to tilt her head into the comet's shadow and out of the dazzling light, enabling her to see what confronted them.

"It's a security droid," she murmured. "A floating sphere about twice the size of a human head. It looks to be armed, though I couldn't say with what. Leave this to me."

Leesa was exposed, in the full glare of the droid's light and still in a crouch where she'd landed after exiting the ship. Jen, on the other hand, was marginally closer to the hull and now partially in shadow; not by much, but enough.

She stepped across. Perception shifted. The night time world was bleached of colour, becoming almost monochrome. Jen flowed up the hull of the ship. The droid was saying something, a command robbed of words by the flattening effect of the shadow state combined with her having other things to concentrate on. Perhaps it was reacting to her disappearance, demanding an explanation. She had to move quickly, before it responded with more than just verbal queries.

She reached the top. From here the hull curved back on itself, so going any further would take her away from the droid, which floated a little below her current vantage but still some distance from the comet. No time to think this through, no time to doubt. Jen flung herself outward, shifting back into physical form as she went.

She stretched her arms with every sinew and felt her fingers close on the droid. Momentum, gravity and surprise all worked in her favour. She pulled the droid closer to her as she hurtled towards the ground, taking it with her.

"Jen!"

She didn't need Leesa's shout to remind her of what a crazy stratagem this was. She already knew. While her shadow form could strike the ground at any velocity and simply step away, her physical self was considerably less durable. Hit the ground at this speed and broken bones were the best she could hope for.

It all came down to timing. The droid was beneath her and so would bear the brunt of the impact. At the last possible instant she shifted into shadow, praying that she'd got this right and closing her eyes for fear that she'd judged it wrongly.

No pain, no part of her body screaming in protest of injury. She opened her eyes to see the droid attempting to wobble up off the ground. The spotlight had gone out, presumably smashed by the impact, but the droid itself was still functioning. Leesa was there in an instant, grabbing the small bot and hurling it back into the sand, stamping on it, kicking. Jen shifted back into physical form and joined in. She drew her knives and attacked a crack that had opened in the sphere's outer casing, slipping a blade through and twisting, then pulling it out to do the same again.

There was a muffled phut of something discharging inside and a spark of energy release, then the droid went still. The two women stood over the fallen machine for a moment, panting and watching for any sign of returning power.

"That leap... That was insane!" Leesa said, thumping Jen on the shoulder.

"I know; but it worked, didn't it?"

"Only just. That energy beam nearly had you."

"What energy beam?"

"The one the droid fired at you just as you slipped into shadow and it hit the ground... You didn't *see* it?"

Jen shook her head mutely, even more glad that she had decided to shut her eyes. "I think it's done for, don't you?" she said after a moment, giving the droid a tentative kick.

"Reckon so. Let's get out of here."

With that, they were off, racing as quickly as they could for the safety of the *Ion Raider.*

"Where the hell did Sanders get a security droid from, anyway?" Leesa called as they pelted between slumbering giants.

"He probably salvaged it from one of the passenger liners that ended up here," Jen called back. "They use security droids, don't they?"

"Couldn't say. I've never been on one."

"You know that schedule you mentioned, the one where we lift off and go in search of the captain sometime late tomorrow?" Jen said. "Maybe it needs moving up a bit."

"Yeah, thanks for pointing that out; looks as if I'll be working through the night."

They arrived back to *Raider* without any further incident. Leesa disappeared to clean and test the filter. Jen made a half-hearted offer to help which Leesa waved away: "You'd only get in the way."

She was probably right. Jen determined to get some sleep while she could, saying to Raider, "Wake me if anything interesting happens."

"Define 'interesting'."

"Use your judgement."

Apparently, nothing interesting occurred until shortly after first light, at which point Jen found herself ushered back into wakefulness by a gently vibrating bed and the pinging of an alarm.

She had no idea what the time was at that point, but it felt early.

"What's going on," she asked, sitting up and trying to shake the wool from her thoughts.

"We have visitors," Raider informed her. That did the trick

She threw on some clothes and hurried up to the bridge. This was another area where the *Ion Raider* scored over most ships of her class: a proper ops room, situated a little back from the original cockpit and incorporating the two pilots' chairs. While still compact, it was a hell lot bigger than your average small trader could claim.

Leesa was there ahead of her.

"What have we got?" Jen asked.

"See for yourself." She nodded towards the image on the screen, which showed the yard outside the ship. Jen recognised the view, and the carcass of the vessel that sat beside their lot. Except now the small strip of sand in between was occupied.

Sanders stood there, along with the gangly kid they'd seen when they first arrived but had never been introduced to. The pair had evidently driven over on a fat-wheeled buggy which looked to be a lot more comfortable than the gurney that had been rolled out for Jen and Leesa.

Arrayed beside them in a truncated crescent were three of the spherical droids, hovering just above head height.

"He must have found a whole cupboard full of droids on that liner," Leesa commented.

"Which liner is that?" Raider asked.

"Never mind."

If ever two men and three metal balls could be said to look menacing, this was it. Sanders was clearly fuming.

"You in that rust heap," he yelled. "You owe me. For a stolen part and a wrecked droid." He counted off on his raised fingers as he spoke. "Not to mention the fucking inconvenience!" A third finger went down. "Come on out here now or we're gonna come in to get you. I could probably kick that piece of junk down myself without workin' up a sweat, but why dirty my boots when I've a pack of security drones here to do that sort of stuff for me, eh?"

"Are those drones capable of breaching the hull?" Jen asked.

"Probably, given enough time," Raider replied.

"Which they won't get, of course."

Having provoked no discernible response, Sanders was evidently losing patience. "Okay, have it your own way," he called, and then nodded to Gangly Boy.

Beams of energy leapt from each of the drones, converging on a single spot on the ship's hull.

"At least they've sense enough to concentrate their firepower," Leesa said, sounding amused.

"Right, I've had enough of this." Jen turned to go.

"Wait a sec; there's no need. All they're doing for the moment is burning off the camouflage, and as the man said, what's the point in having drones and doing the difficult stuff ourselves? Raider, you can hack those drones, I take it?"

"Of course."

"Are there any failsafes to stop them turning on each other?"

"No, they're not that sophisticated. It would be a simple matter to subvert one and have it destroy the other two."

"Sounds like a plan to me."

Outside, Sanders continued to gloat, clearly confident of the outcome. "Well whadaya know? It looks as if this ship is in better shape than I realised. Seems you've been holding out on me."

Before he could say anything further, the drone closest to him abruptly swivelled around, turning its beam on its closest colleague. In quick succession the other two spheres sparked and flamed and dropped to the ground, their energy lances winking out.

Sanders ducked away from the small explosions and glared at Gangly Boy, who shrugged and held up his hands as if to say 'wasn't me'.

"Sanders," Leesa said, her voice transmitted outside the ship by Raider, "you have ten seconds to haul your fat ass into that buggy and get the hell out of here before the drone reduces it to slag and then turns its attention on you."

"You stuck up bitches! Don't think you're getting away wi…" Sanders' rant was cut short as the drone fired a burst of energy into the ground beside him, causing him to jump and curse.

"Eight seconds," Leesa said calmly. "Seven…"

His nerve having evidently failed him, Sanders clambered rapidly into the buggy, where Gangly Boy already sat waiting. The engine whined, wheels spun, and the vehicle sped away amidst a plume of dust, the security drone keeping pace behind in watchful vigil.

Jen couldn't help herself, she burst out laughing. "Now that almost makes being called a stuck up bitch worthwhile."

"I was thinking it kind of suits us. Maybe we could adopt it as our new crew name – 'forget the Dark Angels, they're yesterday's news, we're the Stuck Up Bitches'."

"Try explaining that one to the captain when we find him." Jen glanced at the screens, which still showed the plume of dust thrown up by the retreating buggy. If nothing else, the incident proved they had outstayed their welcome on New Sparta. "How close are we to being ready to leave?" she asked.

"The new filter's in place and working fine, so we're as ready as we're going to be until we can replace the other degraded parts."

"I thought you said those parts weren't vital."

Leesa shrugged. "Compared to the fusion filter they aren't. These things are all relative."

With only two of them aboard there was no argument about who would enjoy the privilege of the pilots' chairs during lift off – they both could. No cling patches bonding them to walls and hands clenched around grips in case the patches somehow failed, not for them, not this time; which was just as well, because Raider wasn't holding back.

No one who used the expression 'it took my breath away' knew what they were talking about unless they'd experienced lift off under this sort of acceleration. She had no idea of the g-force Raider was inflicting upon them but reckoned it had to be upward of six.

"Security presence in and above the atmosphere is concentrated over the capital, which is on the far side of the world," the A.I. informed them. "However, there are still enough ships within reach of our trajectory to present a potential hazard. I've timed things to maximise our opportunity, so there should be sufficient window for us to reach RzSpace before anything can intercept us. It does mean applying considerable acceleration to be certain of this, though."

"No kidding." Even Leesa sounded strained.

For her part, a great weight had settled on Jen's chest, pressing her back into the upholstery of the chair, and she was grateful not to be hugging an unforgiving bulkhead instead; bruises would have inevitably resulted if she had been and this was uncomfortable enough, in seating specifically designed for such manoeuvres.

She would have loved to look back and watch the myriad forms of abandoned spacecraft stranded in the desert spread out beneath them, diminishing as they rose from the planet's surface, but in reality she knew that the flare of the *Raider*'s drives would have blotted that out in any case and, besides, she was in no state to look at anything just then.

"Bet this beats being on a farm, huh?" Leesa yelled across. Was she actually *enjoying* this?

Not in a million years, Jen thought but didn't say.

The punishing acceleration eased as they left New Sparta's atmosphere.

"Nothing appears to be pursuing us," Raider reported. "There doesn't seem to be any reaction to our unscheduled departure."

"Are you sure this wasn't just your way of stretching your muscles after so long on the ground?" Leesa said, standing up from her chair.

"I shall treat the question with the contempt it deserves."

"How long before we enter RzSpace?" Jen asked, freeing herself from her own chair's protective embrace.

"A little under five minutes."

Jen headed to the canteen, helping herself to a chilled juice. While there, she heard Leesa descending into the cargo hold and, curious to see what she was up to, followed.

She found her friend standing in the centre of the hold, staring at the door to the artefact room. Leesa greeted her with a thin, unconvincing smile.

Jen could have left things there and retreated back up the stairs with the matter unsaid, but she decided to be blunt, feeling that the two of them were close enough these days for her to do so.

"Are you going to face your demon or keep avoiding it?" she said, gently.

Leesa hesitated before answering. "Face it, of course, but only when I'm good and ready."

Jen nodded.

"It's funny," Leesa continued. "Over the past year or so I've steadily been piecing together who I am… who I *was*, without her. I existed before Hel N and I existed after her, but once I set her aside I never really felt… complete. It's different for you. When the Angels disbanded you took Shadow with you."

"I didn't have a choice," Jen said softly. "She's part of who I am. When I first embraced the shadow tech, it embraced me as well, becoming a part of me. From that moment, I've never been able to differentiate between Jen and Shadow the way you do with Hel N, there's simply me."

Leesa was nodding. "That's what I'm getting at. Your Shadow tech is fully integrated with your body, inseparable, but I never had that, not with Hel N. No matter how much I *felt* she'd become a part of me, she was just a surface layer, to be shed like a discarded set of clothing when the Angels went on hold… But I missed her, missed *being* her. Desperately. I didn't appreciate until after she'd gone how much I'd come to identify with the persona of Hel N, how integral she'd become to who I was. Not being her was crippling, like having a limb cut off… No, it was worse than that, because at least a limb can be replaced."

Jen didn't know what to say. She'd never heard Leesa open up like this before, and felt flattered to be trusted in this way. At the same time, she felt helpless in face of the anguish these recollections revealed.

"Does it feel different when you're her?"

"Oh yeah, but… I don't know how much of that's down to the Elder tech and how much is down to me, psychologically, you know? The moment I slip into the suit, everything's heightened – sight, smell, sound, even the feeling of a breeze on my skin… It's exhilarating simply being her; I get a real buzz and a sense that I can take on the world, *any* world."

"You're still extraordinary, even without Hel N."

Leesa laughed. "That's one way of putting it. I'm different, that's for sure."

"The last of the auganics…"

"Yeah, that's me. Not a privilege I ever sought, I can promise you that."

"Have you any idea *how* you survived the massacre on Tyson Five?" It was something Jen had always been curious about but never had the courage to ask, until now.

"Not really," Leesa said. "I can only put it down to the fact that I was already augmented to an extent, even before Bruckheimer recruited me to his techorg project. I'd had implants ever since I was born – had to have them in order to survive on Liaise, a world where humans were never meant to live… I think that's what saved me when the government fried us – the fact that my mods weren't purely auganic tech, that Bruckheimer chose to build on what was already there rather than starting from scratch as he had to with the others. I remember how pleased with himself he was after the procedure, how he wanted to impress on me that I was special, though I reckoned even then that he was more concerned with how clever *he* was rather than anything else."

Again Jen wasn't sure how to respond. Thankfully, Leesa filled the silence herself after a brief pause. "The thing is, I've always felt different, like I didn't fit in, but when I was Hel N it was a *good* kind of different."

"And when you stopped being her you missed that."

"More than simply missed it, I *yearned* for it. That's what's holding me back now. Since regaining my memories I haven't felt that craving to be Hel N, that dreadful sense of being incomplete, but then I never expected to be presented with an opportunity to be her again."

"And you're afraid that once you do, you might not cope with losing her for a second time."

Leesa nodded. "Got it in one. Whatever comes next for us, whatever happens with the Saflik, I can't live to a ripe old age as Hel N, but how will I ever cope with setting her aside again?"

"You don't have to, you know," Jen said.

"Have to what?"

"Don't be obtuse. You know what I mean. You don't have to become Hel N again."

"Yes I do, and we both know it," Leesa said quietly. "But… not today." With that, she nodded to Jen and walked away.

Ten

Terry Reese's fears about the situation Drake had gone into were looking increasingly justified. She had yet to hear anything at all from him since he left with Payne for Enduril II and his second report was now overdue. Could that be explained away by misfortune, by messages simply lost in the aether, or were there other factors at play?

New Sparta was one of the core planets, the long-settled worlds that constituted the heart of human civilisation. A series of relays had been established, radiating outward from this cluster of central worlds, devices capable of collecting data squirts via RzSpace and passing them on. The system was prohibitively expensive and, as such, almost exclusively the domain of the mega-corporations. When assigning Drake, Reese had secured a line of credit to carry his reports. This was far from usual procedure and she didn't doubt it would have raised a few eyebrows within First Solar's upper hierarchy, but anyone who had a problem with her actions was welcome to raise the matter with her. No one had.

The system was also notoriously unreliable due to the vagaries of Rz, and Enduril II was at the extreme limits of its reach; had Enduril been any further out or in a less fortuitous region of the ever-expanding sphere of space as you travelled away from the core worlds, they would have been obliged to resort to courier ships, rendering regular contact impractical.

The Rz relays, though, made regular contact feasible, at least in theory. Two messages... It was always possible, of course, that one had gone astray and that Drake had been prevented from sending a second by some technical issue at his end... *Two messages.*

Terry was glad she had taken the impulsive decision to put

Jen and Leesa into play but it was proving insufficient to salve her conscience. She considered her options. She could send a second representative on her own authority, as promised, but that seemed a paltry measure under the circumstances. First Solar did possess more robust remedies but these were very much measures of last resort and way above her pay grade. Her gut, which had always served her so well, kept insisting that more than mere misfortune was involved in Drake's silence, but could she convince anyone else of that on such flimsy circumstantial evidence?

She had to.

Drake was her agent. She was responsible for sending him out there and it was up to her to organise back up if required.

Decision made, she sat a little straighter in the chair and spoke to the air. "Connect me to Senior Partner Åkesson."

After a brief pause a face appeared in the air before her; close-cropped silver hair and beard – the latter an unusual affectation in this day and age – and kind eyes. "Terry, this is a rare pleasure. What can I do for you?"

"Sorry to trouble you, Valter, but could you spare me a few minutes for a face to face?"

She could easily have said all she needed to there and then, but the request to meet in person would impress upon him how serious she considered the matter. She knew how valuable his time was, and he knew she knew. This was the first time she had ever made such a request. There was also the small matter of discretion.

In fairness to Åkesson, he didn't hesitate. "Of course. My office, in ten minutes."

"Thank you."

The partners' offices occupied some of the higher floors in the First Solar building, though the very highest were reserved for board meetings, entertainment, the president's suite, and impressing VIPs. Åkesson's was to be found on the 112th.

Reese timed her arrival with precision, stepping out of the lift seven seconds before the appointed time. She was shown straight in.

"Terry, it's been too long." Åkesson came forward to clasp her hand.

Although he was her direct boss, Reese had little to do with him. Success earned her a degree of autonomy and she was largely left to her own devices, though she didn't doubt her performance was under constant scrutiny, as with all of First Solar's loan advisors.

She refused refreshment and sat down in the proffered seat, a little amused to be this side of the office – which was both larger and more lavishly appointed than her own; the Spartan décor being her personal preference.

"So, what can I help with?" Åkesson asked.

"Valter… I believe we have an agent in trouble."

"This would be your man Drake."

She nodded, not in the least surprised that Åkesson had spent the preceding ten minutes reviewing details of current missions in order to anticipate what had prompted her request for a meeting.

"As I understand it, he's only missed two reports and the latest isn't all that overdue."

"That's correct, but even so."

He watched her, waiting for her to continue, but two could play that game. She stared back, saying nothing, despite his being her boss.

He shook his head and smiled. "Terry, you have the best conversion rate of any of our assessors, but then you know that. You've always had a knack for making the right judgement call on marginal profile scores – a far higher success rate than mere statistics can account for." He looked at her for a moment, as if weighing her up. "I presume your much vaunted gut is telling you that this isn't a simple matter of system failure."

"It is."

"The same gut that, according to your comments on file, caused you to have reservations about the Enduril case in the first place."

"Yes – the fact we can find no record of Payne until nine years ago, his insistence on Drake's involvement, and the contradiction of a reclusive society suddenly wanting to open themselves up to tourism."

"Then why accept the case at all?"

"You've seen the assessment score."

"I have." Åkesson sat forward, as if to suggest this was just an off the record chat between two friends. "Look, Terry, are you sure that your concerns regarding Drake aren't simply a manifestation of guilt at having accepted the case despite your gut telling you there was something iffy about it?"

"Valter, I know myself well enough to answer that one truthfully. Yes, I'm sure. Drake's in trouble, I'm certain of it."

"Very well. I had to ask." He sat back, clapping his hands together and rubbing them. "Very well. What are you proposing we do about this, then?"

"A second agent to be sent directly to Enduril II to enquire about Drake, and... I'd like you to authorise the deployment of a SABRE."

Officially, there was no such thing; unofficially, and known only to very specific individuals within the bank's upper management, First Solar maintained two SABRE units: Special Armed Bank Response. Each unit consisted of half a dozen operatives, drawn largely from special forces, highly trained and fully equipped to the highest spec, ready to be sent in for clean up or when things got messy, as they occasionally did.

A SABRE?" Åkesson didn't look surprised. He must have known from the moment Terry asked for a personal meeting that she was after something like this. "You've given me nothing to justify that sort of a commitment."

"I know."

"But you're asking for it anyway."

She nodded.

Another moment passed in which he stared at her, perhaps in

judgement, and this time she did feel uncomfortable, but she brazened it out, meeting his gaze.

"This is your call, Terry."

Meaning that the buck stopped with her should anything go wrong; he wouldn't support her. She nodded, having expected nothing less.

"Very well," he said. "Here's what I'm going to do. Representative Archer has just returned from a few days off."

Reese knew Archer. A bit too cocky for her liking, but he showed a lot of promise and was resourceful, which had already earned him a good reputation around the department and might be just what was needed now.

"Brief him and send him straight to Enduril II," Åkesson said. "SABRE Unit 1 is currently available. I'll despatch them to the Enduril system, with a watching brief. Once there, they'll be free to assess the situation, intervening only if they judge it to be necessary, and if said intervention is likely to be effective. Unless it becomes unavoidable, neither Drake nor Archer must know of their presence, or indeed of their existence."

"Understood, and thank you."

"Drake is a valuable asset, his record proves that, but I wouldn't normally go to these lengths on such thin evidence. You're going out on a limb here, Terry. I'll hold the branch for you for as long as I can, but your gut had better prove to be right."

"It will," she said, with only a little more conviction than she actually felt.

"And, Terry... Your recruiting of Drake was a master stroke. I've never pried into where you found him or what his background might be, and while he continues to be such a lucrative investment I don't suppose I ever will, but I hope one day we'll sit down, off the record, and you'll feel able to tell me the full story."

"One day, I will," she promised," and with that she took her leave, before Åkesson could change his mind.

ELEVEN

Before heading down to breakfast, Drake set about composing his third message to Terry Reese – having sent one on his return from the cache the previous day, as per the agreed schedule. He knew full well there were no guarantees any of these reports were actually getting through, but he had no control over that. He thought back to the first message, sent from the visitor centre to the port, and then to an orbiting satellite to be squirted through RzSpace in the direction of New Sparta, and knew that it could have been intercepted at any point. There was no way for him to check. He just had to continue on the assumption that they *were* getting through; and, if they weren't...

Reese had spoken of sending in the cavalry if he failed to keep to the agreed schedule. How long would she wait before doing so? Of course, there was also the question of exactly what she had meant by 'the cavalry'; First Solar didn't maintain an armed security force as far as he was aware, preferring more subtle means of achieving their aims – financial and political solutions rather than militaristic ones – so would 'the cavalry' simply entail another agent or two enquiring after his whereabouts and wellbeing, armed with threats of economic sanction as a last resort? Hardly the stuff to strike fear into the hearts of a determined enemy. The bank certainly didn't lack the resources necessary to hire mercenaries if they chose to, but it didn't really fit with what he knew of his employers. Of course, it was doubtful he knew everything.

This third message was something of a bonus, pre-empting the next scheduled report, but he felt obliged to send it following the unexpected progress he had made the previous evening.

As Payne had dropped both him and Ungar back at the hotel

following their introduction to the cache, he mentioned, almost as an afterthought, that there was to be a reception that evening in Drake's honour, with the good and the great of Hamilton in attendance. Drake was finally being given the opportunity to meet some of Enduril II's decision makers aside from the ubiquitous Payne.

Even at the time, Drake couldn't decide whether this was an event hastily organised following his comments about the other officials' continued absence, or if Payne knew about the reception all along and had deliberately chosen to withhold the information.

Governance Hall, the setting of the night's festivities, struck Drake as an odd blend of the decorative and austere, as if the architect had tried to emulate opulence but didn't quite know how to pull it off. The food, on the other hand, was a revelation. Paper-thin leaf parcels made soft by steaming, which fell apart at the first touch of a knife to reveal an unctuous filling of rice, chopped herbs and melting cheese; the cheese, made locally, was tangy and tart. The parcels were followed by a highly spiced broth, bright yellow in colour and loaded with slender, translucent noodles and a generous helping of red crustaceans, or perhaps insects, that resembled tiny shrimps with wings – they proved to be utterly delicious – followed by several types of char-grilled meats, some basted in sticky sauces, others merely seasoned, along with a bewildering variety of vegetable side dishes. This wasn't the subtlest food Drake had ever eaten but was brazenly robust and hearty; every dish, though, was well prepared and flavoursome and there was certainly plenty of it. He supposed that, given the richness of the forest that still covered a good portion of the planet's surface, Endurian chefs had no shortage of ingredients to choose from. By the time dessert came around he was already over-full, and took no more than polite tastings of sugary confections, chocolate gateaux, and melting citrus bombes.

During the meal, he found himself sandwiched between the finance minister – a slender, intelligent woman with a pleasant smile and a politician's knack for evading questions when it suited her, and the wife of a city official whose rank Drake failed to remember. The wife was stout and voluble, and eminently proud of everything Enduril II had to offer, as she proceeded to demonstrate at considerable length. She evidently considered it her solemn duty to browbeat their guest into acknowledging the world's many virtues and her husband, seated on her other side, seemed glad to escape her attentions for a while, leaving Drake to her tender mercies.

Meal aside, the evening had gone well. It was hardly the time or the place for in depth discussion, but he was able to circulate, making enough contacts to keep him busy with the promise of one-on-one meetings in the days to come. Disappointingly, no one attempted to take him to one side or have a word 'off the record'. On the face of it, at least, everyone was presenting a united front and voicing support for the plan to open the cache as a tourist attraction.

An odd attitude for a bunch of people who are supposed to be isolationists, Mudball commented.

Isn't it just, Drake agreed, knowing that Reese harboured similar concerns. Why would a society that had shunned contact with its fellow worlds for generations suddenly be so keen to throw open its gates to hordes of strangers?

Of course, much of this declared support for the proposal may have been for public consumption only. Time would tell if it still held true once he spoke to them individually and in private.

He had managed to maintain focus and do his job for the duration of the reception, but once back in his own room and without such distractions, his thoughts returned to the vivid sense of déjà vu that had assailed him from the moment he stepped inside the cache chamber.

He went to sleep still wrestling with the issue, doing his best to keep his mind closed to Mudball but suspecting the little alien must have sensed some of it.

Ungar hadn't been at the reception and Drake hadn't seen him since they returned from the cache, causing him to wonder if the historian might have left Hamilton to visit one of the other towns whose mines were still active. Drake was pleased, therefore, when the older man joined him at breakfast.

"Good to see you're still here."

"Oh yes, you won't get rid of me that easily," Ungar assured him.

"I thought your principal interest in coming here was the mining communities."

"Indeed it is, but Hamilton *is* a mining community. The mines here may have been unproductive in recent years but they are what the town was founded on, and Hamilton remains the political and administrative centre for an entire planet of mining communities. I'll travel out to visit some of the other sites after I'm done here, but that won't be for a while… Besides, how could I pass up on the opportunity to visit an untouched cache again? I confess I was a little dazzled by yesterday's experience. I hope this time around I can be a little more analytical."

Drake could sympathise, having been more than a little distracted himself. He was curious to see whether the second visit to the cache – arranged for later that morning – would affect him similarly.

After finishing breakfast, Drake nipped back to his room ahead of the day's trip. As he headed back to the front of the hotel at the agreed time, Mudball broke an uncharacteristically long silence. *I think I understand now, about the docile nature of the cache entity.*

Go on.

Well, I'll have to verify some of this when we encounter it again, but okay. To start with, you have to forget everything you think you know about the relationship between caches, the artefacts they contain, and the entities who watch over them.

Okay…

You humans have got things the wrong way round, Mudball said, *always have had. You've assumed that the artefacts are the important things and that the cache entities are there to guard them. Not surprising, of course, because that puts you at the centre of the equation: 'this tech has been left here for us to discover; it's all about us!' Like hell. In fact, the artefacts are incidental. It's the cache entities that are the important components. They're what the chambers are all about.*

What are the cache entities, then?

They're the fractured echoes, the Elders who were left behind.

"What?"

When the Elders transcended, not every member of their race went with them. A handful didn't want to go while others were not deemed suitable, so they remained in this universe. The Elders realised that any members of their race who stayed here would be veritable gods, able to rule over emergent sentient races, interfere with their development, mould them as they saw fit, even cut short a race they took exception to. These remainers would be so far beyond any emergent sentients that they would be seen as gods and able to shape the future according to their whim.

This was seen as undesirable and irresponsible. The Elders, in their wisdom, felt it necessary to safeguard the development of these theoretical sentients, which might or might not emerge, even after they had turned their backs on this realm and abandoned it. So they took steps. They split the remainers' consciousness into myriad partials, Remnants, creatures of diminished capabilities and intellect, of stunted ambition and awareness, and no memory of what they had been. They then scattered these partials across the galaxy, so that there was no possibility of their ever reuniting, entombing each within a carefully constructed environment, in effect a prison. They felt this was the most 'humane' – for want of a better word – course of action.

Hang on a minute, Drake was stunned, and needed confirmation that he'd understood this correctly. *So you're saying that the cache guardians are Remnants of actual Elders?*

Yes – do keep up. Fading over the course of centuries, as the Elders knew they must, some driven mad by their circumstance, others devolving into simpletons, but that's exactly what they are: Elder Remnants.

And the artefacts that fill these chambers, what are they, then?

Ah yes, the artefacts that you humans place such value on. They're toys.

Distractions. After reducing their fellows to such a diminished state and then abandoning them, the Elders salved their collective conscience by lavishing a multitude of trinkets and gadgets upon them, to provide entertainment, to stop the poor dolts growing bored. That's all the cache chambers are: a child's playroom, nothing more.

Drake found himself growing angrier and angrier. *You knew all this and have never bothered saying anything until now?* he thought, aware that the alien would sense his anger but not caring. He'd always suspected Mudball of holding out on him, but this went way beyond anything he could have envisaged.

No, nothing like that. I suspected, yes, some of it, but only now have all the pieces fallen into place…

Is that what you are, Drake pressed, his anger rising with every passing moment, *one of these Elder Remnants?*

Well what did you think I was likely to be? You found me in an Elder cache chamber, remember?

Drake remembered only too well. He'd shied away from considering Mudball's true nature ever since; he knew the little alien was associated with the Elders – member of a client species perhaps… Of course he'd wondered, but had never really stopped to analyse. Thinking about that now, he suspected the alien of subtly manipulating his curiosity.

So when you saved my life back then, that was all a ploy; you were saving me from yourself.

No! Well, sort of, but not in the manipulative way you're thinking. I was different from the other Remnants. I managed to retain a large part of who I was, my identity, but in order to keep from being detected, I had to suppress that aspect of myself. It only started to emerge when you appeared.

Because finally, in me, you had a vector that could take you out of the cache chamber and out into the wider universe, to freedom.

Yes. At least the alien made no attempt to deny the fact. *The entity you fought was the infantile, intellectually stunted Remnant of me. What saved you was the emergent rational aspect.*

Great; a schizophrenic cache guardian.

Not really, no, but if the comparison works for you that's fine. The thing is, describing myself as 'rational' back then is perhaps misleading, and a term that only applies in comparison to that other version. I had the potential *to be rational, but I was damaged, my intelligence crippled and my awareness shredded. I knew that in order to heal I had to get out of there, away from that prison, or lose myself entirely…*

So you hitched a lift.

Yes, that's exactly what I did, by forming a partnership, and look at how it's worked out for both of us. With my help you've become a highly valued employee at a major corporation…

From where Drake was standing, the benefit was in the balance but he clamped down on that thought.

I've only started to piece things together in the past few days, Mudball said. *Time, as they say, is a great healer.*

I see.

I can tell you're sceptical…

I'm not sceptical, I'm livid.

Well set your hurt feelings to one side for a moment and consider the implications in the light of our current circumstances. Because I now recognise the cache entities' true nature, I can understand what this one is about. Whatever the Endurians might think, it isn't attempting to form an alliance of trans-species harmony…

As you did with me, you mean, Drake couldn't resist interjecting, not bothering to hold back on the irony.

It sees you humans as merely another type of toy, Mudball continued, ignoring him, *another form of entertainment that has wandered into its limited world. There to be used or discarded as it sees fit.*

Drake resisted the temptation to repeat his observation. Not for the first time he found himself wondering *why* Mudball had chosen to remain with him for all these years, what the alien gained from their association and its motives for continuing to pursue it.

To avoid being dissected as a test subject or put on display at a zoo, Mudball said, evidently catching Drake's thought. *I know you'll never reveal me to the authorities.* This was the same answer the little alien always provided, but the explanation was wearing thin.

Don't be so sure, Drake told him, *not now that I know you only saved me from yourself.*

Ah, but save you I did. If I hadn't awoken at that point or had chosen not to intervene... The alien conjured in Drake's mind stark images of his gruesome death by various malicious artefacts. The irritating thing was, Drake knew that Mudball had a point, whatever the alien might have chosen to withhold from him subsequently.

We'll revisit this later, he thought, determined not to let his companion off the hook just yet.

With that he strode out to the car, where Ungar already waited. Of Payne there was no sign, which was no bad thing by Drake's reckoning; just Ungar and the unflappably silent Evans. It was apparent that the historian was in a state of considerable excitement, and when they were both in the car he wasted no time in telling Drake why.

"Payne has approached me with a proposition," he explained. "He wants me to write about the cache, on condition that I not release anything until a specified time... Something to do with the timing of publicity?"

At least that explained why Payne had been so accommodating to Ungar. Drake might have guessed the man would have an ulterior motive.

"You've said yes, I take it?"

"Of course I have! Who am I to refuse a commission like that?"

Payne met them in the empty building that fronted for the cache. With him were two government officials Drake had been introduced to the previous evening – Clemens Nowak, the minister for mining, and Feliks Lis, the resources minister. The latter Drake had spent a few minute chatting with prior to the meal, the former he had only met in passing.

"So, Mr Drake," Nowak said, "I gather you were suitably impressed by your first visit to our chamber."

"Oh indeed," Drake said. "How could anyone fail to be impressed, either by the cache or its unique location?"

After the ritual of depositing their perminals in the security box, Ungar, Drake, Payne and the two ministers entered the false elevator, Evans again staying behind with the valuables. Now that there were five of them it proved a far tighter squeeze than last time. They managed, but not easily, and this looked to be the small compartment's capacity.

"We will be enlarging the access room before we open to the public," Payne said. "The aim is to take through groups of up to a dozen at a time plus a guide."

Even though Drake was ready for it, the transition still evoked that flash of intense internal discomfort, gone almost before it had been felt, and immediately afterwards he was hit by a sense of déjà vu, even more forceful than the first time.

What's wrong? Mudball asked, evidently realising that more than just the physical effect of cross-over was troubling him.

Having analysed the phenomenon in private without reaching any helpful conclusions, Drake had decided to share it with the alien in the hope Mudball could offer some insight. *I feel as if I've been here before,* he said.

Really?

Yes... No! At least I'm pretty sure I haven't, not here as such. It just feels that way. I wonder if I've been somewhere similar, another pocket of some sort, maybe even another cache hidden within a pocket; something here feels so familiar. And the transition, I've definitely been through that before, but I can't recall any of the specifics. It's as if I almost remember things but they're not really my memories, as if I'm catching echoes of somebody else's experiences.

Interesting. If these are your memories, they must have been suppressed.

That's what I'm beginning to suspect, though it wasn't an easy thing to contemplate.

And you had no notion before now that this might have been done to you?

No, none.

And the trigger for these 'echoes' seems to be the moment of transition, when you cross into the pocket?

Yes, Drake confirmed. It certainly had been this time.

Okay, I'll come back to you on this shortly. Right now I'm off for a pow-wow with a rather peculiar cache entity.

That's it? That's all you have to say? But he was talking to a blank space, Mudball's presence having already withdrawn.

Drake's thoughts turned outward, to where Payne was holding court. This time, Enduril II's governor was making far more of a show of presenting the cache – either that or Drake was better able to pay attention. He suspected, though, that the presence of the two ministers had a bearing on Payne's approach.

After a brief address in which Payne touched on the initial discovery of the cache and praised the wisdom of those early discoverers for not stripping out its content for immediate profit, the party began to proceed through the chamber. Drake would have liked to hear a little more about the actual discovery. The account Payne gave mirrored those he had been able to access since arriving at Hamilton, all of which held up the Endurians involved as heroes but glossed over the mechanism of discovery. The only way Drake could imagine the cache ever being 'discovered', bearing in mind its location, was if the guardian entity chose to reveal itself and invited folk in. He determined to ask Mudball about it once the alien had concluded its 'pow wow'.

As they progressed through the chamber, at a far more sedate pace than on the previous day, Drake was struck anew by just how big the room was. He didn't doubt there were more artefacts here than in any cache he had uncovered during his time with First Solar, despite their neat arrangement reducing the impression of numbers. For the first time, he began to appreciate how the Endurian cache might actually work as a tourist attraction – even seasoned experts would be falling over themselves to visit an Elder site of this size and significance. To make it work, the locals would need to be educated on the realities of marketing and persuaded to relax their veto on images being taken and released, but that would come. All this, of course, depended on their declared desire to open up to tourism being genuine and the cache entity's willingness to go along with a mass invasion of its domain. Drake had yet to be convinced on either count, particularly given Mudball's revelations regarding the true nature of the cache entities, the implications of which he was still processing.

This time, rather than merely talking about the various artefacts, Payne took the trouble to stop and demonstrate some of their properties – a pile of slender rods which, when triggered by the lightest of touches, would spring to life and commence constructing a three dimensional object – a building in this instance – only to break down to rods again. Touch them again and they would build something different – what looked to be a bridge the second time, though the design was sufficiently alien to leave Drake with the suspicion it may have been something else entirely. Next up was a mesmeric light display emitted by an innocuous-looking cube if you rubbed it a certain way.

They had only gone a short distance into the room, however, when the whole place abruptly started to shake, a rapid vibration that rippled up through Drake's body and everything else, toppling a number of the artefacts, several of which were sent crashing to the floor, and disrupting the room's perfect order. It felt as if the chamber were being hit by an earthquake, which, given its setting, was a nonsense.

Drake was looking directly at Payne as the disturbance began and he could see that the governor was caught as much by surprise as anyone. This wasn't a ploy, it wasn't part of some trick; this was genuine. The vibrations stopped as suddenly as they had begun. Everyone stared at each other, not quite sure what to say or do. Before anyone could decide, the shaking returned, even more violently than before. Payne fell over, attempting to break his fall by holding on to one of the casket-sized artefacts but failing. Drake nearly followed suit, steadying himself with difficulty. He saw Ungar sprawl heavily over another large artefact and Nowak stumble to his knees.

The world stopped shaking for a second time.

"The elevator!" Payne called out. "Everyone get to the elevator."

Lis was already halfway there and no one needed any more persuading. Ungar seemed shaken and was slow to react. Drake helped him to his feet, keeping an arm around the historian's shoulders and guiding him hurriedly towards the exit.

The five of them crammed into the small compartment and... nothing happened.

Payne looked stricken. Drake couldn't see precisely what he was attempting to do due to the press of bodies, but whatever it was he evidently tried again, with the same lack of result.

"It's not working, we're trapped!" he spluttered. His gaze fixed on Drake. "What have you done? This has never happened before. Decades of co-operation, then you show up and all of a sudden the guardian entity stops communicating. What the hell have you done to our cache guardian?"

"I've done nothing," Drake said calmly, able to do so with complete honesty, though he had a feeling he knew who had. *Mudball?* he called in his head. At the same time, he realised that the diminutive alien's form no longer occupied its usual perch on his shoulder, nor was it in the pouch that sat beneath. *MUDBALL!*

TWELVE

Leesa slowed her breathing, drawing air into her lungs in a measured, steady fashion, keeping sound to a minimum as she strained to hear anything out of place. The darkness would have been complete but for a single streetlight around the next corner, which cast its sour yellow glow broadly to reveal wet road and pavement; not the clean wetness of freshly fallen rain, but rather the sodden staleness of water that has sat for too long, gathering in shallow puddles and unable to evaporate due to the muggy air.

The light flickered unpredictably, suggesting an intermittent fault. Leesa refused to be distracted, but would have preferred the damned thing to go out entirely. Darkness didn't bother her.

At last, a sound; the barest whisper of something brushing against the wall behind and above her, but it was enough. She focused on that ghostly presence and waited for the sound to be repeated. It would be, she was confident of that. If the unseen presence were in a position to attack her it would have done so, and now that she knew it was there she'd sense the slightest adjustment should it choose to do so... *When* it chose to do so... There!

Leesa spun around, bringing her handgun to bear and firing in one fluid movement. Only as her target dropped to the ground did she register its nature.

"What the...?"

A segmented bot, roughly the length of her forearm, crashed to the pavement. It was formed of a solid front section from which arose three sets of legs, then a prehensile tail built of layers of overlaid plating and ending in a long, curved sting or claw. Two of its 'legs' on the right side appeared to be damaged and immobile, so presumably her shot must have winged it. Despite this, the thing twitched as if attempting to right itself. She shot it again and this time it stayed still.

As if her second shot had been a signal, a horde of the things erupted from the building before her and the surrounding street, some scuttling across the pavement, others clambering down the sheer wall, all converging on her. Their advance was marked by an erratic tattoo as myriad metallic claws struck against stone and brick.

She backed away, firing coolly, calmly, the part of her that never slept marking the position of each small construct, allowing her to choose and eliminate the greatest threat at every turn. This wasn't a conscious process requiring thought or consideration, it was instinctive. It was who she was.

They kept coming, though, in numbers that threatened to overwhelm even her reflexes, with three, four or five immediate threats arising simultaneously no matter how rapidly she dispatched them. She refused to turn and flee but quickened her retreat. Her greatest fear was that the mechs would outflank her. They tried, fanning out and attempting to establish an arc of attack rather than a front, to catch her in a pincer movement. Were they being actively controlled, were their actions pre-programmed, or did they have enough intelligence to improvise? Something to ponder later; right now it made little difference. She quickened her pace again.

Inevitably, some got through at last. She felt a sharp stab of pain in her left foot and looked down to see one of the bots clinging to her boot. The claw of its foremost leg had pierced the leather composite and sunk into the flesh of the foot, just behind her toes. With a snarl born more of frustration than pain, she kicked out, dislodging the mech which had yet to secure a firm hold and sending it sailing beyond the ranks of its still-advancing twins.

Dealing with that one had cost her, though, requiring a split second of inattention she could ill afford. Even as she kicked that one away, two more had latched onto her standing leg and she felt a sharp blow as another landed on her shoulder from somewhere above.

Without hesitation she sprang into the air, twisting as she did so to wrench the mech from the back of her shoulder and at the same time kicking out to dislodge one of the two on her leg. The other, though, clung on stubbornly.

She landed hard, feeling metal carapaces buckle under the impact as the sea of attackers had closed to fill the position she had jumped from. Sharp claws pierced her overalls as multiple bots latched onto both legs, and she felt heavy impacts on her back and shoulders as more fell upon her from an overhang she'd failed to spot, so focused was she on the threat at street level.

There were too many of them. No matter how she tried, they had her, but she wasn't about to give up and fought with renewed energy.

"Simulation ceasing," Raider's voice said from the air.

Instantly, the bots froze. She stood for a second, absorbing the abrupt stillness and getting her breath back. Then she set about shaking off the bots from her back and reaching down to pick off individual climbers from her leg. One had taken a particularly firm hold, causing her to wince as she pulled its clawed feet out of her flesh. The wounds were all superficial, and would heal quickly enough with a dab of nuskin.

"These segmented scorpion bot things are new," she commented as she left the central area of the gym.

"I had to find some way to pass the time during the years you abandoned me," Raider replied.

Leesa had no idea if he meant that or not. Raider had steadily developed a sense of humour that approximated a human's to an uncanny degree during his association with the Dark Angels, but it wasn't always easy to spot. "I thought you were dormant, in hibernation or whatever," she said.

No reply. Leesa tried a different tack. "Why did you stop the simulation?"

"To prevent you from destroying any more of the bots.

They're not simple or cheap to build, you know. Rebooting their systems once you've shot them with the energy beam is straight forward enough, but after you've stomped and crushed and kicked them around a bit, not so much."

"You shouldn't pit your toys against me if you don't want them to get hurt," Leesa said, peeling off her training suit and heading for the dry shower cubicle.

"Why can't you be content with a standard workout using standard exercise equipment, like Shadow?"

"Boring," Leesa replied, activating the shower and effectively ending the conversation.

She stepped out from the shower a moment later feeling refreshed, her body tingling. She always felt good after a rigorous gym session, and was relishing the opportunity to pit herself against the scenarios Raider cooked up for her once more. A hard workout followed by a dry shower and then the pleasure of slipping into crisp fresh overalls, what could be better? The session had left her feeling energised and ready to face anything

As she left the gym area she paused, her eyes drawn to the closed door of one of the other compartments occupying this part of the hold: the artefact room. She hadn't ventured in there as yet, knowing what was waiting for her. Perhaps now was the right time.

With only the two of them knocking around on the ship it was almost impossible not to live in each other's pocket – the *Raider* wasn't that big a ship – and if she was going to play two-woman-crew with anyone, Jen would be a pretty good choice, but Leesa was glad her friend wasn't present at this particular juncture. This was something she had to face alone, a prospect that simultaneously unnerved and drew her.

Almost without her own volition, she walked across to the room. The door slid open and, with only the briefest of hesitations, she stepped inside.

The first thing she saw was Cornische; or so it would be easy to believe. Facing the door stood a mannequin draped in the familiar dark blue leather coat, the hat, the boots... Screw up your eyes a little and squint and it wasn't hard to see the mannequin's blank face as the distortion field that habitually blurred the captain's features into indecipherable static. The dummy's posture had even been modelled on the captain's. At first glance the resemblance was uncanny, and Leesa had been ready for it; she could only imagine how much it might startle the unwary.

Her awareness expanded to take in the rest of the room. The interior always struck her as clinical – the bright white walls, floor and ceiling Cornische's choice, not hers. There was nothing regimented or precise about the way the room's contents were displayed. Each item, suit, or oddly-shaped artefact had its own stand, plinth, carefully labelled drawer, or in a couple of instances mannequin, but they were positioned haphazardly, as if to counter any suggestion that this was a shrine. It wasn't, though doubtless there would have been those who viewed it that way had they been aware of the room's existence. This was simply how Cornische had chosen to store the various disguises and Elder tech of those Dark Angels who no longer served on the crew, for whatever reason. "Beats sticking them away in a cupboard," he'd once commented when asked about it.

The first artefact stored in the room had belonged to one of the original Dark Angels, Helix, after he was killed during the Six Moon Run, a notorious incident that saw two rival trading ships lost with all hands and the *Ion Raider* take some serious damage. They'd all been relieved to survive that one – those that had – and no one objected when Cornische had suggested setting up the artefact room, which had been smaller in those days. Actually, considered in that light, maybe there was something of the shrine about the place after all.

There was nothing mystical or spiritual about Leesa's mood, however, as she walked towards a plain plinth on the far side of the compact room. Rising seamlessly from the floor like some misshapen ceramic toadstool, the simple stand looked a little out of place – the poor relation standing awkwardly at the back, uncertain of its right to even be here.

As Leesa approached, four letters sprang up to hover in the air above the rounded top of the plinth: HEL N. Appropriately enough, the lettering was silver.

With a sense of resignation and a lack of joy that would have dismayed her earlier self, Leesa reached out with her right hand to place her palm on the curved surface before her. At her touch, a drawer in the stand slid open.

It lay there as she'd left it: shining, silver, looking like a pool of overly bright mercury. She felt the once-familiar tug of its call; this garment, this second skin which had come to define her in the public's perception once upon a time and might yet do again. Part of her rejoiced to feel the skin's lure even as a corner of her mind quailed.

Before actually reaching the podium – as she had crossed the room towards it – she had sensed a faint stirring, as if something was questing for her, responding to her presence. Now the drawer was open that sense of connection struck her with near physical force. She put out a hand – perhaps to steady herself or was she reaching for the garment? Afterwards, she couldn't say with certainty.

The skin rippled, as if the drawer had been shaken, a wave seemed to run across its surface, causing it to rise slightly to meet her fingers. At first touch a jolt of energy surged through her body. She gasped, at the same moment conscious that the river of silver was climbing up her arm, across her shoulders and chest, down her body and along the other arm. It didn't burn, it didn't hurt; instead the cloth's touch was cool, like the softest of silk running over her skin, a kiss rather than an assault. Her neck and head were last, the silver climbing her throat and slipping into ears and nose and mouth – the taste vaguely metallic but not unpleasant, while sound muffled for a moment and then sprang into even greater sharpness, as if someone had adjusted the volume controls and over-compensated. Sense of smell was heightened, too. She became aware of a faint antiseptic scent pervading the room, which she had been completely oblivious to before.

She felt energised, alert – the garment's return stimulating a super-charged version of the buzz her recent gym visit had given her, and she began to remember precisely why she had missed being Hel N so much.

For a moment longer Leesa simply stood there, giving both her body and her mind the opportunity to get used to the differences. Then she had the skin withdraw, feeling it desert her face and exit her eyes and nose, retreating down her body in a co-ordinated wave, to gather beneath the soles of her shoes, out of sight and completely anonymous to any casual observer.

After taking a further moment to reacquaint herself with the duller, more mundane world, Leesa left the artefact room and went in search of Jen.

Jen was in the ops room when Leesa found her. No real reason for her to be there except that it was marginally larger than her cabin and boasted more comfortable seating. Leesa had been hogging the gym and Jen was killing time here until it was her turn to work up a sweat.

One thing she hadn't missed during her ten year sojourn from space travel was RzSpace. Trips through the theoretical non-realm always affected her profoundly. Whereas others seemed able to take the gradual deadening of emotions and the sense of detachment that exposure to Rz evoked, these things never failed to unnerve Jen. She'd heard tales of suicides among those who had remained in RzSpace for too long, and it didn't surprise her. Intellectually, she knew that interstellar travel was only possible due to Rz and that without access to this mathematically described realm, where the laws of physics ran differently, it would take generations to get anywhere, and she had of course come through many dips into Rz unscathed, but she still didn't fully trust the place and had to steel herself every time.

As a distraction from such morbid contemplation, she summoned up a list of news reports and travelogues relating to their destination, just to get a feel for the place. Animated images of another world surrounded her as she flicked through the available recordings, all depicting the city of la Gossa, a major capital on the world of Babylon, famed for its knock-off gadgets and affordable machine parts.

"Really?" Jen had said when Leesa proposed they should go there.

"Where else? We're not about to find the parts any cheaper – and I know all the best places to go to get the very best price, trust me – and it's virtually on route if we're headed for Enduril."

"All well and good, but, in case you've forgotten, the captain is missing, presumed to be in the shit. That's our priority here, so let's go rescue the captain first and *then* worry about engine parts."

Leesa had shook her head. "Without these parts the engines are at little more than seventy per cent efficiency, which means we're going to have to make the journey in two jumps anyway, so we might as well take the break at Babylon. I won't need long – a day or so tops – and once we have the engines back to full capacity we'll make up most of the lost time in any case. Besides, we've no idea what the captain's got himself into, and if we have to grab him and make a quick getaway we'll need all the grunt *Raider* can give us."

Jen hadn't been convinced, still reckoning they ought to go after the captain first, but she couldn't fault Leesa's reasoning. What Leesa had neatly managed to avoid mentioning so far was how she felt about returning to Babylon. After all, this was where she had gone to live after the Dark Angels disbanded and where she had subsequently been subjected to a memory wipe. This was the world she had escaped from at the first opportunity.

Jen realised she was no longer alone in ops and looked round to see Leesa standing in the doorway. She motioned with her hand, dismissing the images that surrounded her – a particularly earnest account of life in la Gossa's shantytown which she should probably have been paying more attention to.

Leesa looked... odd. Jen found it impossible to read her expression. "Are you okay?"

"Yes, I'm fine." As Leesa spoke, a hint of silver glinted on her foot. The glint became a fast-moving ripple that rose rapidly to cover her entire body.

"Wow!" Jen had seen this before but not in a decade, and it never ceased to fascinate her even back then. "So you've finally taken the plunge." At least this explained why Leesa had spent so long in the gym that morning.

The silver coating withdrew, slipping down Leesa's body as rapidly as it had risen. "Had to, really, before we left RzSpace and landed at Babylon."

"Oh, and why's that?"

"There's something I haven't told you about la Gossa..." She looked almost embarrassed, which wasn't an expression Jen was used to seeing. "Kyle's there, on Babylon."

It shouldn't have come as a surprise really, not given their history, and it certainly explained one thing. "So that's why you're so keen to stop off there."

"Yeah, well, partially that, but it doesn't mean the rest of what I said isn't valid as well. We really do need those parts, and Babylon is pretty much on our way... I have to *know*, Jen. How much did Kyle know about the memory wipe? Did he have anything to do with it?"

"You still don't remember what happened?"

Leesa shook her head. "The thing is, when I returned to la Gossa, with no memory of who I'd been, I met Kyle again. I went to the clubs, dealt with his lieutenants, and he didn't let on, didn't give me any clue that he knew me. None of them did. So what does that say?"

"I've no idea," Jen admitted. She felt annoyed at Leesa for not being open about this from the start, but she had never seen Leesa hurting like this, and could only imagine what it must feel like to lose so much of yourself. "But we'll find out, together; and then we'll go rescue the captain. Deal?

"Deal. And, Jen… thank you."

Thirteen

Leesa didn't feel anywhere near as confident as she was trying to appear. Securing the parts for the ship had been as straight forward as anticipated, and she had done so without drawing any undue attention. The next part of the visit was unlikely to go as smoothly. This was the first time she had returned to Babylon since reclaiming her past, which gave her the opportunity to tidy up some unfinished business.

Despite this being the city where she had lived for the best part of a decade, Leesa saw her return to la Gossa as a challenge to be faced rather than any sort of homecoming. Even so, the oppressive heat, the aroma of spices, the smell of leather and native fruit she'd never encountered anywhere else, the pinched nasal sound of the local language as hawkers plied their trade or one neighbour called across the street to another, all evoked a sense of nostalgia she hadn't anticipated. Most of her memories of this city were anything but pleasant.

A matchakai regarded her with doleful eyes from its perch on the end of a vendor's stall. The wizened seller flashed a yellow-toothed grin and held out a skewer of honey-glazed diamond flies towards her. She might have found their sweet, nutty aroma tempting on another day, but not on this one.

"Good, sweet, crispy," the vendor said. "You try, try."

She shook her head and hurried past. The matchakai's gaze followed her. She had always found the diminutive twin-tailed primates vaguely disturbing, especially their eyes, which were too knowing and seemed capable of peering into the deepest recesses of a person's soul.

Leesa had faced more than enough personal demons in recent times as she set about recovering the shattered pieces of her past and coaxed them into the semblance of a pattern, but there remained a gaping hole at the centre of the jigsaw, and she sensed that the pieces needed to fill it were waiting for her here in la Gossa. The prospect of finding them simultaneously thrilled and terrified her.

"Are you okay?" Jen's voice asked in her ear.

"Yeah, I'm good," she intoned. "I'd forgotten how fucking hot this place is, that's all."

She resisted the temptation to run a finger around the neck of her lightweight top. The action would have been no more than a reflex, an affectation. No sweat had gathered there to moisten her fingertips – the auganic part of her saw to that, modulating her body temperature to avoid discomfort – but that didn't supress her awareness of the prevailing conditions.

Babylon's capital was a patchwork of contradictions – a fitting metaphor for the state of her memories. Tourists could loiter here for weeks visiting the glitzy shops and glittering stalls of high streets and markets, dazzled by the abundance of affordable jewellery and low-price tech – the city was a magnet for those seeking to stock up on the latest gadgetry on a budget. They could sample street food and eat at cafés and noodle bars steeped in local 'colour', or dine in air-conditioned splendour at establishments where the waiters didn't so much walk across the floor as glide and every dish was a statement of artistic style, all without ever stumbling across the city's rotting core: the shantytown that sprawled behind the façade and provided the cheap labour that kept the economy running so smoothly. On certain days when the wind was up and blowing in the right direction they might smell it, of course, and wrinkle their noses in displeasure, but it would be impolite to comment or enquire, to acknowledge the truth behind their comfort.

Leesa had slept rough the last time she was here, her few meagre belongings bundled into the corner of a disused railway carriage. Before that, she had enjoyed every luxury that la Gossa could provide, so she was conversant with both aspects of the city and more. She knew too of the nightlife that lurked in the shadows and wore la Gossa's other faces as camouflage: the clubs, the music, the drugs, the sex, the money. This was a side of the city she was all too familiar with because she had lived it, *wallowed* in it. The underbelly of Babylon's capital had once provided her with an easy escape – a world of hedonistic pleasure that demanded nothing in return; a lifestyle that had seduced her into abandoning all responsibility. Enamoured by its charms, by the lure of instant gratification, she had allowed herself to become distracted from what she *needed* to have been doing: searching for the past without which she could never have anchored her present.

At the heart of la Gossa's sleaze sat Kyle, the kingpin of the city's night world, the man whose fingers grasped the threads of shadow that radiated outward to ensnare so many of the clubs, the dealers, the thugs and the pimps, while money flowed back along those threads and into his eager hands. Kyle, who had known her long before her memories were wrenched away and had given no indication of the fact when their paths crossed again.

That omission made him culpable. He was at the centre of the mystery as he was of so much else, Leesa felt certain of it. Now that her memories were largely restored, she knew things about Kyle, things that few others would ever suspect.

They were the keepers of each other's secrets, and it was past time for a reckoning.

She headed towards the river, hurrying across the aptly-named Third Bridge Street with its customary snarl of traffic and into the warren of side streets and alleyways that led towards the old wharves. It was a little cooler here, out of the sun's glare, but no less muggy. She kept her head down, shoulders rounded. This was Jade Warrior territory and she'd had dealings with that particular group of disberos once upon a time. Some among them might still remember her and the last thing she wanted was to draw attention. Clubs such as the Green Gecko and the Siren, twin flagships of Kyle's little empire, lay behind her in other quadrants of the city. Most people seeking him would probably start there, but she knew better.

Her goal was Embargo, the place where it had all started; a club built within the carcass of an old warehouse, the club they had built together.

Embargo faced towards the river and was self-consciously plain – a broad expanse of dark-stained wooden planks without any windows, interrupted only by a simple door above which the word 'Embargo' stood proud upon a white placard, emblazoned in red, and in a font that made the letters look as if they had been branded into the surface of the sign. At night the club's name would be illuminated by two retro downlighters, one of which even flickered intermittently for effect. Never mind that the wooden planks forming the façade were not wood at all, never mind that they were impervious to the ravages of time and weather, looking as fresh now as the day they were first erected... That was the point. Image was everything, and Embargo thrived on simplicity, the lack of glitz to its frontage and the grungy interior of the club itself, a pattern Kyle had abandoned when he expanded his burgeoning empire, preferring to cater for other tastes.

Popularity is a fickle friend, and Embargo was no longer the 'must visit' icon it had been. Other establishments had superseded it in the club-goers' consciousness, but the old place still ticked over, and it remained Kyle's haunt of choice outside of opening hours. At least, it used to be, and Leesa was counting on that not having changed.

Eschewing the front of the building and the large metal delivery door at the side, she headed for the back door, which was even simpler in appearance than the front. White, oblong, inconspicuous and down a short flight of stone steps, its top barely rose above street level.

Security cameras overlooked the door, but they would be unmonitored at this hour and Kyle's people were welcome to pore over the recording of her entry to their hearts' content once this was all over. The door was alarmed too, and boasted a lock that was far more sophisticated than its simple appearance might suggest, but Leesa brought with her a device from *Raider* that took care of both and in a matter of seconds the doorway stood open.

No lights, but that didn't trouble her. The auganic part of her brain supplied an image of a corridor stretching away before her. There were cameras here, too – used to keep a record of comings and goings – but it was the sensor net spread immediately beneath the floor that Leesa focused on. She crouched at the threshold, not yet having stepped into the building, and activated a laser pin before thrusting it into the floor.

"Thank you, I'm in." It was Raider's voice in her ear this time rather than Jen's. "The security net is deactivated and the way is clear. You may proceed."

Now she moved forward, confident in the darkness, hurrying to where a set of wrought iron stairs led up into the club proper. They brought her into the back room behind one of the bars servicing the main dance floor. She stood in a space caught in a strange state of dormancy, suspended between its last useful service and the next. Drone waiters hibernated, stacked neatly against the back wall, while the counter dispensers had been retracted to lie flat beneath the bar top. Still there was no light.
At this hour few people would be about, but that didn't mean the place was completely deserted.

If he was here at all, Kyle would be on the next level up, the mezzanine that sat above this bar and the reception area. Moving stealthily, Leesa ascended again and crossed from the public area into the private. Here she found the first sign of habitation: light.

"Two men approaching from your right," Raider warned.

She moved hurriedly to press herself against the wall, partially hidden behind a buttress, hearing the men before she saw them.

"... So she wasn't after your credit at all?"

"Nah, turns out she was completely genuine."

"You idiot."

"Tell me about it."

Two suits, neither of whom she recognised. They walked past, oblivious to her presence, but that could change at any moment: from this angle she was exposed, and if one of them happened to glance her way... She held her breath, keeping completely still, and relaxed only once they were out of sight.

"Clear," Raider proclaimed.

Leesa stepped away from the wall and hurried to her right, the way the men had come, heading towards Kyle's office and personal quarters.

"Is he here?" she murmured, though she presumed Raider would have told her by now if not.

"Likely. I can't access his private rooms for confirmation. Security, assuming there is such, must be on a second isolated system, completely separate from this one."

Kyle always had been a paranoid bastard, and it made sense that he wouldn't risk his security staff spying or eavesdropping in those rooms. She'd just have to do this the hard way.

If the outer doors to the building were plain, the ones to the boss' inner sanctum were anything but. It had amused him when building Embargo to have two ornately carved and polished wooden doors installed – the sort that wouldn't be out of place in an old world mansion, the sort that could *never* be opened surreptitiously.

Bracing herself, and muttering a quiet, "Here goes," Leesa grasped twin handles and pulled. The doors weren't locked and swung open easily, belying expectation given their obvious bulk. Kyle was waiting for her. Of course he was – whatever security system Raider couldn't hack was bound to display anyone who approached the doors.

He sat behind the heavy wooden desk she remembered only too well – the sharp edge of it digging into the back of her thigh as she lay naked upon it, Kyle thrusting into her...

"Leesa. What an unexpected pleasure."

171

She remembered that smile, too.

He wasn't alone. Jamiel stood in front of the desk and was flanked by Gabon, his minder. Both glared daggers at her. She smiled in response, recalling the last time she'd seen them.

"How's the jaw, Jamiel?" She'd left the two men unconscious then, after Jamiel had tried to grope her once too often.

"You've got a fucking nerve, coming back here…" He took a step towards her but Kyle raised a hand, silencing his lieutenant and stopping him in his tracks.

Leesa's attention switched back to the man behind the desk, her former lover. He still had that aura, that assumption of authority that demanded attention. Was this what had first attracted her to him? If so, she no longer felt its thrall. "We need to talk," she said.

He regarded her, hesitating for a split second before saying, "Possibly."

She held his gaze. "I *know*, Kyle. I remember all of it." A slight exaggeration perhaps, but close enough.

"Ah." Another pause as he weighed up his options. "In that case…" He gestured for Jamiel and Gabon to leave. They did so with poor grace, closing the big polished-wood doors behind them. Leesa drew petty satisfaction from knowing that Jamiel would have given anything to stay.

"So, what is it you think you know exactly?" Kyle asked. "Oh, and you needn't worry, the room is soundproofed, no one can listen in at the door."

She drew a deep breath, organising her thoughts. She'd envisaged this scene repeatedly in her head on the way over here, but now that the moment had come she wasn't sure how to begin. Before she could, every nerve in her body came alive; this wasn't agony, it wasn't even pain, it was more a sense that someone or something was strumming the receptors in her skin to see what tune they might produce. A net of energy engulfed her, emanating from the walls.

She was vaguely aware of Kyle speaking as she struggled to

assess what was happening to her.

"Sorry about this," he said, "but I know what you can do and I'm not about to risk you being pissed off with me after all that's happened, so I had a nullifier installed in case you ever came back. It won't harm you, not in any permanent way; it'll just subdue that part of you which never sleeps."

She could feel it, could sense the auganic element of her mind shutting down in the face of whatever energy this was. She hadn't known such a thing was possible and felt panic rising at the prospect of being crippled like this, even temporarily. Where had Kyle found anyone capable of doing something like this?

As well as panic she felt something else, a pressure against her legs as the silver skin of Hel N which had lain dormant on the soles of her boots responded to the threat, rising rapidly to coat her body, to protect her.

The energy net cut off before the skin could completely seal around her, vanishing as abruptly as it had appeared. Kyle sat rigid at his desk. Jen stood close behind him, holding a knife to his throat.

"Hello, Kyle," she said. "Good to see you again."

Kyle's attention was focused on Leesa, as if neither the knife nor Jen were of any consequence.

"You're... *her* again."

"Yeah."

"How?"

"Long story, and not the reason we're here."

The use of the plural seemed to remind him of Jen's presence. "You can take the knife away now," he said. "I'll behave. I installed counter-measures to protect myself from Leesa in case she turned up itching to settle a grudge, but I know they won't work against Hel N, let alone two of you."

At a nod from Leesa Jen lifted the knife away and took a step back, but she didn't move from behind Kyle.

"Thank you," he said, reaching up to touch his throat where the blade had rested.

"Now," Leesa said, "why the hell did you have my memory wiped?"

"That wasn't me; that was your own doing."

"*What?*" Yet she sensed he was telling the truth.

"I helped, sure" Kyle added, "but only at your insistence. You couldn't cope any more, mostly with the memories of who you'd been, of what you'd done as Hel N; but also, I think, with the knowledge that you could never be her again. It haunted you, all of it, and you pleaded with me to help you forget. I... would have done anything for you. So we tracked down a tech from the original auganics project, a man who had survived the war and escaped the purges..."

"Maitland," Leesa whispered, half-remembering a face peering down at her.

"Yes. He was able to wipe your memories and put blocks in place to prevent the auganic part of your mind from trying to repair the damage and restore what you'd lost."

"It was what I wanted," she murmured, as those memories returned at last and she tried them on for size, "... to get away, to make a new start somewhere else, free of everything I'd been. Somewhere I wasn't known and where there was nothing to remind me."

"Yes. I couldn't stop you. I refused at first but you kept on and eventually wore me down... Maitland warned us both that the blocks might not hold, that the auganic side of you was tenacious and would work tirelessly to reboot your memories."

"It did, through my dreams."

"I nearly had a heart attack when you turned up here again, searching for who you were and not even recognising me."

"And you didn't think to say anything?"

"How could I? I wanted to, of course I did, but that would have undermined everything, and you'd have hated me for it afterwards. I couldn't bear to see you like that so I stayed away, saw as little of you as possible."

"And let me become a stim-head, a bum, living in an

abandoned railway carriage and going nowhere. How *could* you? That was never what I wanted."

"I helped where I could. I tasked Jamiel with looking out for you…"

"Oh he did that all right; fed me drugs and did his best to get inside my pants." Kyle looked genuinely shocked at that, perhaps he hadn't known. "And this energy net you just sprang on me, was that intended to help too?"

"No, of course not. I only commissioned that after you busted Jamiel's jaw and disappeared. Maitland designed it, assured me that if you ever came back it would stun the auganic side of you and give me the opportunity to explain without you flying off the handle."

Leesa let that go. She was shaken by Kyle's revelations, by the memories they stirred, and didn't know how to begin processing any of it, so instead she switched to the other reason they'd sought him out. With a thought, she sent Hel N's silver skin sliding back down her body to its hiding place beneath her feet, so that she faced him as Leesa once more.

"Do you enjoy this life, Kyle?"

"Love it."

"Really? You've no friends worth the name, spend all your time mired in sleaze and rely on scum like Jamiel to do your bidding, while all the while wondering when one of your lieutenants will find the balls to turn on you and make a play."

He shrugged. "Comes with the territory."

"What if we were to offer you a way out? What if we could make you a Dark Angel again?"

He stared at her.

"We've reunited with the *Ion Raider*," she said quietly.

"I'd say thanks but no thanks." He spoke very deliberately. "That was always your dream, Leesa, not mine. I was glad to see the back of Cornische and that damned ship of his."

"You might not have a choice," Jen cut in.

"There's always a choice, and I'm perfectly happy here."

"I can sympathise, believe me" Jen continued. "I was content with my life too, right up until the moment someone tried to assassinate me and blew up my home in the process."

"We're being hunted," Leesa pressed. "A highly motivated and effective organisation called Saflik is tracking down former Angels and taking us out one by one. Spirit, Gabriel, Quill," she counted them off on her fingers. "All gone."

"Quill's no great loss, though I am sorry to hear about Gabriel; but I have to ask what any of this has to do with me."

"Saflik, they'll find you," Leesa said. "Maybe not today, maybe not tomorrow, but some day they'll track you down and kill you, and you'll never see it coming."

"Unless we take them down first," Jen added.

"Ah, so that's it. You're looking to put the Angels back together so that we can kick the asses of these Saflik before they kick ours. Well, good luck with that but count me out. Do you seriously imagine we can do this and then all just return to normal when it's over? If so, you're being naïve. Life doesn't work that way. We could never go back. I *like* what I've got going here, and I'm not about to walk away from it for the sake of some half-baked crusade that'll send me gallivanting across the stars."

"You'd rather just wait here to die?"

"I'll take my chances."

"You're making a mistake," Leesa said, conscious they were losing him. "Don't take Saflik so lightly."

"And we would welcome Ramrod's help," Jen added.

Kyle shook his head. "That's not who I am any more. Thank you for warning me, it's appreciated. Now that I know about these Saflik I'll take precautions, but you're not recruiting me."

She saw in his eyes that there was no persuading him.

"Leesa, I'm glad you've found a way to become again who you always wanted to be, I really am. I hope it brings you everything you crave, whatever that is."

This felt like goodbye, and she supposed it was. She had no intention of pleading with him, though part of her wanted to.

Seeing Kyle again had brought it all crashing back: the memories, the passion, but she resisted the urge to rush across and hug him, kiss him. Instead she stayed exactly where she was.

"Now, if you'll excuse me," he said, "I have work to do."

She'd run out of words, so after a moment's hesitation simply turned and left, with Jen beside her. At the door she paused long enough to say, "Watch your back, Kyle."

He met her gaze for a moment and nodded.

They retraced their steps through the streets of la Gossa in silence, crossing the main thoroughfare of Third Bridge Street, and the bustling marketplace of ScheiKa.

Jen didn't begrudge the lack of communication. She could only imagine what was going on inside her friend's head and respected her need to process everything she'd just learned. Kyle and Leesa had only hooked up in the latter days aboard the *Iron Raider*, and it never occurred to Jen that they might have stayed together once the team dissolved.

By the sound of things, their relationship was far more complicated than her own with Robin had ever been, and she was grateful for that. She'd settle for simplicity any day. She shied away from the comparison, though, preferring not to be reminded of how much she missed her husband.

Instead she focussed on their failure to enlist Kyle's support. After Mosi, it came as a bitter blow. Their first two attempts to recruit another Angel had both failed, for whatever reason. What if everyone felt as Kyle did, preferring to rely on anonymity and choosing not to get involved?

Jen felt deflated – another reason she wasn't in a hurry to chat with Leesa – more than that, she felt angry, a seething rage that had been steadily building since the assassin came calling. Her life had been ripped apart and, as yet, she hadn't managed to strike any sort of meaningful blow in response. What she needed more than anything just then was to *hit* something, and hit it *hard*; which meant getting back to the *Raider* so that she could work out her frustrations in a training session.

She snapped out of her reverie as Leesa froze and held up a warning hand, suggesting that she'd heard something. They had just entered a quiet backstreet not far from the port and Jen couldn't identify anything untoward, but she knew better than to doubt the auganic's acute senses. A split second later they were both blown off their feet, Jen crashing painfully against a wall. For a moment she lay there, dazed, trying to piece together what had happened. A concussion round, she concluded, not fired to kill but to disorientate and disable them.

Jen pulled herself to her feet, her ears ringing, thought processes still stubbornly sluggish. On the opposite side of the alley Leesa was doing the same, and they weren't alone. Six figures, three to either side, all with their faces dyed to a deathly grey.

"Cellothan," Leesa hissed.

"You know these jokers?"

"Yeah, they're a warrior elite sect… Assassins."

"Gloves off, then." Jen focussed as hard as she could on the approaching figures.

"Definitely."

Their attackers were all armed, making a show of brandishing blades and hand-to-hand nastiness, but there wasn't a gun to be seen, which meant that whoever fired the concussion round had put down the distance weapon in order to get up close and personal, or there was another of these grey-skinned ghouls somewhere, hanging back to see how things developed. On the rooftops above them, Jen reckoned. That's where she'd be, to get the best vantage point, but she'd worry about that later. The effects of the concussion round were dissipating already – far more swiftly than their opponents were likely to anticipate. Shadowtech afforded Jen a degree of protection – limited in comparison to what Leesa enjoyed as Hel N, but it helped.

It looked as if she wouldn't have to wait to get back to the *Raider* for that workout after all. With so much of her life recently spent running and dodging, feeling hounded and pursued, it felt good to face a tangible enemy again. As she closed on the nearest attacker, moving lightly on the balls of her feet, Jen realised she was smiling.

He was good, this Cellothan; his movement fluid and professional, his handling of the knife assured. Against most enemies he would probably have been *too* good, but she wasn't most enemies.

The flat of her hand smashed into his larynx after he'd extended too far in an attempt to slash her.

The next opponent carried an energy blade, which merited a little more respect. She backed away a few steps as he advanced, until she felt the solid wall against the back of her shoulders.

She left it until the last possible moment, until she could almost feel the heat of the strike, before stepping into shadow. She came out again as soon as the blade had passed, amused by her opponent's startled expression as she plunged her own blade into his stomach while simultaneously striking at his wrist with the knife in her left hand to send his weapon clattering to the ground.

This was exhilarating, satisfying, exactly the release she needed. The next opponent she teased, slipping in and out of shadow as they fought, seeing the desperation gather on his face as he sought an escape, realising he was outmatched. There wasn't any. Tiring of the game, she put him out of his misery by slitting his throat.

At intervals she'd caught a flash of silver in the corner of her eye and knew that Hel N could handle the rest. That just left the shooter. She spotted him on the rooftop as anticipated, peering down but wary of firing another round in case he took out his colleagues, but that was likely to change as they continued to fall.

Jen shifted into shadow and flowed up the face of the building. She materialised beside him. He had enough time to start to turn, the barrel of the concussion rifle swivelling towards her, before she grasped him and threw him over the edge.

Back on the ground it was all over. Hel N had managed to find one of the Cellothan still alive and, as Jen stepped out of shadow, was addressing the man.

"This stops now. You know who we are?"

The man nodded. The fear in his eyes obvious.

"Good. Your boss really doesn't want us for enemies. Luckily for both you and for him, we've got other things on our mind right now, but if he *ever* sends anyone after us again we'll hunt him down, hunt you *all* down, and we'll put an end to the Cellothan once and for all. Have you got that?"

The man nodded, vigorously.

"Just to make sure, is there any part of you that thinks I'm making an idle threat?"

The shake of his head was equally emphatic.

"Good. I'm so glad we understand one another." She hauled him to his feet. "Now piss off."

With that he stumbled away, cradling his broken arm.

As he disappeared around the corner Leesa turned to Jen and grinned. "Welcome back," she said.

"Sorry?"

"On Callia you were like a woman possessed. This is the first time since we reconnected that I've seen you look like the Shadow I remember."

Jen couldn't deny it, though she wasn't convinced that was in any way a good thing. "I… needed that," she admitted all the same.

Her attention shifted to the dead around them. "So this wasn't Saflik?"

"No." Leesa shook her head. "Purely local. An old score. One that Jamiel doubtless took great pleasure in stirring. I wondered where the little prick had got to. I was half-expecting him to confront us as we left Kyle's, but instead he must have scurried off to alert the Cellothan."

"So who exactly *are* they?"

"Glorified thugs." Hel N's silver skin receded and they started walking towards the port again. "You have to understand that there are at least two aspects to just about everything in la Gossa, including the law. There's official law and street law."

"I get that." La Gossa was hardly unique in that regard.

"Maybe, but here the system is really entrenched. See, the authorities divide the city up into administrative districts, all neat and bureaucratic, but the ghettos, the back streets, the sweat shops... they march to a different beat. It's here that the disberos hold sway, the street gangs, carving the city up into territories all their own: the Red Tigers on one side," she waved expansively to their right, "the Dragon's Teeth on the other." This time she gestured to the left. "The Jade Warriors traditionally claim the area around the docks on this side of the river and the Fire Demons the southern bank, and so on – dozens of small time wannabes jealously protecting their turf.

"They're laws unto themselves, these disberos, but *all* of them have one thing in common: they're all scared of the Cellothan, the Secret Society, the gang of gangs, the crew that got so brazen the authorities couldn't ignore them any longer. They're outlawed, you see. It's a criminal offence even to claim membership of the Cellothan, let alone to actually belong."

"That's obviously done the trick, then."

"It was always going to backfire; you can imagine how much all that official condemnation has elevated their status in the eyes of the other disberos. They were already a gang apart – the ultimate muscle, the killer elite – cloaked in mystery and semi-mystical gibberish. Now they've gone deep underground and are more secretive than ever."

"And they don't like you much."

Leesa grinned. "No they don't, though that's hardly my fault."

"Of course not; I mean how could a meek little thing like you ever get on the wrong side of anyone?"

"Hey, I mean it. This time it wasn't my fault. I was happily going along minding my own business when someone – Jamiel most likely – stuck the Cellothan on me to teach me a lesson.

Two of their enforcers jumped me one morning when I was barely even awake."

"And you killed them."

"Only one of them. The other I sent back with a message to leave me alone."

"Much as you did just now."

"Yeah."

"That worked out well, then. How do you think they'll react this time?"

"One of two ways. Either the prospect of going up against the Dark Angels will put the fear of the devil in them and they'll back off – which wouldn't be like them; losing face isn't in their make-up, or..."

"They'll see this as a challenge and come after us with everything they've got," Jen finished for her.

"Pretty much."

"Then why bother sending them that message?"

Leesa grinned. "Couldn't resist. They've never crossed the Dark Angels before. The Cellothan are legends in their own lunchtime – no one outside of Babylon has ever heard of them. We, on the other hand, are the real deal. If anything's going to scare them..."

Jen shook her head but, realising that exasperation would be wasted, changed tack. "How many of them are there?"

"Fuck knows. Remember the 'secret' bit?"

She had almost forgotten this side of Leesa – the impulsive, reckless side that occasionally surfaced irrespective of the consequences. A number of potential retorts flashed through her mind, but again she quashed them, settling on, "Seems to me the sooner we leave Babylon and its gangs behind the better."

"No argument from me," Leesa agreed. "I'm done with this place."

The girl was sitting cross-legged on the ground beside the ship, at around the point where the access ramp would touch ground when extended. Her clothes looked faded, lived in, though they were of a decent quality and far from threadbare. Her head was bowed, her attention focused on the wafer-thin paintpad that rested on her lap. She passed her hands over it in a controlled and elegant manner, as if casting a spell, long fingers seeming to caress the air above the screen. In their wake a series of abstract patterns appeared on the pad, lifting into the air and dancing at the fingers' beck and call, only to settle back down and rise again in a new form with each successive pass of a hand; every pattern as striking and colourful as the last.

On the ground beside her sat a morphtoy, currently configured as a teddy bear. It sat with head bowed, mimicking its master's posture.

There was something unsettlingly familiar about the girl's actions, the way she choreographed the swirling colours, though Jen could have sworn she had never laid eyes on her before.

At their approach, the girl looked up – how old? Seven eight…? Nine at most. Her skin was a rich golden caramel that almost glowed with vitality, her eyes the deepest darkest brown imaginable. Again Jen felt the jolt of almost-recognition, but again her mind insisted this was a stranger.

"Saavi?" Leesa got there a split second ahead of her.

"Hello Leesa, Jen. I knew you would be here." The girl's smile was dazzling, lighting up her face.

"*Saavi*, but you're…"

"Young, I know."

She uncrossed her legs, rising to her feet in one supple movement without resorting to her hands for leverage. The paintpad rolled up into a slender tube of its own accord, which she squashed, folded, and tucked away into a pocket. The morphtoy shadowed her movements, rising to its feet at almost the same instant she did, to stand as high as her knee.

The last time Jen had seen Saavi, she had been… what, in her early thirties?

"The cloud technology," Saavi-the-girl said. "It changed me

somehow, at the most fundamental level. After we disbanded I started to regress. I didn't realise at first, and when I did I was delighted... But it didn't stop. I've grown a couple of years younger, more or less, with every passing year. It can only be because of the cloud chamber. Ironic, eh? Here's me, a modern day oracle, blithely navigating a path through potential futures... I didn't see this coming in any of them."

Jen stared, appalled and trying to think of an acceptable way to react. "Has it stopped, have you stabilised?" she asked.

Saavi shook her head. "No, it's still going on. Not just my appearance, it's my metabolism, the structure of my cells... Everything is regressing."

"Is that why you've got a morphtoy for a companion?" Leesa asked.

"Oh, no. Thank you for the reminder." She turned to the bear, which was watching her intently, and spoke with deliberate precision. "Jai, this is Jen, and this is Leesa." She pointed to each of them in turn. "They are friends.

"Jai is far more than a mere toy," she explained. "He's my bodyguard. I had him custom built by the T'kai when it became clear the direction my regression was taking. People accept what they expect to see. A young girl with a morphtoy doesn't merit a second glance."

Jen eyed the innocuous-looking bear warily, wondering what it was capable of.

"Your intellect seems to have stayed intact," Leesa observed.

"Thank goodness. I think the accumulation of memories, experience, my knowledge, have enabled me to hang on to that... But I don't know, that's just my rationalisation. I've no real idea how any of this works. The emotions, on the other hand, they can be a real bitch."

"What happens three or four years down the road?" Jen asked. Would Saavi regress to a foetus, requiring an artificial womb to survive? And what came after that? In all her experience with elder tech, this seemed to Jen the cruellest thing she had yet encountered.

"I... I don't know," Saavi admitted. "But it doesn't really matter. I'll be dead long before I ever have to find out."

"What?"

"Not just me, either..." She looked sheepishly at the two women, and Jen suddenly didn't want to know what else Saavi had foreseen. "It's why I had to be here to meet you, why I have to get back aboard the *Raider*."

"You can still do that then, still read the future?"

"Sort of, yes, but nothing like I used to; I only get flashes. It's frustrating – after the cloud chamber everything else is so... limiting, as if that part of my brain has been cauterised, my abilities stunted. There's nothing coherent, nothing from which to build a rational narrative, just tantalising glimpses of possible futures. The paintpad is as effective a tool as anything I've found since leaving, but it's still no more than a pale imitation..." Her gaze slid to the ship. "I have to get back on board, have to immerse myself in the cloud chamber again, to really *see*..."

Jen was unprepared for the desperation in Saavi's voice, and, to judge by the worried look Leesa shot her, she wasn't the only one. Despite her reservations, Jen shrugged in response to her friend's unspoken query. How could they refuse the girl? She was one of their own. They'd come to Babylon hoping to recruit a Dark Angel and it looked as if they had, if not the one they'd intended.

Jen smiled, because she had a feeling Leesa wouldn't and she sensed that this was what Saavi needed just then. "It's good to see you again," she said. "Good to have you with us. Welcome back, Cloud."

"Thank you." The relief on Saavi's face was obvious. Suddenly she looked every bit the bewildered little girl and a long way removed from the slightly aloof and almost mystical savant that Jen remembered. She wondered fleetingly how many futures Saavi had glimpsed in which things had gone differently and they'd refused to let her join them. Then the airlock opened, the

185

ramp extended, and they were walking side by side into the ship, Jen with her arm resting protectively on the shoulder of their diminutive new recruit.

"Hello, Cloud," Raider said as they entered. "Welcome home."

As soon as they were safely on board, Saavi made her excuses and scurried off to the cloud chamber, her morphtoy in close attendance. Leesa watched them go, looking troubled as she turned back towards Jen. "We need to keep an eye on her," she said. "I've witnessed the effects of addiction first hand and Saavi's showing all the signs – the same sort of desperation. Desperate people have a habit of making bad choices."

"Is that the voice of experience I hear?"

"Yeah, you've got me on that one. I can see the very worst of me in her, when I was at my darkest, and that's not a healthy place for anyone to be."

Jen felt awkward pursuing that line of conversation so deliberately switched. "Forget Saavi for the moment, are you okay?"

"Yes... I suppose so. Might take a while to get my head around the fact that I did this to myself, but I'll get there. Besides, if there's one thing guaranteed to take your mind off your own problems it's concentrating on someone else's."

"Are you talking about Saavi or our missing captain?"

"Both, so let's get on with it, shall we?"

"That's fine by me. Raider, could you contact port authority and –"

"I applied for a launch slot as soon as you returned," the ship informed them before she could finish. "We're set to leave in just under twenty-three standard minutes."

"Sounds as if we're not the only ones keen to catch up with the captain again," Leesa commented. "Twenty-three minutes? That should give me time to get at least one of the replacement parts installed. Raider, give me a five minute warning before we lift off. No, make that three minutes. Plenty of time."

With a grin in Jen's direction, she headed for the engine room.

FOURTEEN

Drake was finding it difficult to keep track of time without his perminal. He knew how the mind could play tricks when deprived of a point of reference and when there was little going on to distract it, but he felt confident that more than two standard days had passed since they were trapped in the cache's private pocket of reality. During that time, there had been no contact with either Mudball or the cache guardian. The little alien had never abandoned him like this before, and Drake was starting to entertain the possibility that something had happened to his companion. Could the chamber-quakes they'd experienced have been caused by some sort of titanic struggle between the two entities which neither had survived?

No one had thought to bring any food with them. No one had brought any water. The latter would inevitably be their biggest problem, though Ungar in particular seemed more concerned about the lack of anything to eat, at least for the moment. Drake knew that a few days without water shouldn't be an issue, assuming none of them had any underlying medical conditions, but if that began to stretch towards a week...

He kept telling himself it wasn't yet a problem every time he swallowed on a dry throat or felt the pangs of hunger. It probably helped, a little.

Nowak and Lis had introduced him to a game to help while away the hours – their familiarity with some of the artefacts proving a boon. They called the game spectrum, and it involved manipulating a slow moving beam of phosphorescent particles using paddles. The faces of the paddles were composed of a spongy substance that looked like gauze but, having survived for many centuries without perishing, clearly wasn't. The particles reacted to the paddles, rebounding, their speed increasing and decreasing, depending on the angle and force of the paddle strike. The aim was to push the particles ever faster, the increased speed stimulating a progression through five of the spectrum's colours in ever-shortening wavelengths: red to yellow to green to blue and then violet. When the particles disappeared altogether, the person who had last paddled them was adjudged to be the winner.

"We've no idea if this is how the original game was played," Lis explained, "or even if it's intended to be a game at all, but this seems to work for us so this is how *we* play it. There's also a level that takes the particles into the ultraviolet, which is what happens when they disappear, suggesting that the Elders may have been able to see across a different spectrum to us, including shorter wavelengths."

Spectrum started off slowly and the early stages were simple enough, with both players working together to push the beam faster. The real competition kicked in towards the end, once the particles had turned from blue to violet, the trick then being to control the increase in velocity so that you dictated their disappearance. Drake was surprised at how tactical it became, and by the way his competitive nature asserted itself, relishing the challenge.

The fact that there were only two paddles limited the number of players at any one time, and more often than not it was Drake and Lis who played – Ungar having given it a go once but deciding spectrum wasn't for him and Nowak showing only occasional interest. Of the two ministers, Lis was proving to be the more amenable, Nowak spending much of the time huddled in quiet conversation with Payne.

For his part, Payne still acted as if he held Drake responsible for their current predicament, despite Drake's protestations of innocence and even Ungar pointing out that only an idiot would cause something like this and then trap themselves in the process.

Yes, an idiot! Drake thought into the silence.

Mudball's physical form had been as absent as his mental presence since the 'quake' hit, and Drake *had* looked, doing so under the pretext of tidying up some of the artefacts that had toppled over during the tremors. If anyone else had registered his genpet's absence, they clearly didn't think it worth mentioning.

Drake also noted that Payne wasn't moving around much, spending most of the time sitting on top of a low but long artefact a little to the left of the entrance – a tapering block of non-metal free of any obvious markings but possessing two indentations side by side that looked suspiciously like seats. For that reason alone, Drake would have avoided sitting in them, but then it wasn't his backside that currently did.

Every now and then Payne would get up and go across to the entrance cabinet, only to return to his perch, but other than that he showed little inclination to move. Perhaps the discomfort caused by his exo-legs was genuine after all.

Drake attempted to watch surreptitiously whenever Payne visited the false elevator, and he was becoming increasingly convinced that there was no mechanism involved in the crossing, that Payne was simply repeating a complicated gesture with one hand, presumably a signal to the cache entity that they were ready to be transported either in or out the pocket universe.

Whatever the gesture might be, the cache guardian wasn't responding.

Reminded of his own missing entity, Drake formed the name in his mind, *Mudball*, calling as he'd been doing intermittently ever since the tremors. He didn't really expect a response, but this time he got one.

I'm here.

Thank the Elders. I've been worried that something had happened to you

With good cause. This cache entity is… extraordinary. It's taken me this long to… reach an accommodation with it.

Mudball sounded different – or his thoughts *felt* different? – Drake was never entirely sure of the correct terminology for their unique situation. The playfulness that always been the alien's

190

default had gone; in its place was an altogether more serious Mudball. *Where are you? The physical you, I mean.*

Safe. You've no need to worry on that score.

Good. How soon can you get us out of here?

All in good time. There are other issues that need to be addressed first.

Really? Such as?

You've had some serious memory blocks put in place; deep-rooted and very skilfully applied. I've shared your thoughts for years and never suspected they were there. For some reason, coming here to this cache has resonated with a past experience that lies behind those walls. That's what triggered the sense of déjà vu. I need to find out what's been buried.

So do I, Drake assured him, *but that can wait. Right now the priority is to get out of here before dehydration and malnutrition set in.*

No, I'm afraid it really can't wait. I have reason to believe that what's hidden behind that block in your mind is relevant to our current situation. I'm sorry, Drake, I don't have time to be subtle or gentle, and this won't be pleasant.

What do you mean 'relevant to our current...?' Before he could go any further, a searing wave of agony exploded across Drake's mind. He cried out, or at least he thought he did – he was too busy collapsing to the floor to be certain. The pain built exponentially until, mercifully, he lost consciousness.

Drake came to tasting blood, and realised he had bitten his tongue. Whether he groaned aloud or it was simply his stirring that alerted the others to his waking he couldn't say, but suddenly Ungar was there, offering to help him sit up. He did so gingerly, his head still feeling delicate, to discover that he'd been lying on the floor where he'd dropped, Ungar's jacket scrunched up to cushion his head. He rested now with his back against a knobbly artefact, shifting slightly to find a more comfortable position

"Are you all right?"

"Fine, I think," Drake assured him. "What happened?"

"We were going to ask you the same thing," said Lis, who had come across to stand beside the historian.

"You started screaming," Ungar said, "without the slightest warning, just this agonised scream. It was really quite alarming."

"Then you collapsed to the floor and started writhing, before losing consciousness," Lis added, seeming to enjoying the recollection a bit too much.

"Some sort of fit, by the look of things. Do you suffer from fits?" Ungar said.

"Not usually, no."

Grasping his cane, which lay close by, Drake stood up, very carefully, mainly to prove to himself that he could. Ungar stepped forward to help but Drake waved him away. "I'm all right, thank you."

For a moment, the room threatened to spin, but then righted itself. His head still felt shaky, as if he were running a fever, but he didn't feel nauseous and didn't feel the need to sit down again immediately. All things considered, he reckoned that was a result.

Someone had some explaining to do. *Mudball!*

Predictably, there was no response.

His return to consciousness appeared to have interrupted a game of spectrum between Lis and Nowak. Now that the drama was over, they returned to playing. After a few experimental steps – again accomplished without too much difficulty, Drake sat down.

There wasn't even any water to wash the taste of blood from his mouth, so he contented himself with leaning forward and spitting onto the floor of the cache.

This earned him a glare from Payne. He didn't care.

An exclamation from Ungar alerted him that something was happening. He looked up to find the historian staring at the false lift. Following his gaze, Drake saw the air in the small cabinet ripple and twist, as if viewed through a fairground mirror that was being actively tilted to produce a sense of movement.

The distortion only lasted for an instant, rapidly resolving into two humanoid figures that gained substance almost immediately. Drake had never witnessed the transition from there to here before, or at least not from the outside, and he found the process fascinating. The first of the new arrivals proved to be Evans, Payne's bodyguard. He was bare-armed, dressed far more casually than Drake had ever seen him before, a reminder of how much time had passed since they were marooned here. The second figure was taller and lither than Evans, smartly dressed and bearing a neat shock of blond hair. Drake's hopes soared as he recognised Archer, a fellow agent at Fist Solar. It seemed that Reese had sent in the cavalry after all. He stood up, ready to greet his colleague.

"You took your time," Payne said, also rising to his feet. Drake assumed he was addressing Evans but it was Archer who replied, "Yes, sorry about that. The cache entity has evidently been having a few problems. All sorted now, though."

Only then did Drake make the connection. He stared at his fellow banking agent. "You're Bowman."

There was nothing remotely pleasant about Archer's smile in response. "Well done for figuring that much out, Cornische. Yes, we all know who you are. I can't tell you how long I've waited for this moment."

Drake was still groggy from the mental assault Mudball had unleashed upon him, that was the only excuse he could offer for his lack of response, for not even raising his cane in defence as Archer strode purposefully across. For a moment they locked gazes, and then Archer punched him hard in the stomach, following up immediately with a second blow, this time to the side of his head.

The first punch woke Drake up, and he anticipated the second, turning his head and rolling his shoulders so that it was only a glancing blow, knuckles raking the top of his ear and hairline.

At the same time, he gripped his cane with both hands and swung, so that it rapped against the back of Archer's knee. The angle wasn't ideal and he couldn't put a great deal of strength behind the swing, but it caught his opponent by surprise and must have stung, causing him to straighten for an instant and not press his attack. That gave Drake the split second he needed, and he immediately switched from victim to aggressor. He punched Archer in the stomach – which seemed only fair – putting his whole body weight behind his fist, and then clonked him on the side of the head with his cane, the cane whistling in to deliver a far harder blow than he'd managed earlier.

Archer went down.

A good start, but Drake knew that wouldn't be the end of it. Evans was already advancing towards him, with menace in his eyes and hands at the ready like the pro he undoubtedly was. Drake was confident he could take Evans, but hadn't spared a thought for what might come after that. He wasn't applying a plan here, merely reacting to the situation and winging it. He'd think of something.

Evans dropped into a fighter's crouch, arms close to his body, hands open, legs wide enough apart to give him a solid base and enable him to spring in any direction. Drake was almost tempted to step in and go for it, hand to hand, but there wasn't time. Events were developing rapidly and he wanted to maintain that momentum, to keep his enemies off balance until he could work out how to effect an escape from the cache pocket.

Then an image sprang to life, seeming to peel from the top of Evans' right bicep to hover in 3D above it. A tattoogram, dormant within the skin's natural pigment until triggered by a specific flexing of the muscle beneath it. This one depicted a stylised representation of a war hammer from ancient Earth, said to be modelled on the favoured weapon of a long forgotten deity. Drake knew that badge. It marked Evans as a former Night Hammer.

Drake abruptly revised his confidence in beating Evans hand to hand downwards. He thumbed a control on his cane and was about to raise it when something thudded into the back of his head. A sense of shock was swiftly followed by blossoming pain.

Somebody had hit him from behind. He tried to look round,

even as his knees buckled and his body slumped. He saw a figure there but his eyes refused to focus. Then the figure spoke.

"Honestly, Corbin, is all this violence really necessary?"

Ungar?

"I would have thought, given the setting, that we could be a little more... civilised about things."

Drake didn't attempt to reply. He had slumped to his knees and was bent forwards, hands holding his body off the floor. All his concentration was devoted to not dropping any further and to staying conscious. Blood ran down his face from the head wound. He watched in fascination as the first drip fell from his chin to strike the ground in apparent slow motion. *Ungar...*

He looked up again as another figure loomed above him.

"Not so high and mighty now, eh?" He recognised Archer's voice.

Then the kicking began. His body lifted from the ground and his arms went from under him as the first kick landed. He hit the floor painfully, shoulder first. He drew his legs up and tucked his chin in, trying to curl up into a foetal position for protection, but the blows continued to land. He felt ribs break and then, mercifully, lost consciousness as the fifth – or was it the sixth? – kick found its mark.

FIFTEEN

Pitch darkness surrounded her. She had panicked at first, wanting to scream for help, desperate to escape. Somehow she managed not to, confining her reaction to stifled sobs and tears that flowed freely down her dust-caked cheeks. She was afraid of being trapped, yes, but more afraid still of what might befall her if she were free. Death. The same death that had claimed her mum, her dad, and probably her brother too.

They were still out there, the raiders. Ayella didn't doubt that. They were standing just the other side of the rubble that entombed her, listening hard for the slightest sound so that they could finish the job, stamping out any last vestige of life that might remain here.

She managed to stop sobbing but was alarmed at how loud her own breathing sounded. She imagined it had to be audible outside, the collapsed remnants of wall that surrounded her somehow acting as a drum, amplifying the sound so that no one could fail to hear her. Even the beating of her heart seemed determined to betray her.

The darkness wasn't absolute after all, not quite. Some small element of light must have managed to seep in, though she couldn't discern where. Her eyes had adjusted to this meagre illumination and started to decipher her surroundings, just a little – enough to suggest the ghost of an irregular, tilted surface close to her face, the impression of bulk. All this did was increase the sense of claustrophobia and tip her towards panic once more, so she squeezed her traitorous eyes tight shut, denying their report. Instead she used her hands to explore, running questing fingers over the rough surface before her, which she presumed must be a wall, though memory insisted that all the walls had been smoother than this. For some reason, the close confines seemed more manageable like this, when she couldn't see them.

The pain in her left leg had started to make its presence felt: a deep dull throb, emanating from her shin. She knew she'd been injured when the wall came down, knew the leg was cut and doubtless bleeding. Surely the pain would be worse than this, though, wouldn't it, if anything had been broken? Experimentally, she tried to move the injured limb, curling her toes, flexing her foot. Everything seemed to work as it should, and her efforts brought no significant increase in the level of pain, which she took as a good sign.

Her side hurt too, every time she drew breath, but the leg was worse. She attempted to pull her knee up, draw the leg in, but there wasn't enough room. Something lay across her lower leg, just where the ankle was – her foot bumped against it as she wriggled. It didn't rest on the leg itself, thank goodness, but was close enough to make movement awkward and hold the foot trapped.

It was growing increasingly warm but she wasn't having any difficulty in breathing, not yet at any rate; presumably, if a hint of light could find its way in, so could air.

Ayella tried to listen, holding her breath for as long as she could in order to do so, finally relaxing in a sigh of expelled air, the volume of which worried her all over again, so she only tried it twice. Both attempts yielded the same result: no sound of movement, no muffled voices, nothing to suggest anyone was there. They were playing the long game, trying to wait her out. Never going to happen.

She composed herself, studiously avoiding any thought of what had happened to her family, refusing to dwell on what had brought these men to her home with their mismatched scraps of armour and soiled suits, with grim-looking guns and even grimmer faces. At the same time, she shied away from contemplating the future. None of that mattered, not there and then. All that mattered was staying quiet and winning the game.

Time passed; she had no idea how much, lacking any means

of measuring. She drifted away somewhere, to a picnic last summer, one of her very best memories. Sunshine and laughter, they were the enduring impression of that day. She loved the pink and white dress she had worn – which was too small for her now, alas – and she couldn't remember her mum ever being happier...

Ayella's thoughts were drawn back to the present by the sound of movement from beyond the rubble. She felt a surge of triumph. She had won! Nobody could beat her at hide and seek.

There were no voices, just those faint sounds of people moving about, muffled by the debris, but she had a sense that they were moving carefully. Had the killers finally given up? Were they leaving? She did her best to breathe even more quietly than she had before, determined not to do anything that would give her away and keep them here.

The sounds drew nearer, and then stopped. She held her breath completely now.

Different sounds: closer, louder, and accompanied by a cascade of dust and grit which she couldn't see but could feel against her face. They had found her and were trying to dig her out.

She screamed then – a piercing shriek that cut off abruptly, degenerating into a bout of coughing as she swallowed some of the dust. The dust tasted bitter in her mouth.

"Captain, there's someone alive in here." A woman's voice.

Light suddenly flooded into her world, as a piece of masonry was thrown aside. She squinted upwards to see looming over her a silver figure that literally shone in the light.

"Are you an angel?" she asked.

The question seemed to give the figure pause. "If I *am* an angel, then I'm a dark one." She recognised the voice of the woman who had called out earlier. "What's your name, sweetheart?"

"Ayella. How did you find me when I was trying so hard to be quiet?"

"I'm special," the angel said, and she had the impression that it was smiling, though she couldn't really see its face. "I can see through walls."

"Oh, right. So it wasn't anything I did?"

"No, nothing you did at all. Are you hurt?"

"A bit."

"Can you move?"

Ayella nodded vigorously – the last thing she wanted was for the angel to abandon her here.

"All right then, let's get you out of there."

The silver figure reached in and Ayella found that she trusted her – this was an angel, after all, one that could see through walls – so she didn't resist but instead reached up to meet her. The angel took hold of her upper arms and lifted, shifting her hands to grip under Ayella's arms as she emerged.

"Let me know if it starts to *really* hurt, won't you."

Her side did, quite a lot, but she didn't let on for fear that the angel would put her back. She worried that her foot might not come free but it slipped out easily, now that she was being raised. In no time at all she was in the open and able to cling to her rescuer. The angel's silver skin felt unlike anything she'd ever touched before, but it proved to be soft and warm and comforting. The angel smelled faintly of metal and mint, but in a nice way.

"Have the nasty men gone?" she asked, belatedly.

"Yes, they've gone. You're safe now."

"Thank you for chasing them away. I did well, didn't I, at hiding?"

"You did very well."

The angel stroked her hair. Ayella liked that. Then she tensed. Over the angel's shoulder she saw another figure, a man dressed in a long and weathered blue-black coat, his face completely obscured by a dancing pale grey wash of static. For a moment she thought the raiders had returned and that she was going to die after all, just when she believed she was safe.

Sensing her alarm, the angel looked round, and said, "There's no need to be scared, this is a friend, an angel like me." She then addressed the blank-faced man, saying, "I've found a survivor, Captain."

"So I see."

His voice was deep and smooth and dark. It reminded Ayella of chocolate, her favourite treat, and she surrendered to the angel's embrace once more.

Leesa shot bolt upright in bed. For a moment she felt oddly disorientated, as if the organic side of her brain was having difficulty in meshing with the part of her that never slept, but finally things began to assume proper perspective.

A bead of perspiration trickled down the nape of her neck. The sensation was so unfamiliar that initially she didn't react, simply savouring the experience; she *never* sweated, the auganic part of her mind regulating her body's state and responses to render the process redundant.

What was happening to her?

A memory dream. They always had been vivid, but this was something else. She thought she was done with those a while back, that her past had been fully restored without any gaps, but she didn't doubt that what she had just experienced was a memory, one she had never suspected was missing. Until this moment, she had no recollection of Ayella or the gutted research station and the massacre they'd stumbled upon there.

Knowing that sleep would now elude her for the rest of the night as her mind picked over the implications, Leesa slipped out of bed and padded across to the dispenser, choosing a bulb of chilled juice which she squeezed dry in seconds, discarding the crushed container into the recycler even as she swallowed the last of its contents. She relished the citrus hit for its own sake, refusing to let her aug analyse the blended drink's constituents.

The dream had shaken her. She felt as restless physically as she did mentally, determining to take a brisk stroll around the ship's decks while she analysed the implications. A low level of illuminations greeted her as her door slid silently open and she stepped out into the corridor, suggesting that either Raider had anticipated her restlessness and arranged this for her benefit or she wasn't the only one abroad at this unsociable hour. Judging from the brightness blazing from the galley door, she presumed the latter. Good. A conversation with Jen might be just what she needed. Except that when she reached the room she found...

"Cloud."

The girl/woman sat eating a bowl of what looked to be a mix of cereal and fruit.

"Hi, Leesa."

"Couldn't you sleep?"

Saavi shook her head. "I had to hop on and off at three different systems in quick succession to catch up with you and Jen at Babylon, each with their own time zones. Plays havoc with the sleep cycle, not to mention the bank balance." She put her half-finished snack down on the table. "What's your excuse?"

"Oh, I just had a bad dream."

Saavi looked at her quizzically. "I didn't realise you could have those."

"I don't normally. This was... a specific type of dream."

Leesa had never been especially close friends with Saavi, not in the way she was with Jen, but she found herself instinctively confiding in her now, perhaps sensing that doing so might aid her own understanding, or perhaps because she simply needed to talk to *somebody*. "I recently had a memory wipe," she explained, "but my aug retained everything, and gradually fed it all back to me."

"In your dreams?" No one ever accused Saavi of being stupid.

Leesa nodded, and told her about the vivid encounter she had just awoken from. "I thought that the process was complete, that I now had everything in proper order without any blanks."

"Tonight's revelation has come as a shock, then."

"Just a bit, especially as this one was different. I wasn't *me* this time around. I mean, I was in it, but the whole thing played out from inside someone else's head."

"Wow, and I thought being me was complicated."

"It's never happened this way before, not even remotely. How can you recall a memory from someone else's perspective? It doesn't make sense. I was *there*. I was Ayella. I could feel what she felt, see what she must have seen..."

"Do you think that's down to your aug? Was it trying a different approach with this facet of your past because it had to?"

"I honestly don't know." Could it be that? Had her aug resorted to an extreme method to rekindle this particular memory because the usual approach had failed?

"Have you ever wondered what it must have felt like to be Ayella, trapped and terrified like that?"

"Of course, but that was back then; a long time ago."

"Well there you are, then. Your aug must have seized on that memory and extrapolated the narrative from there."

"I guess." Could the aug even function with that sort of autonomy? It never had before, at least not that she could recall. The prospect disturbed her profoundly.

"Does it all still feel like your own memory?"

"Yes. It does now."

That was true, she realised. Since waking from the dream she could recall those same events from her own perspective, as if the dream had stimulated the process of recollection. She now remembered entering the wrecked station, being appalled at the wanton killing, and then detecting vital signs amongst the rubble when they had all assumed that everyone was dead. She remembered uncovering the terrified girl, her startled face staring up as she cleared a fallen section of wall.

She could remember holding Ayella, who had clung to her like a limpet, and felt again the sense of guilt at the way the girl had idolised her. None of them were angels, they weren't even heroes, or only by accident. They had gone to the station seeking the same research that had drawn the murderous brigands. She consoled herself with the knowledge that the crew of the *Ion Raider* would never have behaved as the first crew had, but their motives were equally as base.

For all that, the legend had grown from this tiny seed. Ayella spoke adoringly to medics and media alike, telling over and over of how she had been rescued from certain death by a group of Dark Angels, who were so incensed by her family's murder that, as soon as they'd ascertained she was safe, they had left her in order to hunt down the perpetrators and bring them to justice.

True, they had gone on to track down the murderers, but not to smite them in noble retribution, merely to claim the research. After all, Cornische already had a buyer lined up.

Quite where her subconscious, or her aug, had dragged up that memory of a picnic baffled her, though. Her own childhood had been spent on an arid oxygen-poor world where humans needed implants simply to breathe, and she had never been on a picnic in her life. Then she recalled a sensi-download she had loved as a kid, one that had depicted a sun-drenched meadow of lush green grass, a family relaxing on a day out and relishing the occasion; a flaxen-haired woman lifting her giggling toddler into the air. The girl had worn a pink and white dress. Leesa had revisited that scene over and over, but the adult her had forgotten all about it until that moment.

"Well, whatever your aug's done, assuming this is your aug, it seems to have worked," Saavi observed.

Leesa had to acknowledge the truth of that, even if she found the method employed disquieting. Something else she was beginning to realise was how easy it would be to underestimate Saavi. There was still a tendency to see a small girl in front of her, no matter that she knew an adult intellect lurked within the diminished frame.

"You're right," she said. "Thank you."

The mood for exercise had deserted Leesa. It was one thing to walk circuits around the ship's deserted decks unobserved, quite another to do so with one of her shipmates looking on while munching on a bowl of cereal. She bid Saavi goodnight and returned to her cabin, deep in thought.

Saavi had surprised her, and she was prepared to admit that perhaps she had misjudged their latest recruit. Throughout their chat in the galley, Leesa had been searching for some sign of the craving she had seen before, of the addict's yearning, but she hadn't seen it. Perhaps now that Saavi had been reunited with the cloud chamber and had her fix, her equilibrium was restored. Leesa could relate to that. Her own craving to be Hel N again had driven her to some desperate extremes – having her own memory wiped chief among them. She couldn't face being simply *odd*, without Hel N's presence to make her special any more. She'd kidded herself for a while, hidden from that gnawing need by committing wholeheartedly to what she and Kyle were doing on Babylon, but that had only worked for so long.

She still couldn't remember making the decision to have the memory wipe, and wasn't sure she really wanted to, but she could understand what had led her there. Those had been dark times back then. The ironic thing was that the memory wipe had worked, in a way. The Leesa that emerged after painstakingly rebuilding her past in order to reclaim her present no longer needed the mental crutch of Hel N. For the first time in a very long while she had been able to stand on her own two feet. She had shipped with a crew, worked the engines, and even saved the day. Her. Not Hel N but Leesa. Then, of course, just as she accomplished that, Hel N came back into her life, when she needed her the least.

This wasn't about her, though; it was bigger than that.

Her thoughts returned to the memory wipe. She might not *want* to recall the circumstances that drove her to take that decision – who would willingly revisit something like that? – but at the same time her inability to do so concerned her; that combined with emergence of the Ayella memory. If one memory had evaded her in this fashion, how would she ever know if there were more?

What other aspects of her past might still lie hidden, waiting to surprise her?

Sixteen

"We've got to change course… Now!"

Jen and Leesa were in the galley, nattering over lunch, when Cloud interrupted them. They were discussing the best way to approach Enduril II – a world neither of them was familiar with. Raider's library had been helpful in that regard up to a point, but the information the ship held was a decade out of date. The file Reese had passed to them on New Sparta did include some more recent background info, but their knowledge of Endurian society remained sketchier than either of them would have liked. Their conversation had soon turned to the client the captain had left with.

"I always got on okay with Donal," Jen felt obliged to mention.

"Yeah, me too, but that was before he had his legs blown to bits and was forced to retire. Goodness only knows how he ended up on Enduril II, and goodness knows how he feels about us now."

"I never pictured him as a miner, that's for sure," Jen said. "So, how do you reckon we should play this? Do we assume Saflik are involved in the captain's disappearance or is this something else entirely, and do we count Donal as a potential hostile or a potential ally?"

"Always assume the worst, so we start by treating him as hostile until proven otherwise."

"I agree. The same goes for Saflik, then. We assume they're involved and work upwards from there."

"Seems the safest way; it would make a hell of a prize for them – two Dark Angels, one of them the captain."

"Wouldn't it just. Okay, so no direct approach. We go in

quietly and see what we can dig up."

It was at this point in the discussion that Cloud burst in, with her demands that they change course. She looked dishevelled, her eyes wild and her hair standing up on end in ragged patches as if alive with unevenly distributed static.

"Saavi, what...?" Jen said, trying to formulate a response that didn't emerge as 'What the hell are you on about?'

"Listen to me," Saavi said, ignoring Jen's attempted question. "If we land on Enduril II as planned it will spell disaster."

"Who for?" Leesa asked, all business, evidently accepting Cloud's credibility despite her reduced physique, something Jen was struggling with.

Jen looked quickly across at her friend but couldn't see in her face any suggestion of doubt or scepticism.

"For all of us," Cloud said, "and I don't just mean those of us here on the ship, I mean everyone, the whole of humanity across every star system, every planet, every habitat."

"Whoa, hang on a second," Jen said. "Are you serious?"

Even Leesa looked taken aback. "That's... quite some claim."

"I know." Cloud seemed to slump, growing smaller still. "Don't you think I realise how it must sound? I've gone over all the potentials again and again, banished timelines and started them again, but no matter how many times I rebuild the possible futures, every variation I pursue, every path I try to explore, they all lead to the same place. That's why this is so urgent – I delayed coming to you until the last possible moment so that I could be absolutely certain, until it was almost too late, and now it *is* almost too late... We've got to alter course immediately!"

"All right, all right, slow down," Leesa said in the face of Saavi's mounting frenzy.

"What's the nature of this disaster?" Jen cut in. "What exactly is this threat you're seeing?"

"I... I don't know," Cloud admitted. "The magnitude of what's coming is so vast that all I can see is chaos, death in millions, *hundreds* of millions, whole planets dying, stars being unbalanced… The details are obscured by the sheer scale of it. At the beginning there's just one death, I know that much. A single death that will make all of this inevitable."

"One of us dies, you mean?" Jen asked, failing to see how something so trivial in the grand scheme could bring about apocalypse.

"No." Cloud shook her head. "I don't know… I just know we have to abort the journey to Enduril. We *have* to."

She stared first into Leesa's eyes and then into Jen's, as if imploring each in turn to take her seriously. "Please, you must believe me. I know I look like a dishevelled kid who's about to have a tantrum, but you can see past that, I know you can. This is me, Cloud."

Saavi took a deep breath. She looked tired, as if she hadn't slept in days. "I can tell you this much, in all the years I've spent in the cloud chamber I've *never* known anything like this before. Potentials converging relentlessly in such a terrible way… All leading to the sort of Armageddon that religious doomsayers have been predicting since, well, forever."

"And you honestly believe that we can stop this? *Us?*" Jen swept her arm out, indicating the three of them and the ship.

"I'm not sure," Cloud said, frustration evident in her voice, "but from everything I can see we're the only ones who might, *if* we change course now."

Jen looked across to Leesa, who met her gaze but gave a small shake of her head. Clearly she was as uncertain of how to react as Jen was.

"Is there nothing more you can tell us, Saavi? Anything that would help identify the threat?"

"Raider," Leesa said, "how long until we emerge from RzSpace on current schedule?"

"Twenty-two minutes and thirty-three seconds," the ship replied.

"So we still have a little time."

"No, no we don't!" Cloud insisted. "We have to act *now*."

"Act how, though" Jen asked. "Where are we supposed to go?"

"I. Don't. Know!"

"So find out for us," Leesa told her. "There's no point in our coming out into normal space only to hang around because we don't know what we're supposed to do next. Identify a course for us, a destination."

"Leesa's right," Jen said, before Cloud could object. "If you want us to follow your lead on this, it has to actually *lead* somewhere, and you're the only one who can unravel where that is. At the moment, we know where we're going. There's no point in changing that until we have somewhere else to go."

Cloud nodded. "Okay, okay, you're right," and with that she turned and sprinted from the room, looking much the same as any other girl in a hurry to be somewhere.

As soon as she had gone Leesa said, "What do you think?"

"I'm really not sure," Jen admitted.

"I know what you mean, but as the lady just reminded us, this is Cloud, and this is what Cloud does."

"Is it, though? I mean is this really the same Cloud we shipped with back in the Dark Angel days?"

"Raider says so," Leesa pointed out. "Besides, you and I both *know* it's her."

"Oh, I don't doubt that the Saavi we knew back then has become the Saavi who's with us now, but people change, we've all changed in the past ten years, and none of us more than her."

"Can she still cut it, you mean, can she be relied on?"

"Exactly. We've never seen anything like this from Cloud before. She was invaluable in telling us the best way to avoid pursuit, where to find someone or something we were hunting, that sort of thing, sure, but end of the world stuff? Never. Don't you find it a little bit odd that she comes back to us so drastically altered, so much *younger*, and starts spouting off about star-spanning calamity?"

"I'd find that odd however old she was."

"But you were the one who had doubts, remember, worries about her need for the cloud chamber. An addiction you called it. And she told us herself that she was struggling with the emotions of this younger version, wouldn't that influence her state of mind? And who knows how that might affect her interaction with the cloud chamber?"

"That's a heck of a jump, isn't it?" Leesa said. "From saying that Saavi's struggling to adapt to her new physiology to suggesting we can't trust her as Cloud any more. Think about it, Jen, what if she's right? What if we ignore this and by doing so bring about the collapse of human civilisation in the face of whatever the hell her prediction's warning us about? Personally, I don't see that we can afford *not* to believe her."

"So what are you suggesting, that we abandon the captain? That is what we're supposed to be doing here, remember – trying to save him."

"I know, I haven't forgotten, and no one wants to get the captain back more than I do…" She sighed, obviously as conflicted by this as Jen was. "Let's just see what Cloud comes back with, okay?"

Jen nodded.

The wait couldn't have been much more than a quarter of an hour but it seemed far longer. Jen couldn't concentrate on anything else and she was pretty sure the same held true for Leesa. Finally they heard Saavi running along the corridor towards them, slowing as she approached, and then she was there, looking more composed, more rational, than the last time, though Jen could sense her pent up anxiety and the effort she was making to appear that way.

"All right," Saavi said, "I've been able to discern a little more detail, but I have to warn you, it's still pretty vague."

"Have you got a destination for us?"

"Yes, and I even know why we have to go there, but I'll come to that in a second. The threat is… alien."

"I knew it!" Leesa said. "An Xter invasion. War at last."

"No, no, that's not it at all," Saavi was quick to say. "This is much worse."

"What could be worse than war with the Xters?"

"The Elders are returning."

"*What?*"

"Are you sure," Jen asked, all her concerns about Saavi's mental health resurfacing.

"Yes, and they're not coming in peace or as benevolent teachers or anything like that. They're coming in fire and death to subjugate the lesser races – humans and Xters both. They're coming back to be worshipped, to rule over those few of us who survive the conquest. They're coming back to become our gods."

Leesa and Jen stared at each other.

Leesa snorted, clearly on the verge of laughing.

"This is *not* funny!" Suddenly Saavi sounded like the indignant child she appeared to be.

"I'm sorry, Saavi," Leesa said, "but *seriously?*"

"Saavi," Jen said, as gently as she could, "are you certain that…"

"Look, Jen," Saavi interrupted, "Don't you think I realise how crazy this must sound? *Of course* I'm certain. I wouldn't be here trying to convince you otherwise. We're facing the end of human civilisation as we know it, and nobody even suspects it's coming."

"Except us," Jen murmured.

"Jen, I apologise, you were right," Leesa said. "I was all ready to back you, Saavi, but how am I supposed to support this?"

"But it's *true*." Saavi sounded close to tears.

Jen could see by the slump of Saavi's shoulders that she thought she had lost them, which was when her cause received support from the most unexpected of quarters.

"I fear that what Cloud is telling you may indeed be the case," Raider's calm tones declared.

Suddenly Leesa wasn't laughing any more. "Seriously? Shit."

"Even if it is," Jen said, "what can *we* possibly do about it?"

"Nothing," Saavi replied. "There's only one being who can."

"Who?"

"I've no idea, but I do know where to find her, him or it."

She gave the coordinates, which Raider helpfully projected onto a star chart.

"That's…"

"The middle of nowhere," Leesa said, finishing Jen's aborted sentence.

"A location very close to the galactic rim," Raider clarified. "Far beyond human space, Xter space, or any known space."

It was Leesa who broke the silence that followed. "Raider, could we even get there and back?"

"Yes."

"Then I don't see we have a choice."

"Of course there's a choice," Jen said. "Remember what we agreed before we touched down on Babylon? You'd take care of what you had to at la Gossa, then we'd head straight to rescue the captain. I'm all for following up on this, but let's get the captain first. We're on the door step of his last known location in any case."

"Please, Jen, we can't afford to delay," Saavi said. "Really, we have to act *now*, or it will be too late."

"I know what we agreed," Leesa said. "But if what Cloud has seen is true, it changes everything. The captain can take care of himself, after all."

"Can he, though?" Jen asked. "His employer doesn't seem so certain, and she's seen a lot more of him over the past decade than either of us."

"He's still the same man, trust me, and can we really afford not to take Cloud at her word?"

"You've changed your tune."

"I know, but with both Raider and Cloud telling us this… I want to save the captain too, of course I do, but I honestly don't see we have any choice."

"Thank you," Saavi said quietly. "Jen, I'm not delusional, and I'm not wrong."

Jen wanted to argue the point further, to say 'let someone else save the universe, let's just concentrate on what matters to *us*', but she knew she'd lost the debate. It was two against one, three if you included Raider, and Leesa had always been Cornische's lieutenant back in the Dark Angel days; not that she'd made any attempt to pull rank since they'd reconnected, but the knowledge was there.

"Okay," she said reluctantly. "I still think this is a mistake, but okay."

Running through her mind was the thought *what if the captain needs us desperately?* But she had already used that argument, and had lost.

In the brief minutes between the *Ion Raider* emerging in the Enduril system and slipping back into RzSpace on its new heading, Jen found herself thinking, *I'm sorry, captain. We will come back for you, I promise.*

Three very focused individuals sat hunched over the equipment in the ops room of *Sabre 1*; among them, Deepak Thapa, the unit's commander. The ship had ghosted into the Enduril system unobserved and the team were working in shifts, three off, three on. Built for speed and stealth, there was very little else to the ship apart from ops, sleeping quarters, and engines.

On arrival at the Enduril system, they had found a military vessel already in orbit around Enduril II, a Night Hammer ship, which was enough to give even the toughest among them pause. The Night Hammers were a discredited commando regiment with a bad-ass reputation. Disbanded after a well-publicised series of atrocities had been traced back to them, their senior officers were put on trial and imprisoned; some of the Night Hammer units had gone rogue, commandeering their ships and disappearing to the fringe to become mercenaries. Official word claimed that the rogue units had been ruthlessly hunted down and dealt with. Apparently, not all of them.

Sabre 1 was equipped with all manner of stealth technology, including the new generation PTARMIGAN cloaking system, and the ship was currently running on silent, with minimum power output – Thapa wasn't about to take any chances.

To date, they were maintaining a watching brief as assigned, observing the planet and specifically the capital Hamilton with every means at their disposal. They had found no trace of First Solar's agent Drake, but had observed the arrival of the second agent, Archer, and followed him from on high until he disappeared in an unremarkable sector of the capital. Presumably he had gone down into the old mines, deep enough to block their surveillance.

They were working on the basis that Drake was down there with him, if he were still alive, but at this stage it was pure conjecture. They didn't have enough information to consider an extraction attempt and Thapa wasn't prepared to sanction a recce to the surface, not when it ran the risk of exposing them and offered little chance of achieving anything.

"Skip, a ship has just entered the system from Rz."

Thapa looked up. "Another military vessel?"

"Doesn't look like it, no. A trader, I'd say, maybe an old comet. It looks as if she's going to pass pretty close to us as she approaches Enduril II."

Thapa grunted. The trader could come as close as she liked, her crew would never know they were there.

"That's odd. She's not shedding velocity and... Oh."

"What?"

"She's gone again."

"Gone where?"

"Back into Rz."

"Is that even possible?" Thapa wasn't certain even *Sabre 1* could go in and out of RzSpace that quickly.

"I wouldn't have thought so, no, but... Shit!"

"What now?"

"I managed to ping her for ident before she disappeared."

"Well?"

"According to this, that ship we just saw is the *Ion Raider*."

Thapa sat there for a moment, not quite knowing what to make of it. Night Hammers, disappearing bank agents, and now a ghost ship. *What the hell is going on in this system?*

SEVENTEEN

Drake's first awareness was pain. He tried to shy away from it, to return to the comforting oblivion of unconsciousness, but he was fighting against the tide and lacked the energy for the struggle. Slowly but inexorably, he found himself carried towards wakefulness.

Voices; indistinct and muted, as if heard from underwater or beneath a heavy layer of blankets, but they toyed with him, snagging his awareness and demanding his attention so that he had to strive to work out what they were saying, he couldn't help himself.

There seemed to be a lot of voices and movement, suggesting more people than had been here when Archer administered his pummelling. Drake tried to open his eyes. The right one, which rested almost on the floor, refused to respond at first, the lids stuck together, most likely gummed up by dried blood from his head wound. The left one reported feet and boots and legs.

Pain overrode everything and seemed to emanate from everywhere. His head was the first to demand attention, a deep-seated thudding pain that intensified when he attempted the slightest movement, but it was his torso that hurt the worst. There was heavy bruising, he could feel it, all across his chest and stomach and sides, but also broken ribs that sent sharp agony lancing through him as he tried to shift position.

He lay there for long minutes, gathering his strength, knowing that he had to sit up, for the sake of his ribs, no matter how much it hurt to do so. It was as he put this plan into action, slowly, painfully, that he realised how badly his left leg was injured as well. Finally, he was more or less upright, propped against one of the larger artefacts. No one took any notice of

215

him, barely even glancing his way, though there was indeed a lot of movement: uniformed men and women shifting crates and in some instances larger artefacts unboxed, loading them into the lift cubicle and then stepping back to watch them vanish.

Were they emptying the entire chamber? Given the limited space in the gateway cubicle, that would take days, even with a team working constantly and efficiently.

No, not the entire chamber, just a few cherry-picked artefacts, said a familiar voice in his head.

Mudball, you bastard, what are you playing at?

Not playing – the time for games is long over. This is where the serious stuff begins.

Drake shifted position, sending hot agony shooting through his side.

Yes, I'm sorry about that, Mudball said. *I never did like that Archer character, even back at First Solar. Too shifty by half. You'll be glad to know we've sent him elsewhere, to oversee tasks more suited to his psychotic tendencies.*

'We'? Drake asked.

Ah, about that… Turns out that I have a lot in common with this Saflik group – that's what they call themselves – enough for them to be extremely useful to my cause from here on in.

Meaning that you no longer need me.

Sadly, no. I'm sorry, Drake, during our time together I've grown quite fond of you in a peculiar sort of way, but it was never going to last. I'm way out of your league.

So this is divorce, then, Drake said, doing his best to be flippant while feeling anything but. *Could I at least have some water?* In addition to all the physical injuries, his throat was as raw as gravel.

I can arrange that much.

One of the soldiers came over and held out a canteen. There had been no spoken order, no signalled instruction, and Drake couldn't help but wonder how many heads Mudball was now inside. He accepted the canteen gratefully and took several deep gulps.

The soldier returned to his duties, leaving the canteen with Drake.

I have to go as well, Mudball told him. *No telling what this lot will choose to load if I'm not there to supervise.*

Drake felt the alien's presence withdraw.

He sat and watched the continuing movement of artefacts and crates for what must have been well over an hour, ignored by the soldiers responsible throughout. At last they appeared to be done, milling around the area in front of the gateway before stepping into it in groups of four and disappearing back to the wider reality of Enduril II. As the last quartet squeezed into the cubicle, one of them – a young lad – met Drake's gaze. He almost smiled before vanishing, the only interaction Drake had shared with any of them since accepting the water bottle.

The chamber was silent. He was alone. For a moment he wondered if this was to be his fate: abandoned here to waste away of dehydration or his injuries.

Mudball?

No reply.

Or perhaps there was. Even as the thought formed, he saw movement in the gateway compartment. Figures started to emerge, five of them: Payne, Ungar, Evans, Lis, and Nowak.

Maybe being on his own hadn't been so bad after all.

Ungar looked across, nodding and smiling as if he were greeting a dear friend. Immediately the five had stepped away from the cabinet another group came through, and then another, with more after that, arriving in fours and fives. Drake guessed they must have assembled in the big empty building, waiting for the soldiers to finish and leave the cache before venturing through themselves. He recognised many of the faces – people he had been introduced to at the reception, which may only have been a day or two ago but now seemed a lifetime to him. They were all smartly dressed; no, more than that: they were *flamboyantly* dressed, as if attending an official function, another reception; as if they had something to celebrate.

He slumped back against the artefact, trying to look beaten and feeble. No point in squandering any last vestiges of strength by sitting up or acting defiant.

Soon the normally clear space in front of the gateway was packed with the great and the good of Hamilton's society; though, strangely, an unoccupied bubble surrounded Drake, as if a force field held the crowds at bay. That, or a consensus of distaste.

Once the migration into the chamber had ceased, Payne stepped forward and addressed the gathering.

"Welcome, one and all. Welcome to a historic day for the people of Enduril II and for the whole of humanity. I promise you that we are here to witness something extraordinary, the like of which no one has ever seen before. This is a day we will all look back on and be proud to say, 'yes, I was there'."

If Drake hadn't been in so much pain he might have laughed at the man's pomposity. As things stood, it was still a struggle not to.

"What are we humans like, eh? Isn't it typical of us that when faced with something miraculous such as the caches, these wonders of the modern age, we put ourselves at the centre of the equation? We've done that since the dawn of time, of course. When astronomers first looked up and noted the stars, it was assumed that the Earth, our original home, was the centre of the universe, and every model of the solar system put forward started with that assumption. It took a genius – Nicolaus Copernicus – to see beyond the accepted theories, to step outside the boundaries set by perceived wisdom and surmise that the existing way of thinking was wrong! He threw out the rule book and started to work on a model that placed the *sun* at the centre, with the Earth merely one among a number of planets that orbited around her.

"We have done much the same today when it comes to Elder artefacts. We discovered the first cache and instantly *assumed* it had been put there for our benefit, can you imagine that? We blithely took it for granted that these storehouses of knowledge and technological marvels had been left for us to find by a benevolent race that has moved on, so that an intelligent species in the future – us – could follow in their footsteps and aspire to the greatness they achieved. How typically *arrogant* of us! It never even entered our narrow minds that the Elders hadn't spared future races a second thought when they built their caches, that any benefit to humanity is no more than an accidental side-effect. We simply leapt in, killed the guardian entity and helped ourselves. We've been doing much the same ever since!"

A few mumbled 'hear hears' rippled through the crowd.

"We're nothing more than lowly scavengers, opportunists taking advantage of a resource we've blundered into by chance. It's taken someone of vision to see that, though, to realise that the Elders intended the artefacts for the benefit of their *own* people, the ones who were left behind, not us. Ancient Earth had their Nicolaus Copernicus. Contemporary humankind has Theodor Ungar!"

Ungar's loving this, Drake thought, *standing there and basking in Payne's praise*. He stopped himself, realising with a mix of amusement and dismay that he was filling in for Mudball's absence by making the sort of aside the little alien might have made himself.

Ungar stepped forward to join Payne. "You're too kind, Martin," he said in that gentle narrator's voice of his, which still managed to carry to everyone. "All I did was question perceived wisdom. Yes, I suppose in the same way Copernicus did in his day, but to compare me to such a great man..." He tutted and shook his head, smiling at Payne. "No.

"It is true, however, that the burden of proposing that the caches might have been intended for a different purpose fell to me; true also that I set about investigating the theory when others dismissed it. People have long debated the presence of cache guardians – why leave a bounty of technological wonders for future sentient races only to place a lethal intelligence to watch over them? The idea that these 'guardians' were there to filter out the unworthy never sat comfortably with me, and from there I started to question our whole approach to the caches and determined to visit as many sites as I could – including a couple that you had been involved with, Cornische, in your Drake persona." Ungar actually paused to smile at Drake before continuing. "I studied the recordings and accounts of people who had discovered caches and even interviewed one or two of them as well. All despicable individuals I have to say, those that I met at any rate.

"The more I looked into the matter the more I realised that these 'cache guardians' didn't behave like lethal killers put in place to repel all boarders. Instead, it seemed to me, they were more akin to mother hens protecting their young. That's when it began to dawn on me that we'd got everything the wrong way around. These Elder chambers don't just happen to have guardian entities in attendance, they were never built to house artefacts at all; they're all *about* the entities, and it's the artefacts that are the incidental aspect.

"These aren't treasure troves left for future races, they are boxes of exotic toys meant to entertain alien intelligences. In many instances senile, diminished intelligences by the time we stumbled into them, meriting care and consideration… And how do we react? In typically heavy-handed fashion, we break in, kill the intelligences and steal their toys.

"You can imagine how excited I was when I learned of a place called Enduril II, where a cache had reputedly been discovered and not desecrated. Of course I came straight here, how could I not – a chance to experience an intact cache chamber, the first such I had ever seen? What I found here astonished me: a world where people *understand*; an enlightened attitude I scarcely believed possible."

A rumble of applause ran around the audience.

"And in you, Martin, I met a natural ally, a man who

appreciates the true wonder of the caches and is as horrified as I am by the atrocities perpetrated against the innocent Elder entities who claim them as their home. And so Saflik was born!"

Ungar's final pronouncement was greeted by a crescendo of enthusiastic applause from the assembled dignitaries that dwarfed the previous half-hearted efforts, and even a cheer or two.

A repetitive chant of, "Saflik, purity, Saflik, purity, Saflik..." started up spontaneously, only quieting as Payne stepped up to speak once more.

It's almost as if they've rehearsed this, Drake thought before he could stop himself.

"By murdering Elder entities, vandalising cache sites and helping ourselves to the contents," Payne said, "humanity has been systematically desecrating the realm of gods whose shadows we're not even fit to walk in. Once I began to appreciate the full extent of our crimes, I looked back in horror at my own past and realised that I had been part of the worst group of defilers of all – the Dark Angels. Those infamous brigands, notorious for stripping caches of their most valuable resources and using them for their own gain."

Hardly an accurate summary, but fully in keeping with all the other nonsense being spouted. Drake had been prepared for almost anything when he set out from New Sparta with Payne, but not religious fervour. Payne and Ungar were zealots, *all* these people were, following a faith of their own devising.

"I sought forgiveness from the Elder entity that resides in our own cache and swore to make amends. The entity heard me, delivering to us Theodor Ungar! And here I must thank all of you, the people of Enduril II, for embracing the path that Theo and I devised and for joining in our mission. Without your support, we could never have flourished as we have, could never have reached out to like-minded people across the human worlds, and could never have hunted down and delivered vengeance to the Dark Angels. We are Saflik, we are purity, destined to cleanse human space of its shame."

"We are Saflik, we are purity!" the crowd dutifully chorused, with one or two fists punching the air.

Drake thought he understood now: Payne's budding fanaticism had entwined with the injustice he felt regarding his injuries. The hatred that had festered in him towards those he held responsible provided a focus for this newly fashioned instrument, this Saflik. Each Dark Angel oblivious, vulnerable in their ignorance and their isolation. How many were already dead?

I did that to them. I left them as easy targets... Tempting though it was to wallow in the feelings of guilt that realisation inspired, he suppressed it. His situation was bad enough without the debilitating effects of self-doubt and guilt. Hindsight is a wonderful thing. Nobody could have foreseen the emergence of a threat like Payne and Ungar and their murderous cult. At the time, scattering the Angels and allowing them to assimilate, giving them the chance of a normal life in their own fashion, had seemed the best option.

Did you miss me? Asked a familiar presence.

Sod off, Mudball! Back to pillage my brain again?

Oh no, there's no need for that. I have everything from you that I could possibly have asked for. Who knew that all this time the location of Lenbya was there, hidden in the recesses of your memory?

What?

Lenbya – the motherlode, the mythical cache of caches that all hunters joked about finding and all the professionals dismissed as a prospector's wet dream. It was the Shangri-La of cache hunting, the El Dorado; said to contain more artefacts and more unique items than all the other Elder hauls combined. Lenbya was a place that nobody would admit to believing in but everybody secretly hoped to stumble upon one day.

With a start, he realised that Mudball was right. He *did* know. How was that even possible?

It's ironic don't you think? Mudball said. *All these years I've spent slowly gathering my strength, absorbing the enfeebled echoes of Elder remnants bit by bit, cache by cache, when the answers I sought were right in front of me the whole while, there in your mind, buried beneath the subtlest of blocks. It makes sense, really, I mean, where else would the crew of the* Ion Raider, *an unexceptional trading ship grubbing out a living like so many others, have found artefacts powerful enough to turn them into the Dark Angels?*

It did make sense, Drake realised. Why had he never seen this, why had he never suspected?

Oh don't beat yourself up about it, Mudball advised. *As I say, the blocks were subtle, and strong. I was in there with you much of the time and even I never twigged.*

Mudball had been playing him all along, Drake now knew, using their assignments as a means to marshal his own strength, biding his time until Drake had outlived his usefulness. A point that had now been reached.

None of which came as a great surprise; he'd always sensed there was more to the alien than met the eye – or mind – and had done his best to hold part of himself back, but, even so, it was a blow to appreciate the extent to which he had been duped.

Did you ever stop to wonder how Payne, an outsider, came to such pre-eminence in a society that has such a strong mistrust of outsiders? Mudball asked.

The cache guardian, Drake replied. *It communicates with him, much as you've always done with me, and it responds when he wants to travel between this pocket and the outside universe.*

I'm impressed. When did you work that out?

The moment Payne had looked so stricken and announced that the entity had stopped communicating, but Drake saw no reason to point that out.

The entity deigned to speak to only two individuals in Enduril society, Mudball explained. *One of whom died shortly before Payne washed up on Enduril II and, to the consternation of everyone here, the entity chose Payne as the replacement. That put him in a position of pre-eminence from the off, and he's worked to further his influence ever since. Presumably the entity saw something in him, though I've yet to work out what. Still, he's proving very useful, so who am I to complain?*

There was still no sign of Mudball's physical form, which

223

puzzled Drake.

All in good time, Mudball assured him. *It turns out Payne has a penchant for the melodramatic.*

You don't say.

He's building up to the grand reveal.

What, of you?

Yeah. You see, I've convinced him that I'm still his precious cache guardian and that the guardian has seized control of your cute little gen pet and adapted it to house its mighty intellect. In fact, of course, I've defeated and absorbed their strong but docile guardian and I'm about to reveal my true physical aspect – I don't have much choice in that, by the way. Maintaining the diminished form of Mudball had become a strain even before I absorbed the Enduril entity. Now that I have, I doubt I could ever compress myself sufficiently to cram into that fluffy little scrap of a body again. Now watch, you're going to like what comes next.

"And now the moment of truth," Payne was saying, "the reason we've gathered here. As you all know, through our efforts justice has been brought to a number of the defilers. Thanks to you, thanks to all of us, the self-styled Dark Angels formerly known as Spirit, Gabriel, Taranis, Quill, and D Mon are no more."

Five, Drake realised, five of his former crew dead.

"News of these victories has always been brought to you from afar. Not today. In a moment, you will witness first-hand the execution of the greatest defiler of them all, the man who led the Dark Angels in their folly. Here, in this very chamber, Captain Francis Hilary Cornische will meet his just end and pay for his crimes!"

This inspired the most enthusiastic round of cheering and applause yet. Drake didn't much like being the centre of attention at the best of times, let alone under these circumstances. He regarded the crowd, staring into the faces of individuals he had dined with, and in many instance he could see in their eyes burning anticipation, the lust to witness another human life snuffed out.

Payne was looking at him now, speaking words that were apparently for his ears but in truth were intended for the audience. "The others, the former members of your crew we've brought to justice, died without ever knowing why, but you're different, Cornische. You're the captain, and with rank comes privilege and responsibility. It's only fitting that you should be made aware of the crimes you have perpetrated, the reason for your execution. It's only fair that you face the truth of your failings and be offered the opportunity to repent before you join your shipmates in death."

Our shipmates, Drake wanted to say, *you were one of us*. But he kept quiet, not wanting anyone to suspect him capable of defiance. Instead, he mustered his strength and his anger in the hope of one moment, one chance to make them count.

"But first," Payne said, openly addressing his audience once more, "we are about to witness something very special, an event unique in human history. Cache entities, the last vestiges of the once mighty Elder race that have lived on into our times, have always been tied by location, slaves to the chambers that support them. That has been their weakness and the only reason we puny humans have been able to systematically murder them. Not any more.

"When we lured Cornische here, we hadn't anticipated that he would bring with him a genpet, but his doing so has proved to be a boon. Our cache entity, the benevolent being who has so graciously allowed the people of Enduril II to visit its home and benefit in so many ways from its presence, has succeeded in subsuming Drake's pet. In doing so, it has cut its dependence on this chamber and is now free to join us in our endeavours wherever they may lead!

"Do not be alarmed in any way by what you are about to see. The genpet's body proved too slight to contain the full magnificence of an Elder entity, so it has been enlarged and adapted to provide a more suitable home, and, remember, the entities, the Elders, are alien and so do not conform to our own aesthetics. Bearing all that in mind, please welcome our friend, our benefactor, and the first ever mobile cache entity!"

The applause that erupted in response was enthusiastic enough to begin with, but it steadily faltered, to be replaced by mutterings of dismay and consternation. Everyone was staring in the same direction, at something – presumably the reconfigured Mudball – that was out of Drake's line of sight. He strained to see, but was blocked by the mass of the artefact he rested against.

People started to back away, despite Payne and Ungar's attempts to reassure them with "Don't be alarmed" and "Remember, this is still the same benevolent entity who has always been with us."

Somebody screamed, somebody tripped over, and then panic threatened to take over, as those at the back broke and rushed towards the small compartment that represented their only way out.

Drake had no idea if what happened next was simply a panicked reaction or if it was to some extent pre-planned, if one of those attending had come here with the intention to disrupt. Of course these people were all trusted, influential, and wealthy; of course they wouldn't have been checked for weapons.

Somebody had brought a gun, a projectile weapon. Drake saw the pistol raised in a man's hand, pointing in the direction people were fleeing from. Two shots rang out, and then chaos erupted in earnest.

This was it, the opportunity he had been waiting for. Nobody was paying him the slightest attention. In pulling his battered body upright he had brought himself marginally closer to where his cane lay – if only he had thought to reclaim it earlier, before Payne and his cronies returned, but he had been in pain and hadn't anticipated a pressing need. Summoning every scrap of determination, he now rocked so that all the weight shifted to his left buttock, ignoring the pain the act sent lancing through his thigh. Scrabbling for purchase and added momentum with his right foot, he flung himself towards the cane, stretching out with his left hand. He had to stifle a scream of agony as his torso hit the ground. All that mattered was the cane. Agonisingly, he was just short of his target. He squirmed and wriggled towards it, striving to reach further, spurred on by the shrieks of terror from his captors.

What are you doing?

Mudball! Despite all that was going on, the alien had somehow noticed, and he couldn't shut Mudball out, not entirely, but he refused to be distracted.

I can hurt you, you know that.

This time Drake did cry out, as all the pains in his body multiplied towards excruciating.

Why make this worse for yourself? the alien continued. *There's no escape. What do you seriously think you can achieve even if you do reclaim that stick of yours? Injure one or two, buy a few more seconds? I'll soon have this situation under control, and once I do… There are too many of them. All you'll be doing is staving off the inevitable.*

Drake refused to listen to either the alien or his protesting body. His whole being was focused on reclaiming the cane. He reached further, knowing that he was over-extending, feeling his shoulder throb – just one more aspect of hurt. Then he had it; the tips of his fingers rasped against the shaft; one final effort and he was able to drag it a little towards him, then close his hand around the smooth cylinder and reel the cane in.

He would have liked to sit up, to adjust his body and seek a better position, but at the periphery of awareness he sensed that Payne was reasserting some degree of control over the panicked mob and knew that the slightest hesitation would mean his chance was lost. Thankfully, he didn't have to think, instinct took over. He had rehearsed this a dozen times while Payne prattled on. Now all he had to do was act. He swung the stick round, willing his suddenly clumsy arm to obey him. Then he had it, his hand closing on the familiar handle and activating the appropriate trigger. He tilted the stick upwards even as a figure loomed above him. Evans. He ignored the security man. Aiming as best he could, beyond Evans, he squeezed his eyes shut and fired.

One advantage of being involved in so many cache hunts was that Drake had gained a degree of familiarity with some of the more common types of artefact. Oh, every cache had its share of unique items, and this one had more than most – the Endurians were justified in considering it to be special – but there were still plenty of objects here that he was able to recognise, at least by general type.

He knew, for example, that the small neatly stacked pyramid of multi-faceted spheres at which he had just aimed were highly unstable – not actually spheres at all, but fifty-sided polygons which, for some ridiculous reason, he remembered were called 'pentacontagons'.

Drake had seen one explode when dropped during a mission some years back, injuring the man who had dislodged it and concussing two others close by, while everyone present had been temporarily blinded by the brightness of the blast. None of those affected had been seriously hurt, but they'd all been caught unawares and incapacitated for a brief time.

That had been just one globe; thanks to the neat tendencies of the Enduril cache entity, there had to be a dozen or more gathered here. The effect when the energy beam from his cane struck the cluster was as spectacular as he'd hoped. Even with his eyes tightly shut and head hastily turned away, he could sense the glare as a wave of heat and light washed over him, while the sound reverberated through his head…

He started to move at once, daring to open his eyes as he did so. There was no sign of Evans and the chamber now resembled a war zone, with figures sprawled on the ground, caskets knocked over and burst open, and a cloud of smoke rolling out from where the mirrored spheres had been.

Blinking away afterimages, Drake struggled to his feet, using the cane for support. The pain from his broken ribs was intense – he didn't want to think about the damage that his lungs might be suffering. Every movement sent daggers through his body, his left leg really didn't want to support his weight, his shoulder felt as if it was on fire, and if he tried to draw anything beyond a shallow breath the pain became unbearable. Apart from that, he was in pretty good shape.

Drake sensed movement from beyond a stack of objects which his mind hadn't the time or capacity to identify, but which stood above head height. He didn't know who was there, he didn't care. Putting his weight on his good right leg, he lifted his cane, jabbed at the artefacts that separated him from the unknown enemy, and activated the repellor field. The whole mass of stacked items shifted and jerked away from him, propelled by the wave front produced by his cane, before collapsing down on top of whoever was on the far side. A brief yelp of surprise sounded, to be drowned out by the crash of heavy objects, and then silence.

Drake had neither the time to pause nor the capacity to draw a deep breath. Leaning on his cane for support, he started to run as best he could – little more than a clumsy, limping shuffle – having to move around two unconscious forms to do so. When the faceted spheres had detonated, his position on the ground and close to the blast point had enabled him to escape the full force of the explosion, but he knew it wouldn't be long before Payne and the others began to recover.

Right on cue, a familiar voice spoke in his head: *A noble effort, but why are you bothering? There's nowhere for you to go.*

Drake didn't reply. The only effect Mudball's comment had was to spur him on. He redoubled his efforts, ignoring the burning in his side, the throb of his shoulder, the constant pain in his leg. It wasn't far, just a little way across the chamber.

I can do this.

Do what?

Mudball had caught the thought. He had to be more careful, couldn't afford to disclose his intentions – it was the only edge he had. Drake clamped down on his thoughts, determined not to let the alien in. Logically, the treacherous creature was right, where could he go? But one thing it had failed to appreciate, even after so many years of inhabiting Drake's mind, was the survival instinct: the dogged tenacity with which all humans will cling to life even in the face of impossible odds. When he'd first spied the globes, Drake's plan had extended only as far as detonating them and getting away from his captors, but by the time an opportunity to do so arose the next step had fallen into place. He now knew exactly where he was going; the only place he *could* go.

Nearly there.

Nearly where?

Damn! He had to be more guarded.

Sounds from behind him could only mean that Payne and the others were waking up, regrouping. Surely they would need a few precious seconds to get their bearings before coming after him. He didn't look back, didn't want the distraction. He could see it now, his goal: almost there. All he had to do was stay ahead of them for a few more seconds...

DRAKE!

Never had Mudball's voice sounded so loud, so strident in his head. It caught him by surprise, banishing his sense of purpose for a split second, but then he focused once more and went on.

I SEE NOW, I UNDERSTAND YOUR POOR EXCUSE OF A PLAN – IT'S A DESPERATE MOVE, DRAKE, BUT EVEN SO IT'S ONE I CAN'T PERMIT.

Get out of my head!

Mudball was right about one thing: Drake *was* desperate. *Just a little further...* He determined to refocus, to achieve that state of tunnel vision that admitted nothing else, but the noise behind him had intensified. It sounded as if a whole army were chasing him and trashing the place as it came.

He did look back then, and it almost proved his undoing. Coming towards him down the central aisle of the chamber and covering the intervening space with alarming speed, was a thing out of nightmare. He could see a vague resemblance to the creature that had perched on his shoulder and shared his life for so many years, but this was a Mudball grown huge and distorted, a sinister caricature of the being he'd known. The little alien's eyes had always been prominent – the effect in a small genpet-sized creature was cute, endearing. They had grown in proportion to become bottomless pools of ebony malevolence. Beneath lay a slitted mouth that opened to snarl or perhaps roar, revealing rows of pointed carnivore's teeth. The most impressive aspect, though, was the sheer size of this apparition. It towered above all else in the chamber, reaching a good way towards the high, vaulted ceiling. Supporting this dreadful, improbable creature was a rolling mass of thick tentacles, which undulated to carry it across the chamber floor, spilling or crushing precious artefacts with abandon. No wonder the Endurians had panicked.

All this, Drake took in at a single backward glance, though it lingered longer than anticipated, so outlandish and horrific was the sight.

The momentary distraction was enough, his shoulder and good knee catching the protruding edge of a bulky artefact. He stumbled, his injured leg threatening to buckle, and he almost went down. Somehow he kept to his feet, the cane again coming to his aid. After a couple of staggering steps he was able to limp on, trying not to think of the monstrosity behind. He heard it constantly now, and knew it was gaining with frightening speed, but the artefact he sought was just a few steps away.

TURN AROUND, DRAKE, TURN AROUND AND LOOK AT ME! THERE'S NO ESCAPE, SO WHY FIGHT THE INEVITABLE?

Drake felt the hairs on the back of his neck rise and there was no mistaking the gloating in Mudball's thoughts. He sensed that the alien was right behind him now, ready to snatch him up at the last moment, just as he dared to believe he'd made it.

No! In a final act of defiance, Drake threw himself at the artefact. In the process, his cane naturally lifted from the floor. He exaggerated the lift, angling the cane so that it pointed backwards and not merely down. He fired, doing so blind and without any idea of what effect, if any, the cane's meagre energy discharge would have on something the size of the creature behind him. He just hoped it would buy him the precious seconds he needed.

His lunge carried him to the artefact. He clutched it with both hands, hugging it to him. The surface felt warm beneath his fingers and textured, as if embossed with an intricate design or perhaps script that was invisible to the naked eye. The warmth spread rapidly, coursing up both arms to encompass his whole body.

No! Mudball's roar, echoing his own denial a second earlier, seemed diminished, no longer filling his mind. He didn't look round, not wanting to acknowledge how close the creature was, but continued to focus on the odd, perfectly formed triangle with the hole in the middle. The artefact had begun to shine the instant he touched it. The intensity of illumination rose in a split second from modest glow to a blaze, forcing him to squeeze his eyes shut. He might have cried out as that flare of energy swept through his body – he couldn't say for sure. The shock of it ignited every corner of his being.

Did he merely imagine the faintest touch of something heavy and rope-like on his trailing ankle, or was that real? No matter. His mind had barely registered the possibility when he was gone.

EIGHTEEN

He was… somewhere else.

Red. That was his first impression. Everything here seemed limned in shades of red or ruddy brown. That observation was immediately followed by the realisation of tightness in his chest. He was finding it difficult to breathe, as if he were at high altitude where the air was thin. He still clung to the triangle, or its twin, which he hastily flung aside, not wanting to risk being pulled back to where he had come from.

Payne had been right, then, a transport device, but to where? And how did the presence of such a thing marry with Mudball's claim that the caches were secure playpens for fragmented Elder Remnants? Why equip a prison with a way out?

The question was moot; there were more important things to worry about, such as where the hell he was. It looked dead. It *felt* dead. A barren wasteland of reddish sand. The night sky was almost devoid of stars – a scattered sprinkling, individual pinpricks of light that stood out in isolation here and there. Had he been transported through time as well as space? Was he witnessing the last stars, the death of the universe? No, that made no sense and the end of the universe wouldn't look like this, surely; it wouldn't look so… *normal*, an extension of the familiar. More likely he was somewhere towards the galactic rim – a staggering distance to have been transported, but more plausible than time travel. No, not transported, he realised, but reconstituted. This wasn't like a trip through RzSpace. The only feasible way of achieving this would be to break down his body, his mind, everything that constituted *him*, and reconstruct it perfectly at the other end. How could he ever know if it *was* perfect, though…?

A stab of pain interrupted the thought as he drew another breath.

Even the starlight was tinged in red – and there was no apparent moon, yet he could make out his surroundings. Everything seemed suffused with a wan light – red, naturally – which he could only think must emanate from the sand itself.

There was no sound beyond his own laboured breaths, the pervading silence heightening his sense of isolation. Breathing really was becoming an issue. He was having to suck in great lungfuls of air, every intake a fresh shard of agony. The air tasted flat and stale and overly warm in his throat, as dead as this world.

He knew the truth even before he discovered the body. He had shuffled away from the arrival point, only for his foot to knock against something solid. He cleared away sand to uncover first a hand and then an arm.

The air here was too thin, the oxygen content marginally too low to support human life. Already he was feeling lightheaded and sluggish – the latter might have been a reaction to his recent exertions and the battering his body had taken, but he knew better. He wanted to move, to escape this latest threat, but where to and how? Why trouble to go anywhere when even breathing was such an effort? Without intending to, he slumped to a sitting position, his injured leg giving way and the rest of him following it down.

Ironic that he had escaped from one form of death only to succumb to another, but at least by doing so he deprived Mudball of the satisfaction of *knowing* that he was dead, and he could hope that Payne, Ungar and Archer would always wonder, never quite certain that Drake was gone for good. In that way, his ghost might at least haunt the bastards.

His mind had started to wander. He was finding it difficult to hang onto thoughts. Even to his hatred. His eyes were going now. For a moment the world rippled and swam out of focus before regaining definition. Breathing had progressed from being difficult to impossible. He was gasping, irrespective of the stabbing pain the act induced. His chest heaved with the effort, his whole body given to the task of sucking in precious air.

He toppled over, his face struck the sand and his left cheek nestled into its cushioning warmth. *One day, will some other stranded traveller scrape away the sand and discover my buried body, even as I did whoever came before me?*

The thought thinned and drifted away.

He was hallucinating. He saw a figure striding towards him, wavering in and out of focus. As it came nearer he could see just the boots and the bottom of the legs, trousers tucked into the boot tops. A knee then filled his view, sinking onto the sand right beside his face. *Ridiculous! They're not even wearing a suit.* Was this the best his imagination could muster?

The last thing imagination conjured was the hand reaching out to descend upon him, though it was hazy and the impression of anything being there at all slipped away even as it formed.

His vision contracted. The world rushed away from him. For a moment he felt as if he were floating, then everything went blank.

About the Author

Ian Whates lives in a quiet cul-de-sac in a sleepy Cambridgeshire village with his partner, Helen. A writer and editor of science fiction, fantasy, and occasionally horror, Ian is the author of six novels (three space opera and three urban fantasy with steampunk overtones), the co-author of two more (military SF), has seen sixty-odd of his short stories published in a variety of venues, and is responsible for editing around thirty anthologies.

His work has been shortlisted for the Philip K Dick Award and twice for a BSFA Award. The first novel in the Dark Angels series, the Firefly-esque space opera romp *Pelquin's Comet*, was an Amazon UK #1 best seller. His short fiction has been collected in three volumes to date with a fourth – his first publication in Spanish – due out later this year.

In 2006 Ian founded multiple award-winning independent publisher NewCon Press by accident. He still wonders how that happened and was bemused to see his 'hobby' celebrate its tenth birthday in 2016.

Ian would like to extend his thanks to the members of the Northampton Science Fiction Writers Group, who workshopped several chapters of *The Ion Raider* in their early stages, and in particular to Donna Bond, who cast her keen eye over the text before it went to print.

Book One of The Dark Angels:
PELQUIN'S COMET
IAN WHATES

In an age of exploration, the crew of the freetrader *Pelquin's Comet* – a rag-tag group of misfits and ex-soldiers – set out to find a cache of alien technology, intent on making their fortunes; but they are not the only interested party and find themselves in a deadly race against corporate agents and hunted by the authorities.

Forced to combat enemies without and within, they strive to overcome the odds under the watchful eye of an unwelcome guest: Drake, agent of the bank funding their expedition, who is far more than he seems and may represent the greatest threat of all.

"A two-fisted SF adventure, space opera as it should be written!"
– *Gavin Smith, author of 'Veteran'*

Pelquin's Comet
BOOK ONE OF THE DARK ANGELS
IAN WHATES

#1 Amazon UK Best Seller in 'Science Fiction Books'
The cover, by Jim Burns, won the 2016 BSFA Award for Best Artwork

"Classic space opera at its finest, a satisfying and enjoyable novel in its own right and an intriguing introduction to a story universe I want to visit again. Thoroughly recommended." – *SFcrowsnest*

"A natural story-teller, Whates works his material with verve, obvious enjoyment, and an effortlessly breezy prose style."
– *The Guardian*

NewCon Press Novellas, Set 1

Alastair Reynolds – The Iron Tactician

A brand new stand-alone adventure featuring the author's long-running character Merlin. The derelict hulk of an old swallowship found drifting in space draws Merlin into a situation that proves far more complex than he ever anticipated.
Released December 2016

Simon Morden – At the Speed of Light

A tense drama set in the depths of space; the intelligence guiding a human-built ship discovers he may not be alone, forcing him to contend with decisions he was never designed to face.
Released January 2017

Anne Charnock – The Enclave

A new tale set in the same milieu as the author's debut novel *A Calculated Life*". The Enclave: bastion of the free in a corporate, simulant-enhanced world…shortlisted for the 2013 Philip K. Dick Award.
Released February 2017

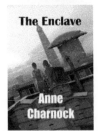

Neil Williamson – The Memoirist

In a future shaped by omnipresent surveillance, why are so many powerful people determined to wipe the last gig by a faded rock star from the annals of history? What are they afraid of?
Released March 2017

All cover art by Chris Moore

www.newconpress.co.uk

IMMANION PRESS

Purveyors of Speculative Fiction
http://www.immanion-press.com

The Lightbearer by Alan Richardson (May 2017)

Michael Horsett parachutes into Occupied France before the D-Day Invasion. He is dropped in the wrong place, miles from the action, badly injured, and totally alone. He falls prey to two Thelemist women who have awaited the Hawk God's coming, attracts a group of First World War veterans who rally to what they imagine is his cause, is hunted by a troop of German Field Police who are desperate to find him, and has a climactic encounter with a mutilated priest who believes that Lucifer Incarnate has arrived...

The Lightbearer is a unique gnostic thriller, dealing with the themes of Light and Darkness, Good and Evil, Matter and Spirit.

"The Lightbearer is another shining example of Alan Richardson's talent as a story-teller. He uses his wide esoteric knowledge to produce a story that thrills, chills and startles the reader as it radiates pure magical energy. An unusual and gripping war story with more facets than a star sapphire." – Mélusine Draco, author of "Aubry's Dog" and "Black Horse, White Horse". ISBN: 978-1-907737-63-3 £11.99 $18.99

Dark in the Day, Ed. by Storm Constantine & Paul Houghton

Weirdness lurks beyond the margins of the mundane, emerging to dismantle our assumptions of reality. Dark in the Day is an anthology of weird fiction, penned by established writers and also those new to the genre – the latter being authors who are, or were, students of Creative Writing at Staffordshire University, where editor Storm Constantine occasionally delivers guest lectures. Her co-editor, Paul Houghton, is the senior lecturer in Creative Writing at the university.

Contributors include: Martina Bellovičová, J. E. Bryant, Glynis Charlton, Storm Constantine, Louise Coquio, Elizabeth Counihan, Krishan Coupland, Elizabeth Davidson, Siân Davies, Paul Finch, Rosie Garland, Rhys Hughes, Kerry Fender, Andrew Hook, Paul Houghton, Tanith Lee, Tim Pratt, Nicholas Royle, Michael Marshall Smith, Paula Wakefield, Ian Whates and Liz Williams.

ISBN: 978-1-907737-74-9 £11.99, $18.99

9 781910 935385